Fighter

KATIE CROSS

KCW

Contents

To Husband
My favorite fighter.
And the one that's shown me my own power.

Chapter One

SERAFINA

The moment I walked into the MMA Center, I knew exactly what would happen: snap judgments, a stare of concern, and maybe even annoyance. But I walked in anyway, because desperate times called for desperate measures.

This fat lip wasn't going away fast enough.

On purpose, I stepped inside at 8:50 pm, ten minutes away from closing. Easier to avoid a conversation I didn't want. My old black backpack was slung halfway across my back and my maniacal brown curls tamed into something of a ponytail.

Ready for this.

There weren't many people left here, which wasn't surprising. The MMA Center was a place for athletes across the country to train in mixed martial arts, not an everyday gym. But Benjamin Mercedy, the owner and founder, had been forced to pack it with weight machines and treadmills and ellipticals for the average mortal to use to pay their mortgage.

Or so the small-mountain-town rumors said, anyway.

The giant mats taking up most of the room, however, belied the casual jogger's attitude. This was a serious place.

A girl across the room spritzed down gym equipment with a

bright spray of cleaner, then wiped it with a cloth. A heavy-set guy huffed away on a treadmill below a TV with the news streaming across it, ticker-tape style.

My gaze honed in on the girl. Medium height, just like me. Strong, but unassuming. She was way wirier than me. I had thighs thick enough to be proud of, as Mom said, but I sensed an understanding soul in this girl. She'd get me. No judgment from a fellow woman. I turned toward her, but stopped when a deep voice to my left asked, "Can I help you?"

The hairs on the back of my neck stood up. I paused midstep. Just the man I *didn't* want to encounter. Benjamin Mercedy himself.

"I just had a question about classes," I responded without looking his way. Maybe I could slip in and out of here without him seeing my swollen face.

"We have a full schedule on the website."

"Yep. Saw it."

Silence answered. I closed my eyes and sucked in a slow breath. Obviously, this was awkward. He had to see the lip. I couldn't talk to the mats on the other side of the room without looking like a total weirdo.

Finally, I turned to face him.

As expected, Benjamin stood behind a counter, both of his hands on the desk. He peered at me through golden eyes framed with eyelashes thick enough to flutter away. Dark hair framed his face in a short cut that, only a few weeks ago, had been shoulder length. The absence of hair gave him a swoony, chiseled facial structure. His neck coiled with muscles all the way across his shoulders and down his arms. Said muscles probably rippled down his back, too.

His Adam's apple bobbed as our gaze collided. I stared right at him to avoid looking at the rest of him and forced my voice to remain normal. "I . . . I just wanted to see if you offered self-defense classes."

His gaze immediately dropped to the fat red line down the middle of my lip. Maybe I could have passed it off as dry skin or some weird condition, except for the swollen state of the lip beneath it. Two days later, it still stung.

When his eyebrows crashed together, I realized I'd lost the game. I dropped all sense of pretense to lean on the counter in an intentional mimicry.

"Look." I leaned forward and waved a hand around my face. "I know what this probably looks like, particularly considering my need for a self-defense class. But I'm not an abused woman in a relationship with a crappy boyfriend. That's not what this is. That's not my jam."

A flicker of amusement traveled through those honey-gold eyes before he nodded. "No, we don't offer self-defense classes right now. We tried, but no one came."

"Well that's stupid," I muttered.

He lifted an eyebrow.

My tense body felt like I was preparing to meet a blow to the stomach. That wasn't the case this time. I was just preparing myself for his inevitable judgment. The quiet talk about what my resources were and how I deserved better. Um, no. Not again, please. I'd already been through this with Bert, my boss.

This wasn't that.

Except . . . it wasn't far off from that, either. I was potentially one more bad situation away from being a statistic, which was why I just needed someone to teach me the basics.

"Do you need some help with whoever did this?" he asked with a nod to my fat lip.

There was an underlying promise of vengeance in his words that sent a little chill through me. This guy didn't even know me, and I'd very intentionally not allowed myself to know him for the last eight weeks. What could *he* possibly want retribution for?

"Nope," I replied cheerily. "Tiptop over here." I leaned

forward again, affecting a casual air. "Do you have any plans for opening a self-defense class in the next week or two?"

His gaze narrowed. "What do you need?"

The blood of my enemies, I wanted to say. *What do you think I need?*

I quelled the burst of inner sarcasm. My bad mood had nothing to do with Benjamin Mercedy. Actually, scratch that. It did. The quiet power in the way he held himself, his muscular frame, and the unassuming way he lived his life was all way too attractive for me to deal with constructively. Here was a human that never had to worry about defending himself.

Instead of answering, I glanced back to the equipment sprinkled through the gym. My gaze lingered on the lifting equipment, treadmills, and a few other things against the far wall, near the mirrors.

Actually, his question had been a fair one. There were different types of self-defense, from what my quick online perusal showed. What *did* I need? Confidence. I needed confidence. Power. Quick reflexes. I needed to be a fighter, and all of that sometime before 3:00 pm tomorrow when Amber showed back up.

"Safety," popped out of my mouth instead.

He lifted the other eyebrow.

"Wait, stop. I take that back." I waved my hands in the air, thoroughly annoyed now. The smell of marinara and chicken carbonara wafted through the air as I tried to fix this. "Ignore my dramatics. I'm in a safe . . . well, mostly safe . . . situation. I just need to be able to defend myself for a few more weeks." My voice elevated a pitch too high. "Not a big deal!"

He stayed cool when he asked, "The one that hit you already?"

"Yes, if you must know," I ground out, then pointed to him. "And he is *not* my boyfriend or my fiancee or my husband so don't even go there. I'm not a victim. He's not . . . an attacker either. It was all an accident. I think," I tacked on, then regretted it when his lips tightened.

Except I *was* sort of a victim in the way that any woman would be against a much larger man she couldn't exactly escape. Or his crazy girlfriend, but that was a whole other bottle of worms. The murky details didn't matter.

Benjamin frowned. "Look, our roster is full. There's literally no mat time available to host a self-defense class."

A curse word slipped out under my breath, but before I could back away, he held up a hand.

"But maybe you and I could figure something out."

"What does *figure something out* mean?"

He tilted his head to the side. "I'll teach you a few things. Self-defense isn't that hard to get started with. We'd need an hour, tops, to cover the basics."

"That fast? Really?"

He nodded. Despite having a larger-than-life presence with his body, he had a calm way about him. Quiet. Just the way he lived. Powerhouse on the mat, quiet as a calm summer day otherwise. Coming in here had been one of the hardest things I'd ever done, and some days, that was saying something. I appreciated the calm mein more than he'd ever know.

"Why?" I asked.

He shrugged. "Let's just say I'm a sucker for a damsel-in-distress."

Three seconds passed while I comprehended that comment. Then my blood boiled. For three more seconds, I saw the world in shades of red. Is this how Talmage felt? Is this why I had a big fat lip? Some genetic predisposition to instant rage when helpful people were just trying to help?

Maybe I had too much pride.

Or maybe that was just a dumb thing to say.

Without realizing it, I had taken a step back sometime

between the word *distress* and my indrawn breath of rage. His eyes widened.

"Then find someone else to rescue," I snapped. "This damsel can save herself . . . with a few well-placed self-defense lessons from someone that isn't you," I added for good measure. "I have some pride, no matter what you've judged of me."

I spun and shoved out the door.

Cool spring air washed down my face as I headed for the mountain bike I'd parked close to the back, out of sight. My bike had been stolen before, and thankfully recovered, but I couldn't afford another fallback. It was my only transportation.

My cheeks had exploded with heat in the ten seconds it took to tell him off. Humiliation had a way of coloring me bright crimson, and I hated it. Damsel-in-distress? *Seriously?* I wanted to throw his own arrogance back at him. I wasn't sitting at home, waiting for the next fist *and* prince charming, thank you very much.

Geez.

Fuming, I jerked the backpack on the rest of the way, grabbed the bike handles, and had one leg almost over the bike when a hand grabbed my leg to stop me.

On reflex, I kicked back with a grunt. Whoever had my leg shuffled at the shifting weight, but didn't budge. They released me. I whirled around to find Benjamin there. My helmet swung from my hand as I wheeled it toward him, but he dodged the flying foam missile like a featherlight ninja, then took a step back and held up two hands.

"Sorry," he quickly said, "I shouldn't have touched you."

Chest heaving, blood thumping, I let my hand rest at my side. The helmet hit my thigh uselessly. Embarrassed at my over-reaction—but seriously, he touched me?—I took a deep breath.

"What?" I snapped again. "You made your position very clear."

"I want to help."

In the dimming spring light, shadows bathed his face. A glimmer of something showed in his eyes, and he tucked his hands into his front pockets. He normally stood with his arms at his side, like a god come to life. His face was usually analytical and serious. Now it was . . . concerned.

Faaaantastic. I engendered pity in the man I'd secretly tried to ignore for months now. And maybe—just maybe—that whole stomping out had been a bit of an overreaction. Mom always said that defensiveness meant there was truth in what the other person said.

So . . . there was that.

"I'm sorry," he said. "That came out as arrogant and it's not entirely true. I don't see you as a damsel-in-distress or whatever. I just . . . I want to help you better your situation however I can. I want you to be safe."

My racing heart calmed. I studied him for another short eternity. "I overreacted," I said. "I'm sorry too."

He lifted his eyebrows. Was it a surprise or a follow-up question? Going with the latter, I stumbled over my own thoughts. Did I want to trust him? Yes.

Could I?

Also yes.

At least I could sense *that* much beneath the layers of vulnerable bravado and muscle that held something of a charming man. He was coiled quiet. Deadly precision. Probably moved faster than I could think.

Not probably, he definitely could.

I'd seen the videos of his last fight where he'd destroyed his opponent in a crushing career-builder, then retired and left the MMA world in a sense of reeling shock. No explanation. Just walked away at the top of his career and disappeared into a quiet mountain town bubble.

There was nothing *normal* about Mercedy, but something told me that everything in him wanted to be.

"I just need someone to teach me the basics in case I need them." I ran a hand through my hair, which had fallen from the loose ponytail and gone full-curl-powered-frizzy at some point. "Like poking eyes or groin kicks or something. I'm pretty open in the afternoon. I work from six to three at the diner Monday through Thursday and noon to closing on Saturday."

His gaze followed my gesture to The Diner across the way. For several moments, a machine seemed to move behind his eyes.

"Come at 9:00 tomorrow," he finally said, "just after we close. I'll teach you what you need to know. But it's not going to stop someone that's determined to hurt you. If—"

"You'd do that?"

"Yes."

I rolled my eyes. "Because you want to be the hero?"

"No," he said softly. "Because I want you to be."

My natural snarky response froze in my throat, and all I could do was nod. Geez, what was I doing? Giving Mercedy—it was easier to picture him as a non-god if I called him by his last name—attitude. Not only that, but I'd be alone with him.

For an *hour*.

"Okay, I'll take that." I nodded, hair waving around my face, and held up a finger. "But wait. Can I pay you?"

"I don't need the money."

"Great! Then I'll bring food. Dinner is on me. And it won't be from the Diner. I'll make it."

A hint of amusement appeared like a crack in his veneer. "It doesn't matter where it's from. And you don't have to bring me food."

I tilted my head back and forth. "Yes, I do need to give something back. I demand it. Do we have a deal?"

Feeling a sense of euphoria for the first time in weeks, I stuck my hand out. It had been too long since I had a real win, and I wanted this one more than I thought. Only a few seconds passed before our hands came together. Then I comprehend that I'd likely be touching him tomorrow.

Him.

Mercedy.

Whom I had quietly stalked from behind the Diner windows and tried to ignore all at the same time. When he gripped my hand in his, tiny little fireworks erupted under the skin of my palm and electrified the rest of my body. His hand seemed to swallow mine. I adored the physical response and tried to soak it up. The pooling collection of heat in my belly caused another shiver through me.

Falling was always the best part.

He gave me a short nod, and I couldn't help but wonder if he ever smiled. "Deal," he said.

"Thank you. I appreciate it. Oh! Do you have any allergies?"

"Nah." He took a step back, our hands falling apart. "I eat just about anything."

Like a madwoman, I wanted to rush forward and snatch his hand back. To cradle his in mine. To imagine what that thrumming touch would feel like on my shoulders. My neck. My cheek. Instead, I let my hand drop back to my side.

"You got it, Mercedy."

His head tilted back in amusement, as if he didn't know what to make of me. He certainly wouldn't be the first. I climbed on top of my bike, one leg bent as I put a foot on the pedal.

"What's your name?" he asked.

"Serafina. You can call me Sera."

I shoved off, my bike tires humming on the pavement as I pedaled away.

Chapter Two

BENJAMIN

My six-year-old daughter Ava snored like a rockstar.

When I pulled the inflatable mattress out from under the front desk, the lights in the gym were already dim. It was 10:00, and I'd managed to finalize everything just an hour after closing. A new record. Everyone else had left, and now we could finally go home.

Ava stirred in my arms when I managed to get her up on my shoulder. Her head lolled around, she smacked her lips, and settled back into sleep. The braid that I had spent almost thirty minutes on this morning had slipped back out, and I cursed it silently. I draped her fuzzy pink blanket around her shoulders and headed out the back door. The alarm beeped as I left it behind, my SUV only a few steps away.

While we drove through the quiet, dark street and into our very small neighborhood on the edge of Pineville, the end of work buzzed through my mind. Bert McMahon had dropped twenty pounds, which was a new record for the old guy. Good for him. Supporting locals in their weight loss goals wasn't where I saw my life going, but hey.

Whatever.

Mackenzie, my employee, reported that one of the treadmills wouldn't lower off its elevation. Needed to fix that in the morning. I mentally put that on my list for tomorrow. The day laid itself out slowly until I pulled into the garage and it whispered closed. One of these days, I needed to hire someone else for all this crap. The only thing I wanted to do was train the fighters coming in.

For just a moment, I closed my eyes and leaned my head back. The silent garage held no sound except a slight whistle when Ava let out a breath. Silence. Blessed, rare, golden, silence. I let myself enjoy it until I started to nod off, so I jerked myself awake and glanced back to Ava. Her head was pressed against the door, her mouth half-open. I stared at her and sighed.

Maybe this life wasn't any better than what she'd had with her Mom. Maybe I just told myself it was, but I was just as big of a mess. What other six-year-old had a blow-up mattress under her Dad's desk?

While I carried Ava to her room, I ignored the mess from breakfast. The forgotten milk on the counter and the pile of laundry in front of the washer. Ava struggled to wake up while I had her go potty and slipped her pajamas on, then tucked her into bed. A little hum came from her as I shut her door, a bright pink night light illuminating her messy room.

A hot shower cleared the sleepy cobwebs of my mind and finally allowed my body to relax. Business was good. Numbers looked great. Trainees doing well. Had some PR opportunities lined up that would get us further into the places I wanted. All that worked great.

My house? Shambles.

My personal life? Empty as the Sahara.

My body? In shape, but nothing on the horizon.

My relationship with Ava? Tense as a harp string.

My goal to give her a better life than her mother did? To be determined.

The checkboxes filled my mind with an ugly reality. Maybe *having it all* wasn't as much as I thought it was. My brother, Maverick, accused me of what he called the *curse of all the gold.*

"You have it all, brother," he'd said to me yesterday when we'd grabbed lunch at the Diner. "Others would kill for your life. You have money. A beautiful, well-behaved daughter. Women literally fawn over you still. You could beat the hell out of anyone you wanted. Now you are your own boss. All the gold, Benny. You have all the gold."

Then again, did I have it all?

The house was still empty. Dark. Unlived in. Ava felt more at home with Maverick's wife, Bethany, than she did with me. My daughter was sort of well-behaved because she tolerated me. She clearly didn't love living with Dad.

It has only been a year, I thought.

Still, I must be doing something wrong.

The bathroom steamed up when I stepped out of the shower, wrapped in a towel, and sat on the edge of my bed. Unexpectedly, Serafina rippled through my mind. A short laugh worked its way out of me while I thought about her wild hair and wrathful gaze. It sobered quickly when I recalled that fat lip and her condemning stare just *waiting* for me to make a comment.

Okay, defensiveness was one thing, but she had something else on her mind entirely.

I'd been in Pineville for eight months now. Once the gym was finalized, Ava and I bought a house on the outskirts of town. Hell, in a small place with only 300 people, *everywhere* was the outskirts. But I couldn't remember Serafina here in the winter. No, she must be recent. So who gave her the lip?

Not a boyfriend.

Father, maybe?

With a weary sigh, I slipped into my pajamas, dropped onto the covers, and promptly forgot everything else when sleep closed over me in a fast wink.

Chapter Three

SERAFINA

The creak of a floorboard sounded like a bomb in the early morning stillness the next day.

With a wince, I paused. A little snort, then a gentle shuffle, came from the room to my right. I crept farther down the dark hall, a distant clock on the coffee machine illuminating enough of a path for me to slip over to my shoes and slide them on. The bright green letters on the clock announced 5:35 am.

Right on time.

Sunrise was a vague promise on the horizon as I slipped into a coat, then grabbed my backpack. My phone buzzed against my thigh with a text message and I sighed. Only one person would send a text at this time of the morning.

Mom: How was he last night?

Not wanting to talk to my parents yet, I sent a quick reply. If more than two minutes passed, Mom would just call. She knew I was awake and getting ready to go to work.

Serafina: He went to bed early. I haven't spoken with him in a day or two.

Mom: Has he apologized yet?

I sighed again. Yes. Profusely.

Serafina: Of course. He was horrified when I talked to him about it.

Mom: That's something.

Serafina: I set the boundary, Mom. If anything happens again, I'm gone.

Mom: Of course. That's fair. We're talking to a counselor now to see if we can get him some help. I'm concerned that this is more than just pain control issues now.

How to tell your Mom that her son was addicted to prescription drugs and his sketchy girlfriend could be feeding him something else?

Certainly not over text.

Halfway out the side door, I paused. Speak of the devil. A beater car was parked on the road at the end of my brother's scraggly lawn. The lawn had once been lush and well-cared for. He lived in a quiet neighborhood on the periphery of Pineville, where the edge of the reservoir gave way to fields and grazing land. Ranches dotted the hillsides and mountains in the distance. His little house had been an ideal place to stay when he worked at a nearby ranch, but now . . . well, it might be a bit isolated for his needs these days.

That beater car, however, meant trouble.

Serafina: Good luck with that, Mom. He got defensive last time I brought it up. By the way, Amber is back. Apparently, she spent the night.

Mom: Great.

I could picture Mom's annoyed eyebrow lift. *Yeah,* I wanted to say. *Feel you there.*

Amber, his new girlfriend, was nothing but trouble. I'd asked Talmage where he found her, but he'd been vague. She ghosted in and out at odd times. She'd been territorial, at best, when we'd first met. A snarl here and there if I showed too much sway with my brother. As if a sister posed any threat to her.

Serafina: Riding to work now. I'll keep you updated, but no news on my end.

Mom: Can we please buy you a car? You shouldn't be riding around the mountains on a bike.

Serafina: I love my bike, and, I'll have you know, work is only a few miles away. Besides, I'm almost there on the down payment savings, but thanks, Mom! Love you!

I tossed the phone into my backpack, grateful that I hadn't stopped to pack lunch and dinner. Amber slept like a sick baby, which meant hardly at all. The last thing I needed was a confrontation with her before a long day at work.

Chilly spring wind brushed against my cheeks as I stepped outside, wiping away the last signs of sleep as I headed into the burgeoning mountain light. With summer on the way, I wouldn't need a car for months before the snow came again. I'd probably hold off on buying one for a while. A rent-free summer in the mountains, helping my older brother while working around delightful people and tourists, was *exactly* what I wanted.

And then?

Who knew. Something spectacular would come along.

Because spectacular things always did.

* * *

The day passed with surprising speed. Too much of it slipped by in a nervous spiral of concern about my upcoming time with Benjamin that night, which set me off balance. I'd accidentally dumped hot coffee on a diner, mixed up three orders, and fielded eight different calls and fifteen text messages from my brother asking if I'd picked up his prescription.

Talmage: Need it, sis. Today.

Talmage: Do I need to send Amber after it?

Talmage: The pain is getting worse and you already know I used my last one.

I sent him the mental bird halfway through my shift, responded once, then turned my phone on silent. Bert let me go half an hour early. When I left at 2:30, my friend Dagny waved me off to take care of only three customers, and I headed to the pharmacy.

Talmage was agitated when I got home after work but he quieted when I passed his pain pills over. By the time I finished baking a chicken, gravy, and biscuit dish that tasted like home, he lay docile on the couch. I blasted music and cleaned to my heart's content. Talmage had always sucked as a cleaner, and since his shoulder injury, it had gotten worse.

Let's just say that fridge probably hadn't been cleaned since my preschool graduation. The grimy work kept my nerves at bay for the rest of the afternoon, but when I approached the side door to the MMA Center that night, I had to quell a rush of butterflies.

Go away, I silently muttered to them.

The last thing I needed to deal with today, of all days, was the brutal attraction. If I wanted to defend against Amber, or Talmage again, I needed to focus.

Just outside the door I stopped, drew in a deep breath, and let it out. When I finally found my courage, I stepped inside the gym to find the lights over the main desk turned off. Only the mat was still illuminated, and the radio off. The clock ticked toward 9:10. After I set the tinfoil-covered dish on the counter, Benjamin appeared out of a back room.

"Hey," he said.

He walked over in bare feet and loose workout pants that sent twin shivers down my spine. That t-shirt fit his shoulders a little bit *too* well. Since I hadn't verbally attacked him yet, like last night, he seemed more at ease.

"Hey," I said. "Thanks again for doing this. I brought my favorite dish from home. It's a chicken biscuit kind of thing with veggies."

He glanced at it. "Great, thank you." Then he nodded toward the mat. "Let's get started."

Riiiiight, I thought, letting my backpack slide to the ground. No casual friendliness here. Unsure of what to expect, I'd dressed in a pair of black workout pants and an old t-shirt with YMCA written on it. If I ever did workout aside from riding the bike around town—which was so close to *never* it paralleled the likelihood of someone living on the sun—I would have worn this.

Seemed fitting.

He'd already headed for a bright blue mat with a red circle around it, so I followed him, but I had enough sense to take my shoes off and leave them with my backpack. Once he stood in the middle of the mat, he turned to face me. Those stupid butterflies resurrected themselves.

"You ready?" he asked.

I took two steps onto the mat and paused. "You're not going to, like, come at me are you?"

To my greatest shock, he cracked a smile. Weary. Exhausted. But there. I accepted it as his first sign of humanity and tried not to notice the way it illuminated his face.

"No. Not that. You ready to get started?"

"Teach away, coach."

"The first thing to work on is confidence. For the most part, I think you have that down."

I reared back. "Say what?"

"Confidence." He readjusted his stance, planted his feet, and kept his shoulders broad. "Being aware and confident in any given situation will automatically deter some people. If you're paying attention, they may pass you by. Most attackers want an easy victim. Don't make it easy for those idiots, all right?"

But what if that attacker is your rage-filled brother and you never know when he's Dr. Jekyll or Mr. Hyde? I thought but nodded instead. A solid wind could knock Amber over. Likely, if I growled at her, she'd back off.

"Confidence. Makes sense."

He held out a hand, stopped, and said, "Can I touch your shoulder?"

I nodded again, this time with a gulp. He reached over, grabbed my shoulders, and pulled them back. It automatically made my chin tip up a little. He lifted an eyebrow.

"Feel the difference?"

"Actually, yes."

There was a sort of power there in the rearranging. Seeming pleased, he nodded and stepped back again. At least he didn't take a quick glance at my chest, which stuck out farther than ever. Not that I had so much to brag about there. If my hips could share a little of the love, I'd be far more even. The smell of his cologne distracted me, and I wanted to follow the trail back to him.

"Next, remember that you're powerful. Use that power. Make them afraid of *you*, okay?"

"Sure."

"We're going to practice a few things, and I want to feel it from you. The confidence *and* the power. A self-defense situation is not the time to hold back. Snarl like an animal if you have to, just use what you've got."

The realization that this may have been my worst idea occurred to me then, particularly when the words, "I'm going to teach you how to fight off an attacker when they have a hold of you," came out of his mouth.

Dear heavens, I thought. *He's going to have his arms around me.*

Ten minutes later, after reviewing things that jumbled in my brain like *groin kick* and *hammer punch* and *use your car keys,* that is exactly what happened. He came up behind me, wrapped his arms around me, and said close to my ear, "This is a bear hug. Someone could come up behind you and stop you like this. How do you get out?"

If you are my attacker, I thought, *I may not want to stop it.*

His arms had clamped around me like a steel vise, my spine pressed into his chest. Those butterflies flapped around helplessly, drunk from the overwhelming smell of aftershave that followed him.

"Think," he chided, no doubt misreading my silence. His arms tightened. "What are you going to do?"

Instead of flipping in his arms and laying a kiss on his lips, I stomped my foot with a grunt, thankfully missing his toes. Then I whirled to the side with my elbow high, the way he'd told me. I tried to shove it into his neck on one side, then the next. It gave me room to spin, and I mimicked a knee to the groin with my knee.

"Good." He stepped back. "You're quick."

Breathless too, but I managed to smile. Praise from a guy like him felt a lot like basking in holy light. Rare, warm, and stupefying. The obnoxious ring of a cell phone crashed through the room, breaking the moment.

He rolled his eyes. "Just a second."

Grateful for the chance to recover my wits, I ran a hand through my hair and peered out the far window on the other side of the desk. A reflection of a rectangular light, like a tablet, and a slight shuffle of pink, caught me by surprise. It looked like it was under the desk if I understood the backward reflection correctly.

Was that . . . was there someone under the desk?

Benjamin spoke into the phone in monosyllables, his back to me. I almost walked over there to see who hid, but a little shock caught me by surprise when I heard a quiet voice say, "Who was it?"

Benjamin replied in a quiet murmur as he shut the phone off, then frowned as he looked at the screen again.

Instead of gasping, I yanked my hair out of my high ponytail. It spilled down my shoulders and relieved a sudden banging in my head. Or maybe that was just the clanging of alarms.

Did he have a *kid*?

In all my months of pretending not to watch his every move, I'd never seen a little girl. Had I?

A little pang hit my chest. I missed little kids. Mom had run a daycare out of our house for the entire eighteen years that I lived at home. There had always been chaos and children and messes and grubby hands and sticky goods. Without it, everything seemed a bit empty. I wanted to walk over there and talk to her, but I had a feeling Benjamin would lock up the *very* tight, minuscule sliver of friendliness this had opened up between us. The questions ran rampant through my mind anyway.

Why keep her hidden back there?

How old was she?

Where was her mom?

Was she even his?

He complicated my questions by returning, so I hastily yanked my hair out of the way again. He stopped several feet away with an apologetic expression.

"Sorry."

"No problem." My arms dropped back to my side. I tilted my head back that way. "Do you need to go?"

"No, we can finish." He ran a hand through his hair, and I caught a glimpse of a tattoo on his left bicep. "Where were we?"

You were hugging me and whispering in my ear and I think we should start there again, I thought.

"You had mentioned a side headlock?"

"Oh, right."

With a shake of his head that seemed intended to get his mind back into the game, he proceeded with instruction. Seeing him a bit distracted by the call made him seem even less godlike, and I relaxed. Instead of focusing on the fact that Benjamin Mercedy was touching me, I tried to picture Talmage coming at me in the darkness again. The unhinged desperation. The wild strength I didn't know he had in him, shoulder injury or not. It brought a ferocity out of me that I hadn't been aware of before.

By the time we finished, I felt surprisingly more confident. Benjamin moved fast as lightning, but treated me like a piece of delicate china. He never once jostled too hard or touched me without asking. At least I'd had a chance to practice the moves, and I made a mental note to buy a lanyard for my keys. Painful weapon, indeed.

"You got this." He nodded once as the lesson faded to an end. "Really. You have natural confidence. Just let it show more and stay aware."

No, don't let me go! my heart cried. *Keep me locked in those arms forever!*

"Thanks," I said instead. "I feel like dinner isn't enough for taking up an extra hour of your time, especially so late. Can I do anything else? I mean, you potentially saved my life tonight."

He waved that off. "I'm glad to help. And if you ever need anything else, just let me know. Hand me your phone? I'll put my number in."

"Really?"

He nodded again.

"Ah . . . well. Thanks."

With a hesitation I couldn't explain, but probably had something to do with the child under the desk, I handed the phone over. Such an offer felt like an egg about to hatch. Trembling, fragile, and quaking in my hands, I wasn't sure what would come of it. Could be beautiful, could be terrible, but the gamble was half the fun.

Just being a gentleman, I told myself to talk down the excited squeal. Benjamin. Mercedy. In. My. Phone.

Seconds later, he returned my cell, and I glanced down to see *Benjamin Mercedy* as a new contact. Would he do that for any woman that had clearly just been nailed by someone in the face?

Definitely.

He was that kind of guy.

The cold reality of that calmed the raging, giggly shrew I'd allowed out of her cage for too long.

"Well." I cleared my throat. "Thanks again. The same goes for you if you ever need anything. Not that you'd need saving on a dark night. But, you know, I do pretty good meals."

He cracked a pity smile. "Night, Sera. Oh, and thank you for dinner."

"Anytime."

The sound of my name off his lips gave me a delicious shudder that was difficult to hide, so I turned away. As I headed for the door, the glare of a screen under the desk had faded, and I thought I heard a gentle, quiet snore.

Chapter Four

BENJAMIN

"She's been fantastic, as always."

Bethany ran her head over Ava's hair. Ava ignored me as she walked past me to go around the desk, a tablet already in her hand. Behind me, three men stood on the mat. One of them barked out instructions while the other two grappled. Ava ignored them, slipped around the desk, and crawled underneath.

"Thanks," I said with a sigh. "I appreciate you bringing her by and feeding her dinner."

"We're always happy to help. I think she may be a bit bored at our place, so I'll try to find her some new games."

"I'm so grateful for all you've done."

Bethany's brow wrinkled. "She'll come around, Ben. You're a single dad, you're doing the best you can. She's . . . having a tough time after her Mom died."

Bethany bounced my nephew, Shane, on her hip. He drooled a soggy grin at me. Two teeth jutted out of his bottom jaw as he smiled, gnawing on a toy. The first time I met her was when I drove her brother's bike to the Frolicking Moose and watched my brother propose filtered through my mind. How far they'd come. Now, Bethany wore a pair of heels and bright lipstick, beautifully navigating her upscale real estate job with the real-life turmoil of parenting.

"It's been a year since she died," I said quietly. "I just . . ."

"Yeah, and Ava's *six*. It's not something you just get over. You know that as well as anyone, and you weren't six when your Dad died. "

Frustrated, I ran a hand through my hair, unable to fight with that. Yes, I knew how to lose a parent, but not at six. Ava never spoke about Sadie or what life was like with her. Rarely spoke at *all*, really.

Was I just being impatient? Did time really heal all wounds? Would Ava recover? Maybe Ava was like her Mom: destined to hate me forever.

"She's lucky to have you," Bethany said as if she could read my mind. She put a hand on my arm, and the warm touch was soothing. I didn't agree with her, mostly because I thought it was all a contrived crock of crap. I sucked as a father. Ava had big emotions that I didn't know how to deal with, loved nail polish, and the best I could do with all that hair that she wouldn't let me cut was a braid and a ponytail.

Yeah, I loved Ava. I was happy to provide a roof over her head. But she didn't love me, and sometimes that really sucked.

"Thanks again," I said, done with this topic.

Bethany opened her mouth to say something, decided against it, and smiled half-heartedly instead. Then, clearly on an impulse, she leaned forward and gave me a quick hug. For a moment, I melted into the warmth. It had been a long time since anyone had touched me. Then again, I rarely touched anyone else, so maybe it was my own damn fault.

Like many things.

"Hang in there, Ben. You're doing a great job."

With another little wave, she disappeared out the door with a quick shout. "Love you too, Ava!"

No sound issued from under the desk. I headed around it

and crouched down to find her on her tablet. When my shadow darkened her little hovel, she looked over at me with a teenager's annoyance. She'd been like that at three, but I'd been more of a novelty then. A passerby that came when he could and her Mom probably talked smack about all the time. She'd tolerated me then because I brought her gifts and we did fun things together whenever Sadie allowed it, which wasn't often.

Now she had no choice but to endure me.

"Hey," I said, and thought of reaching out to push her hair out of her eyes, but she was prickly as a cactus. "How was school?"

"Fine."

"Any homework?"

She turned back to her tablet. "Nope."

"What did you have for lunch?"

"Hamburger."

"Was it good?"

She shrugged and tapped on the screen. Well, that was scraping the bottom of the barrel, wasn't it? Talking to my daughter about school lunch. I tugged on her headphones cord when she didn't look back at me, and her eyes turned back to me with a silent *what*?

"We'll go home earlier tonight, all right? You need more sleep."

Her teacher had called me about her sleepiness in class and plummeting grades again, last night during the lesson with Serafina. As if we hadn't already talked about it and discussed the very not-ideal circumstances of single parenting. Unfortunately, I had an idea that her teacher, a single woman, just liked to talk and tried to find excuses to get on the phone with me, a single man with more money than Pineville had seen in a while. No teacher should call at 9:30 at night.

"Okay." Her expression brightened slightly. "Can we have that biscuit stuff for dinner again?"

"The chicken thing?"

"Yeah." Her eyes widened. "It was so good."

"I'll try to figure out how she made it."

"Who made it?"

"Serafina."

She seemed to ponder that for a minute, then said, "I like that name. It's pretty."

Well, that was a first. Didn't know she was capable of liking anything. "We'll try to make it together?" I asked.

Ava's nose wrinkled. "Nevermind."

"Listen, hater," I said, attempting some levity, "I'm great at cooking."

Her expression suggested otherwise, and a shout from the gym called me away. "Good talk," I said and patted the blow-up mattress she'd thrown herself onto, but she'd already turned back to her screen. Maybe the tablet was the issue. It had been loaded full enough when she came, as if Sadie let her be on it all the time. Restricting her to an hour of use a day certainly hadn't helped our relationship.

With a sigh, I let myself get drawn back into the new trainee who had just moved here for the next three months. Work called, and so did the oblivion that followed a rigorous mat routine.

While walking past the big, open wall of windows that faced Main Street—technically the only road in Pineville except for neighborhoods, and it didn't even have a stoplight—I glanced across the street to the Diner. Serafina stood out there, a dirty black apron across her rounded hips. Her hair trailed out on her back behind a hat, and she laughed, eyes bright, while talking on the phone. Did she work in the evenings? Knowing her, she went back to work to visit a friend or something.

Last night recalled into my head. Her soft body in my arms. The way she seemed so trusting. Occasionally distracted. Confident, but quiet. Her lip had healed somewhat but still seemed a bit sore. It still puzzled me. I thought she might tell me more about how she got a fat lip during the lesson, but nothing had come out.

Brother, maybe?

Friend?

I turned away, already unable to get her off my mind. Why it mattered, I didn't know. With great effort, I forced myself to focus on the mat.

The last complication I needed in my life was another woman.

* * *

The clock over the desk glared at me several hours later.

9:30.

So much for that early escape.

With a sigh, I shoved away from the paperwork my accountant, Stella Marie, had requested from me. She lived up the canyon with her boyfriend Mark and had to finagle some final paperwork back together to get our payroll running. I'd put it off too long already to accommodate the new trainee.

My eyes were bleary as I rubbed them. Ava had fallen asleep a few hours ago, or else I would have left early. Seemed stupid to wake her up too soon because then she'd be awake for hours, singing in her bed, banging her feet against the wall. I could crash here. We had a few blankets in the back.

Or maybe I just didn't want to go back to that stupid, empty, still-dirty house. I hated that house. The ringing hollow of it. It felt like a lifeless tomb. It sucked my time, energy, and mental capacity after an already long day at work, and it never felt like home.

Frustrated, I shook my head and straightened up just as a little *tap tap tap* came from the side doors. My head lifted, startled, to see a head of brown hair standing outside. Three seconds passed before I comprehended that it was Serafina. She'd come here in the *dark*.

In a few steps, I'd crossed the space and yanked the door open.

"Come in," I said. "What are you doing here? It's late."

She held another pan in her hands, and I realized, stupidly, that I hadn't even thought of cleaning and returning the other one. We'd finished it off for breakfast this morning.

"Hey." She smiled wide, but there was a hesitant tint now that I'd barked at her. "I ended up with some leftovers. Thought I'd bring them by. They're a bit more kid-friendly than the other one."

"Oh."

Her vague non-mention of Ava startled me so that I just stared at her, holding out a dish, before my mind caught up. Had I mentioned Ava to her? No. Ava had been asleep last night. Hadn't she?

"Right," she whispered and smiled wider. I realized I'd been standing there an awkward amount of time. Color swept the tops of her cheekbones. "I'll just . . . I'll just put this over there."

My brain caught up with my mouth then. "Thank you. I'm sorry, it just took me by surprise. I . . ."

"It's good. No worries." She set the dish down. "Spaghetti with little meatballs, and my secret is brown sugar in the marinara. Not much." She held up a hand as if I'd protested. "I get that you 'fit' types are kind of above sugar, but you will thank me for this one."

Her air quotations made me crack a pathetic smile. Totally lost, I ran a hand over my head and just said, "Thank you. Seriously. The chicken thing was delicious."

"It's the carrots," she said with a funny self-assurance. "And the peas. They're sweet veggies. See? Sugar. Transforms stuff, especially with kids. Anyway, I included some chocolate chip cookies. I'm not a heavy-on-the-chocolate-chips kind of girl because they take over the cookies, but whatever. They're cookies."

As if I'd protested again.

"At any rate," she continued, "both of you should love them and carb up tomorrow. Enjoy!"

Both of you should love them rang through my mind. How did she know? She turned around to leave, and I almost reached out for her but stopped at the last minute. A hint of something both feminine and heady wafted behind her that I couldn't place. Citrus? No. Coconut.

"How are things?" I asked instead. "Are they okay?"

Should I just ask who smacked her across the face and if they were going to do it again? I hated insinuations, but I also didn't know what to do with this woman. Like trying to capture moonlight in my hands. I felt this way with Ava all the time. Totally taken aback and equally tongue-tied. Put me on a mat and I could beat just about anyone. But these girls gave me twenty thumbs.

And those tight black pants she wore again weren't helping matters.

She paused at the door, pasted on a smile, and said over her shoulder, "Great! See you later!"

Just like that, she disappeared back outside. Before I could follow her out and offer her a ride home, Ava woke up crying. By the time I woke her from her bad dream and had her calmed down, Serafina had gone.

Chapter Five

SERAFINA

"Y-your brother just called again," Dagny said. "N-n-not sure what he w-wanted."

I rolled my eyes.

"Thanks."

Dagny paused at the edge of the swinging door, where she always peeked out to see who had come in and who she had to prepare herself to talk to. The comforting bustle of the Diner rang in the air behind us. Better than a movie soundtrack some days. Behind me, the smell of freshly grilled chicken wafted by.

"W-w-why do the attractive ones always have to be married?" Dagny murmured. "Meanwhile, all these other j-jerks are trying to grab my hips and slap my rear, but they have like three t-t-teeth and hair as oily as my lawn m-mower. I h-hate waitressing."

Dagny leaned against the wall and peered out on the main area through slits in the swinging wooden doors. Her green eyes were so light they were almost pastel. She was lovely, but quiet, and reserved because of a childhood stutter. Working at the Diner was an active attempt to fight through her social anxiety, and I loved her for her courage every day.

"Who are you creeping on?" I asked, dumping some ice into a cup.

"M-maverick. Oh, Benjamin just walked in too."

My heart seized. First, what? Benjamin had actually taken time off of work to go somewhere else? That rarely happened at this time of day. Second, my hair looked terrible today. I hadn't washed it in seven days. My record was fourteen, but that had been in the middle of France, and it needed some help. A salon had dolled me right up after that.

"Where is he sitting?" I asked and slipped to her side. Wasted effort when the door swung open, thankfully *not* revealing us. Frantic, I yanked my hair out of my face so it rested on my shoulders in a hasty ponytail that fluffed out all over the place.

"Y-your table," she grumbled. "They always sit at your t-t-table."

I screeched under my breath, then calmed. No, I couldn't do this. A plethora of boyfriends in my past had started this exact way. Butterflies, lonely longing, and a hint of them needing saving. No boyfriends. I had to focus on Talmage. Geez, I still had places to travel that I hadn't even visited yet.

But then . . . why not?

There was something magical about the start of a romance. Besides, none of the other boyfriends had been Benjamin. In fact, some of the butterflies in my past had been conjured out of loneliness and desperation.

After-the-fact butterflies don't count. This guy caused the real-deal butterflies.

With that reality, I could *totally* do this again. Falling hard was a heady feeling in the beginning. The ending sucked, but I hadn't had butterflies like this ever.

Besides, Benjamin was the safest bet I'd ever have a crush on. That man loved nothing but the mat and hopefully whatever child lurked under his desk at night. Nah, he'd be nothing but an innocent flirtation.

Like a stalking panther to keep my eyes on and enjoy their power.

Besides, he'd looked so lost last night when I brought the food over. Whatever soul lurked beneath all that brawn was broken. I felt for him. Mom would make him a pie and pat his arm without a word and probably heal half the mistakes of his past with one bite of her crumbly crust.

I needed that pie recipe.

"Wish me luck," I murmured.

"G-g-get his num-m-mber," Dagny whispered conspiratorially, her hair pulled away from her eyes with a few expertly-placed pens. Her eyes widened. "I d-dare you."

I smirked, said, "Already have it," and flounced out.

After checking on an older couple in a back booth, I pulled my writing pad out and approached. Thankfully, Maverick sat in the chair facing me, though I had little doubt that Benjamin knew I came up behind him. He didn't seem like the type to let his guard down, even at the Diner.

Maverick grinned as I approached. The two were clearly brothers, but Maverick had a softer expression. Benjamin appeared to be chiseled from stone, with sharper angles. The man needed a lighthearted conversation or a walloping kiss. I'd be game for both.

"Hey Mav," I cried. "My favorite Mercedy."

He laughed. Ben scowled.

"Just kidding," I sang as I pulled menus from my pocket and handed them over. "It's great to see you too, Ben. How was the spaghetti?"

"Amazing, thank you again."

He lifted two clean, empty containers from the seat next to him. How could returning plastic dishes cause a flutter in my chest? No, not the dishes. He'd remembered and brought them back. Swoonworthy, right there. *No finer man than the one that brings your dishes back,* I imagined Mom saying. She'd be halfway in love with him.

"Glad you liked it," I said, putting them beneath one arm, against my hip. His gaze went there, then skated away.

"We loved it."

The *we* was a win. At least he acknowledged that he didn't live alone, whoever the small child with him was. So far, my subtle inquiries around town pointed to a daughter named Ava, but that was all anyone knew about her. Not even Bert, who owned the Diner and worked out at the MMA Center daily now, had seen much of her.

Maverick glanced between us, brow high, but said nothing.

"What can I get you?" I asked.

Mav ordered a fresh cup of coffee, Benjamin stuck with water—no one was surprised with a body like that—and both settled for sandwich and salad specials. I darted away before my urge to linger and learn more about their lives and secret hopes overcame my common sense.

A new lunch rush started to move through, and I lost myself in the usual rhythm and movements of waitressing. Every now and then I felt eyes on me, but ignored them. Men's eyes followed me all the time.

It's your hips, my girl, Mom would say. *Be proud of those.*

She'd certainly given me enough to be proud of. I wasn't brave enough to figure out if it was Benjamin looking or not, so I pretended to ignore it. Pretended my heart didn't flutter in my chest every time.

"Oh. Em. G-gee." Dagny sighed when I stepped through the swinging door to grab a basket of biscuits. "H-h-he has been staring at y-you this whole time!"

"He's in love with my cooking," I said, but felt a secret thrill. "The man is so broken he probably can't even make mac and cheese."

"I'd fix him," she whispered, breathless. Then she sighed.

"No, I wouldn't. I w-w-wouldn't even be able to speak to him. He's t-terrifying."

"He's a teddy bear."

She shook her head, utterly unconvinced.

When I slipped back out, delivered the biscuits, and made my way back to the Mercedy table, Maverick and Benjamin stood up. Empty plates and salad bowls littered their table. Maverick tossed some money on the table, but Benjamin dropped more.

"Hey." I smiled at both but spoke to Maverick. "We still haven't finalized where we're putting my name on your arm."

He laughed, glancing at his left arm, where a sleeve of tattoos colored the skin. All of them were some version of a niece or nephew name with varying colors and designs, supposedly to reflect the child.

"That's right," he drawled. "Serafina is such a short, easy name to manage. And your subdued personality will make it even easier."

"You're right! We'll scrawl it across your chest."

"Bethany won't mind," he said.

"Not at all! Another woman's name over your heart? Sounds entirely innocent." I turned to Benjamin with a warm smile. "Glad you enjoyed the spaghetti. I bake a pretty mean ziti casserole. It's all up in the cheese, I'm just saying. I mean, if you have something against cheese then you can get over it for one night. It's *cheese*."

A desperate look came to his eyes. "Sounds great," he said. "Tomorrow?"

The moment the request slipped out, I could tell he regretted it. But he didn't take it back because that would have been even *more* awkward, so I rolled with it.

"Tomorrow sounds great. Brownies this time?" I asked.

He nodded, relief clear on his expression. "Brownies are an excellent choice for a very picky eater that also ate every single cookie, as well as two helpings of spaghetti, and then again for breakfast."

A thrill warmed me all the way to the bones. Why did I suspect that said picky eater rarely had a home-cooked meal? Or that his relief had something to do with a happy, well-fed child? Hungry children were cranky buggers.

Although I was a bit disappointed that he wasn't asking for it just to see me, I could appreciate a father's desperation.

Feed 'em, Mom always said. *That'll bring them in just like the cows.*

"I'll drop it off tomorrow." I tilted my head to the side, one eye narrowed. "Maybe a little earlier, though. 9:30 is kind of late for little tummies. I'll text you."

Maverick's puzzled expression cleared when I thanked them and they walked out without another word. Once they left, I let out a long breath, grateful the pressure in the air had gone with them. Benjamin carried weight with him everywhere he went.

"B-boy," Dagny whistled as she walked behind me. "That man is *intense.*"

"Tell me about it," I muttered as I grabbed their plates, plucked the cash off the table—they'd left me a $30 tip—and swept into the back, my mind whirling.

* * *

"Where have you been?"

The next afternoon, several bags spilled out of my arms and onto Talmage's rickey table. The house I had cleaned so meticulously had fallen into ragged tatters. He paced back and forth across worn carpet, hair standing on end. The exhilaration of going shopping up the canyon to the local "big city" with Dagny faded. I mean, I'd even found a black dress with pockets.

Best day ever.

But all that faded with Talmage's obvious irritation.

"What's up?" I asked, monitoring my tone. Just to give me something to do, and in case I needed something between us, I slipped behind the counter in the kitchen. The charged air was a warning. I should get out of here.

But first, I had to just grab the dinner I'd made for Benjamin and his daughter.

"I'm in pain!" he cried, hitting a book off a shelf. He winced when it slammed into the wall. His breathing was fast. I grabbed my phone and slipped it into my back pocket.

Talmage was two years older than me. We were born close enough that we'd hated and loved each other deeply while growing up. Despite being from the same family, he towered over my five-and-a-half foot tall frame at a stocky six feet. His once thick shoulders had made him even more frightening, but he'd lessened in muscle since the injury at work that had put him into multiple surgeries. That didn't lessen his sheer brawn. Like Daddy, he was a big guy. He was twenty-seven, and I was twenty-five, but he looked more like fifty these days.

"Tal," I said and propped a hip against the counter. "I'm sorry. Let's get this figured out, all right?"

"Get my meds."

"I just refilled them a few days ago. Did you lose them?"

"No." His nostrils flared. "They're gone."

"Gone?"

"Gone!" he shouted. "Gone. They're gone, gone, gone. I'm a big guy. They're not prescribing me enough."

My mind spun, startled at this new argument. I found my keys in my pocket and threaded them through my fingers, just in case, the way Ben had taught me. Did I want to use any moves on Talmage? Of course not. He was my brother. He loved me. I loved him—had once adored him like a hero. He'd always protected me from the mean kids at school, had kept me safe when our parents were gone on a date and I was scared in the house alone.

But right now I could also recognize the monster that had given me the fat lip last week. The same one that had no similarities to the brother I once knew. The brother I came to live with two months ago to help through what should have been his final surgery.

Calm Talmage was nothing like this guy. Dr. Jekyl had returned.

I swallowed a flurry of panic. With every jerky movement he exhibited, I wanted to wince. He'd always had anxiety as a kid. Hated closed spaces, big crowds, or any type of peer pressure. The last few months with unemployment and continuous surgeries had only worsened it.

Today, however, something else had him on edge.

"Have you called your doctor?" I asked.

"Yes."

"What did they say?"

"That I can't have anymore," he spat. "What do you think? You think they hand that stuff out? I'm freaking useless. Can't work. Can't pay my bills. Can't . . . can't deal with this pain. I just . . . I just need a few more to get me through today."

He didn't stop moving, but rubbed a hand across his chest now. Sweat beaded on his brow. My gaze dropped to a pile of papers on the counter. One of them was a torn envelope. The red lines of an overdue hospital bill decorated one of the papers that spilled out. My throat tightened.

"Let's get you some ibuprofen."

He scoffed, wiping at his forehead. "Waste of time. You know it doesn't do anything."

His last surgery had been six weeks ago. He should have been weaned off the meds in the weeks after. The first surgery had been much easier. The second had been the worst, with the longest recovery time and the hardest pain management. After that came a fast third, now fourth surgery.

And Talmage was a totally different person.

"Tal, maybe we should call and get some other help. Maybe this is something else?" I said the words gently, but he turned on me anyway. His eyes were unfocused as he barreled toward me.

"You don't know what this feels like!"

I ducked the first clumsy blow, an open slap likely meant to punt me out of his way, but the swinging fist that followed caught me right in the ribs and robbed my breath. I dropped to my knees with a gasp.

Benjamin hadn't covered this. Or had he? My mind suddenly fractured, and all I could think about was air.

He stomped a foot onto my side and shoved me to the ground. Pain wired through my body, hot and fast as lightning. I struggled to regain breath, too weak to shove him off when he pressed a foot into my chest. An audible *crack* sounded seconds before pain shot through my body again. My breath rushed back all at once, exacerbating the heat. I slammed a fist into his calf to get him to move, but his leg was too heavy. He leaned too much weight into it.

He didn't even notice.

"You know nothing," he growled.

Seconds later, I was pinned against the fridge by my throat while he screamed. Emotion built in his eyes. Were those tears? No. Rage? He screamed incomprehensibly. Whatever came over him was dark. Foreign. Something else. The anxiety. The meds. A combination of all of them.

Or something worse.

He released me and I scrambled away with a desperate gasp, but he grabbed me by the hair and hauled me back. A backhand across the face sent stars across my vision. Somewhere in the blur of pain and disbelief came another voice.

"Talmage!"

Had I imagined it? Was Amber here?

Whoever it was, the voice distracted him. He paused, hand poised to strike again, when a semblance of humanity came back to him. When he glanced over his shoulder toward the front door, his grip on me loosened. I grabbed my only chance.

With a cry, I drove my fist into his knee. The unexpected blow took him by surprise and he dropped with a grunt. Then I hammer-punched his injured shoulder with the keys in my hand so I could clamber over him. He squealed like a pig, and it gave me the space to get out of his reach. Amber let out a cry and dropped to her knees.

"That's his injured shoulder!" she cried.

Panting, I backed away. My back slammed into the door as I fumbled for my phone. My head swam, dizzy now.

"Talmage!" Amber's too-thin body was visible beneath a dirty tank top as she put her hands on his bright red face. "I'm here. I'm here."

"Sera!" he gasped, the word lined with terrifying rage.

My side on fire, I bolted outside. No one followed me as I slipped out of sight into a grove of trees, grabbed my phone, and called 911.

"911," answered a voice. "What's your emergency?"

"My brother is going to kill me," I panted. "Please send someone now."

* * *

"You going to be all right here?"

Jayson Hernandez, a county deputy, stood in the doorway to the small hotel room I'd managed to rent. His shoulders shadowed the room as he stepped inside, then frowned. He had thick forearms and a quick smile. With his short black hair and warm hazel eyes, he was a charmer. He'd come into the Diner several times after his shifts, and always tipped well. To have him witness all of this was . . . embarrassing, at best. But his serious mein and professional manner kept me from wanting to fold in on myself as I scanned the hotel room.

The bar that housed these hotel rooms lay in the heart of Pineville, just next to the pizza place, and a short walk from work. If I moved to the front of the building, the Diner would be visible just down the road, by the MMA Center.

More importantly, it was smack dab in the middle of everything. People added security. Talmage wouldn't come here.

Which was a good thing.

My hastily packed bags lay on the hotel bed, which had a headboard made of thick wooden logs and a lamp with an adorable bear peering around the back. It seemed impossible that only a few hours had passed. That the world still moved on. That no one else had noticed my entire life shifting a bit more to the wrong angle.

"Sera?"

Jayson's quiet question pulled me from my spiraling thoughts. I nodded, my voice scratchy when I turned to face him.

"Yeah," I said. "I'll be good here. Thanks for the ride and for all the help."

"I'll talk to the owner," he said. "Make sure you're good, just in case. If you need anything, just give me a call."

He pushed my bike the rest of the way into the room.

"Thanks, Jayson."

"My pleasure," he said. His brow furrowed over his blue eyes. "He's in custody for the night, but call if you have any problems after that. Anytime, Sera. You're sure you don't want to go to the hospital?"

A small smile seemed to reassure him. "I'm fine. The paramedics looked me over. Really."

With a quick nod, he was gone. I wondered what he thought of me. Did he judge me as dramatic and wild because of my brother? Did he know that my upbringing was as middle class and stable as anyone's had a right to be? That the only drugs we'd ever known as children were kid's Tylenol? Our parents hadn't raised us to this. We were functional, emotionally healthy people from a normal family.

But my brother was still a monstrous mess anyway.

Tears bubbled up behind my eyes, but I sniffed them back. My side ached with every breath, sending spirals of lacy pain through my back and ribs. If I didn't breathe deep, and no one jostled me, I'd manage. Didn't need an x-ray to know my rib was broken. The skin over my left cheekbone was swollen and tender. With any luck, it wouldn't bruise too badly. Even my hair hurt. My neck a little, too.

Grief, but I looked like a *Loveline* movie actress.

My mind skipped over the whole event again, the thoughts unstable and unsettled. I'd have to call Mom and Dad soon. Have to tell them what happened and explain it and let them know that I still didn't know if I'd press charges or not. Didn't know what Talmage would be like after this settled.

Would Mr. Hyde ever return?

Probably.

The four walls seemed especially close all of a sudden. I couldn't just sit here and think and stew and *feel* and cry when my rib hurt so much. Even crying was too painful. Instead, I shoved my phone back into my pocket, carefully pulled on a jacket, and shoved the rest of the cash that I'd earned from tips today into my other pocket.

I still owed Benjamin dinner. If nothing else happened today, Ava would get a delicious meal.

I could do that much.

The sound of sniffling met my ears when I stepped into the MMA Center an hour later. I shuffled inside, two grocery bags hanging off my right arm, and set them on the counter. Moving that way sent another shot of irritation through my side, but I breathed through the yelp it almost caused.

No one else filled the strangely empty interior, especially considering it was 7:00 at night. Darkness ebbed in from outside, filling the space with quiet.

The sniffles continued.

"Hello?" I called.

A little girl came into view as I walked farther into the room. She sat with her back against the main counter on the left, her knees tucked into her chest. She wore a pair of jeans and a dirty baseball t-shirt. Her hair had come out of a braid in awkward lumps. Definitely the work of a desperate father. This had to be Ava.

Slowly, I approached.

"Hey. You okay?"

She peered up at me through reddened eyes. Adorable pink flip-flops clung to her feet. She stared morosely at me. Slowly, with poor attempts to hide my wince, I lowered onto the floor next to her.

"Hard day?" I asked.

She nodded with cherub cheeks. Probably six years old, if I could guess through the tear tracks on her face. She had adorable dark hair in curls, not unlike my own thanks to the braid. Her eyes were a gentle olive color, unlike Benjamin's, which were a honey color. I tucked a piece of hair behind her ear, grateful to find someone whose day had been as crappy as mine. The gentle touch didn't seem to bother her.

"Want to talk about it?"

She shook her head, but a new round of tears started again. Wordless, I held out both arms. She climbed inside with another deep wail, threw her arms around my shoulders, and laid her cheek on my shoulder. I held my breath, my eyes scrunched shut, until the rocketing pain around my ribs calmed down several moments later. Then I managed to reach a hand up and rub her back.

"Let it out, honey," I murmured, the way Mom did for me. Secretly, I hoped I'd get some sort of relief from my own pain by watching her let go of hers. "Just let it go."

Her soft cries continued into my shoulder. Eventually, her tears seeped through the fabric of my shirt and tugged at my heart. What would Ben say if he found us like this? Where was he anyway? Why was she alone here? No girl should be alone with heartbreak like this.

But was I thinking about her or myself?

Several minutes later, she pulled away. Her hands remained on my shoulder as she peered at me. Then she reached up and a gentle finger touched my throbbing cheekbone. Likely, the bruise was even darker now.

"You have an ouchie."

"I do."

Her head tilted slightly. "Do you have bullies too?"

"I do."

"But you're an adult."

"I know." My nose scrunched. "There are adult bullies too. Isn't that the worst? It's hard enough being a kid, isn't it?"

Soberly, she nodded. Her shoulders lifted with a big breath, then fell. I glanced up at the counter, then back to her.

"Hey, you know what helps bad days?"

She reached out, fiddling with the edge of my slate jacket. Despite the warm spring night outside, I still couldn't get warm.

"What?" she asked.

"Brownies."

Her eyes instantly widened. "I love brownies."

"Me too. Let's have some, what do you think? I brought you some dinner, too. I think you'll like it, but I didn't make it this time."

"Are you Serafina?"

"I am. Are you Ava?"

She nodded, then reared back a little, suspicion thick in her gaze. "It's not a peanut butter and jelly sandwich, is it?"

I laughed. "No. You'll see."

She stood up. Gently, I followed. If I held my breath and braced my side, it wasn't too bad, but several moments still passed before I could breathe normally again. If she noticed, she gave no sign.

"Come on." I motioned her onto a nearby bench, then patted the counter next to me. Phones and paperwork cluttered the other side, but this space was empty. "Climb on that, then sit here."

"Dad doesn't let me sit up there."

I winked. "Dad isn't here, is he? I'll keep you safe."

Probably a false promise. With a broken rib, I wasn't even sure I'd be able to carry a tray anymore. Still, I couldn't deny her the pleasure of a minuscule rebellion on a hard day. Beaming, she obeyed. Five minutes later, I'd sliced her a few pieces of rotisserie chicken with a plastic knife I'd nabbed at the deli counter, broke off a wing, and stuck a spoon in packages of warm mashed potatoes and corn. I bought all of it at the deli inside the grocery store, but she didn't seem to notice the containers with price tags on them.

"Brownies?" she asked hopefully.

"After dinner."

She stared at the spoons. "Where's a plate?"

"Didn't bring one. You can eat it just like that."

She blinked. "Really?"

"Really. It won't spread germs. Just you and your dad eating it."

Once she took a tentative taste of the mashed potatoes, her eyes lit up, and she dug in for more with a happy little squeal.

"So," I leaned against the counter on my good side. My hands still trembled a little, but comforting Ava had an oddly soothing effect on me. "Want to tell me more about your day? Who had you in tears?"

She shook her head, her mouth full of corn.

"You don't want to talk about it?"

Her eyes widened to an alarming size. She shook her head more urgently now. "Fair," I said as flashes of Dr. Jekyll Talmage flashed through my mind. "Sometimes it's hard to talk about bad days."

She nodded again, then turned her attention to testing the corn. Like the potatoes, she dove in with gusto. Just as my phone buzzed with a text, a shuffle came from the far side of the room. A voice followed it.

"Ava? Sorry, I'm off the pho—Oh. Hey."

My heart raced as Benjamin appeared, carrying a box. His startled expression was a little bit relieved. I forced a smile. Halfway across the room, he slowed. His eyes locked onto something. Maybe it was my posture. Maybe the bruising that had surely intensified on my face. My head throbbed like a wild thing as the adrenalin left me and I might be in a perma-grimace. Suddenly, I felt weak as a rag doll and gripped the cool counter beneath my hand.

Whatever clued him in, he'd taken full notice now.

"Sera?" he murmured quietly. His voice was thick with a question, and I saw a flash of the rage that had been there when he first saw my fat lip. I tilted my head slightly to Ava, then shook my head. He closed the last few steps between us and set the box aside.

His nostrils flared as he regarded me up close, but he reluctantly nodded a quiet assent to not talk about it yet. His gaze lingered on my cheek.

"Ava's had a rough day," I said, "so I told her that if she had some dinner, she could have brownies." My voice caught and I felt stupid for the rush of emotion that followed. Carefully, I swallowed it back. "Brownies fix every bad day," I finished in a small voice.

Ava had another chomp of chicken, her feet swinging on the edge of the counter as she hummed to herself.

If possible, Benjamin's expression hardened even more.

"Of course they do," he murmured in a silky voice. He didn't take his eyes off of me. "And how was *your* day?"

"Here." I reached into my back pocket and handed him a folded pile of papers from the deputy that took Talmage away, as well as the initial receipt from the hotel. "This will answer most of your questions."

Without question, he shuffled through them. The tension in his neck ebbed slightly. Ava had another dainty bite of potatoes, then stuck the spoon back in the container and brushed her hands off.

"All done!"

Benjamin spoke before I could. "Why don't you take your brownie to the window and eat it?"

"Can I have my tablet?" She clasped her hands together. "Pleeeease?"

His gaze flickered to the clock. "Fine. You haven't had it all today. You have one hour, all right?"

With a squeal, she snatched a brownie from the open box replete with colorful sprinkles and disappeared under the desk. So there *was* a sanctuary there. Benjamin turned to me then, eyes full of concern. I shuffled to change my position a bit, winced, and his gaze narrowed further.

"What happened?" he asked quietly.

I swallowed and repeated the most minimal details necessary to get the story across, and avoided descriptions of the actual blows that landed. I ended with what I hoped was an easy, "I'm staying at a hotel while we sort all this out. I won't go back there," I added quickly. "Not even to check on him. My parents will probably come to town now and try to reason with him.

Maybe talk with his doctor. But I'm . . . pretty much out of the Talmage picture for the time being."

"Good."

He said it with all the inflection of a rock. I swallowed and motioned to the food. "I brought you dinner."

He frowned. "You still brought this after all that?"

"I promised that I would and Ava needed it," I said quietly. "Maybe I did too."

His stark expression shook me. "Yeah," he finally murmured. "I get that."

We lapsed into an eternal silence that had all my nerve endings firing. He stared off in space, his jaw tight. Meanwhile, I wandered into the deep quagmire of doubt I should have visited a while ago, perhaps before I came here.

Why was I here? Had this been a mistake? Benjamin saw me as that strange person that kept dropping off food. The waitress who joked with his brother about tattoos. And what did I see him as?

A safe place, maybe?

Was this some sort of subconscious attempt for me to feel safe after all that had happened? I should be laying in bed, watching stupid TV shows on ancient cable while sleeping this awful day off. Instead, I stood here trying to act like I wasn't in pain. Like I didn't want his comfort when I did want it. In fact, I wanted it so desperately tears burned my eyes. So why didn't I call my parents? Why didn't I call Dagny? They would comfort me.

Heck, even watching a funny show would comfort me.

But no one could keep me safe like Benjamin.

The realization came with a hearty sense of shock, maybe embarrassment. We weren't even friends. Hardly acquaintances. But I couldn't help the way I felt, or the utter truth behind it. Benjamin was safety personified. And maybe, on some small level, a sort of friend. If he even had those.

Unfortunately, I couldn't just jump up and haul out of the MMA Center the way that I wanted, because my ribs already ached just from holding back the sobs. So I did the only thing I could to save my pride.

"For heaven's sake," I whispered thickly, "can you just say something please? I can't stand this silence."

He looked at me then, his expression so serious. His gaze dropped to my cheek before a gentle hand lifted to my face. His warm palm touched my skin, thumb hovering over my bone where the pulsing had become angry. He touched it softly. I held my breath as tears welled in my eyes.

"I hate this for you," he whispered.

The tears dropped down my cheeks, sliding over his thumb.

"Me too."

Free now, I couldn't stop the tears. My face twisted as a sob peeped out, jarring my ribs. His arms tensed and a moment of indecision crossed his face while I wrestled to gain control of the agony. My arm braced against my side uselessly. It only made it worse, and I sat there for a moment, a ball of twisted pain, before I could get a hold of myself. For a breath, I thought he'd pull me into his arms—I so desperately wanted him to—but Ava's voice broke through the room.

"Dad! These brownies are *so* good."

Properly reminded of where we were, the strange moment ended and I turned away. This had definitely been a mistake. He owed me nothing and I'd revealed far too much already. Without his intense scrutiny on my face, I was able to quell the sobs and wrest them under control. His hand fell back to his side as I carefully wiped the tears off of my face.

"I'm sorry," I whispered. "I didn't mean to drop this on you. I just . . . I didn't want you to think I'd forgotten and I didn't want to be in that hotel room alone right then."

"Are you . . . do you . . ."

The words stuttered in his throat, as if he didn't know what to say, but wanted to say something. Time to save him, then.

"I'm okay." I gave a watery smile. "I promise. I feel better. Ava was . . . amazing. She helped me feel better just being with her. And thank you for listening. It helps. I'm going to go back to the hotel now."

And die in a puddle of mortification, thanks, I finished silently.

I stood up too quickly and swayed. With one arm braced on my side, the other reached for the counter. He clamped a hand on my arm immediately.

"I'm good now," I whispered once it passed.

But his frustrated expression hadn't lessened, and he clearly wasn't fooled. "Let me drive you back to the hotel. Is it the cabins down the road, by the river?"

The thought of climbing into that monstrous SUV sent another whirl of pain through me. No way. Besides, I needed to grab things at the store and that was practically next door. I'd gone through the grocery store with the single-minded focus to get them food and had forgotten a new toothbrush. Packing my stuff had been haphazard while Jayson waited for me and the other officer took Talmage away.

Amber had conveniently disappeared before they even showed up, the skunk.

"No, it's the hotel at the bar."

"That place?" he cried. "That's so sketchy."

"It's just until I find a place to rent."

"Do you feel safe there?"

"Of course," I snapped.

He didn't like it, obviously. But as his gaze darted to Ava, his weird spot became blatantly apparent. No doubt he needed to get her home and in bed. And who was I to him anyway?

"Thanks." I forced a more confident, certain tone. The same he'd tried to teach me to take. I should just be grateful he didn't ask for an accounting of my self-defense moves. Which hadn't, at the moment, deterred much of Talmage's wrath, as Benjamin had mentioned. Not until I got ruthless and hammer punched Talmage's injured shoulder.

Straightening my shoulders sent another twinge through me but I ignored it. "I've got this and appreciate the distraction. See you later?"

"Wait, Sera—"

But I sent another wave, called goodbye to Ava, and disappeared out the door as fast as my legs would carry me. Which, admittedly wasn't fast enough to avoid the silence that remained in my wake.

Chapter Six

BENJAMIN

My hand hovered above the hotel door, ready to knock.

Behind me, a dim street light cast shadows on the balcony where I stood. They'd given Serafina a room on the second floor, which kept her above, but not away from, the bar patrons below. Drunken shouts already drifted out on the night air, which was still cool as the sun set.

I ran a hand through my hair, then forced myself to just knock already.

Seconds later, my knuckles wrapped on the door. Too late, it occurred to me that she might be sleeping. Maybe she had just gotten the pain under control and slept and I'd just woken her—

A chain jangled, then the door opened no more than an inch. Bleary eyes looked out at me from a tear-stained face.

"Sera?"

A moment of confusion registered next before she shut the door, slid the chain free, and opened it again.

"Benjamin?"

Below, a shout surfaced from a bar patron that stumbled into the parking lot at my back. Sera reached out, grabbed my arm, and pulled me inside. When she shut the door, she immediately flipped the lock on it. I stepped back to give her some space, and she beckoned me farther inside.

The hotel room wasn't as dingy as I'd expected. All the lights were turned on, and a television ran a black-and-white show in the background so quietly I couldn't hear much of it. Her phone lay on top of the only bed's duvet. Numbers ticked across it, and a woman's voice called out.

"Serafina, honey? You still okay?"

"Yeah, Mom." Serafina slid past me and grabbed the phone, which was clearly on speakerphone. She carefully sat on the bed. "It's Benjamin, not Talmage."

"Hi, Benjamin!"

Startled, I managed a broken, "H-hey."

"I'll let you go, Sera," she said with the dripping warm tones of a mother. "Call me later?"

"Yeah. Love you, Mom."

"Love you more."

The phone clicked away, which left us with an awkward silence. Sera crossed her arms over her chest and gazed up at me. She wore a pair of loose sweats and a black, fitted shirt that went all the way to her wrists.

"Sorry." I tucked my hands into the front pockets of my jeans. "I won't stay, I just . . ."

The words stuck in my throat. I wasn't good at this. I could win the award for the most nervous tongue on the planet. It didn't make any sense at all that I was here. Sera and I weren't even friends. At least, not by definition. Which, at the moment, I couldn't actually define anyway.

"Where's Ava?" she asked, saving me from myself.

She sniffled, clearly trying to clean her face off without making it obvious. Her left cheek had become more bruised in the hour or so that had passed, and the tears made the skin an angry shade of red. By morning, she'd have something of a black eye.

"I took her to Mav's. She's going to stay the night there."

"So you could come here?"

I nodded. She softened, then scooted back and motioned to the bed next to her. First, I reached just past her, grabbed a pillow, and tucked it under my left arm, like my arm was a wing.

"Splint your injured side like this when you have to cough or take a deep breath. I've had so many fractured ribs it's not even funny. It helps."

She blinked. "Oh. Thanks."

"Fractured ribs can turn into lung issues pretty fast. Injures the lung tissue a little if it's severe enough, so you have to cough. It sucks but . . . pneumonia is worse."

This time, a hint of a smile found her. "Thanks."

Maybe it was the coach-like tone I'd used. Or the severely awkward way I just tried to teach her something as a means to get a conversation rolling when I had no idea what I wanted to say.

Or why I was even here.

Following a hunch based on the amusement in her eyes, I asked, "You already knew that, didn't you?"

Her widening grin broke the tense air. "My dad is a doctor. He's already given me the lecture."

"Oh."

"Have a seat, Mercedy."

She reached to the side where a mini-fridge lingered beneath the bedside counter. When she peeled it open a few water bottles waited inside. She tossed me one.

"Thanks," I said.

Underneath all her forced bravado, she looked exhausted. The lid cracked when I twisted it off, and the cool drink helped settle me. But that sober air had returned and I didn't know what to do with it.

She spared me the pain of finding a discussion point.

"I'm surprised you came."

"Me too."

My response had been immediate, and I mentally berated myself the moment it slipped. Her amusement curbed my embarrassment.

"Why *did* you come?"

My brow grew heavy. This is where women and I didn't work well. "I'm not sure," I admitted, rubbing the back of my neck. "I was worried about you, for one. You didn't look great back there. And . . . I didn't want to . . . I don't know."

She softened, and for some reason, it eased my tension. When she reached out and put a hand on my arm, something deep inside me twinged. Like a rope being cut free. No one touched me unless they were family, and even then it was awkward. Like I carried an invisible wall around me and everyone sensed it there, so they didn't get too close. Normally, that was fine. I preferred it that way. But lately . . .

For her to make it so simple to touch me made me wonder if I complicated things too much.

"Thanks," she said, then her hand slipped away. I wanted it back.

"I went into work after I dropped your dinner off," she said, and I sensed that conversation was a calm place for her. She picked at the edge of the water bottle label with her fingernail. "Bert gave me the rest of the week off. There's no way I can lift a tray right now and Dagny wanted some extra hours. Besides." She waved a hand toward her left cheek. "People are going to ask and I don't want to deal with it. Although, I could make up a superhero story or something. So . . . I guess that it's good I don't have to work for five days."

"You don't sound happy about it."

She frowned. "I'm grateful. It gives me some recovery time and time to find a place to stay."

A heavy *but* lingered in the air. She didn't give it words, and it seemed out of character for her to *not* voice a thought. I looked at her then, really looked at her, and saw the buried fear beneath the layers of bravado. Serafina bubbled over with life and energy and gentle sarcasm, but today she seemed downtrodden. Exhausted. Maybe more than a little frightened.

How could she not be?

"What can I do to help you?" I asked.

Startled, she blinked and tucked a wild strand of hair behind her ear. For whatever reason, it seemed to be the last thing she expected me to say. My own fear kicked in next when tears sprang to her eyes, but I schooled it down. Ava cried all the time, and we'd survived all of those. This would be fine.

"You really want to know?" she asked.

I nodded, startled that I didn't feel a rush of panic for whatever I'd just pushed myself into. She wasn't Sadie. Sadie would never come back, but her legacy lived on all the same. Serafina hesitated, but I could tell that all her guards were down. Any usual social etiquette would be shoved to the side, which was exactly the way I felt comfortable in a conversation. When all the crap I wasn't supposed to say didn't hang over my head.

"Will you stay?" she asked.

Before my eyes could even widen, she quickly continued. "I just . . . the first time Talmage hit me, it was at night and I didn't see it coming and really could have been an accident. So darkness has been a bit weird. Today was . . . not that . . . and the thought of trying to sleep is a little overwhelming. It's stupid but—" Her gaze dropped and she sighed. "It just feels like I'm not safe. Tomorrow, when I have a clearer head, I'm sure it will be fine. But tonight it's all a little fresh."

"Yes."

The reply came before I knew it was there, but I didn't regret it. For several moments, she just stared at me. Relief spread through her entire body then.

"Thank you. You don't have to stay all night, just . . . until I fall asleep?"

There were so many questions that surfaced right then. Why me? Why did I make a difference? Sure, the whole professional-MMA-fighter thing likely played a part, but I had a feeling it went deeper than that. Serafina had been taking care of herself for years if all the travel stories Maverick had relayed to me meant anything. If I hadn't stopped by, she would have figured it out and been fine.

So why did she ask?

"I'll stay, Sera."

Something passed through her face then that I couldn't read. "Thank you."

Before things could get awkward, she slipped off the bed, turned off the TV, and flicked the lights off. I pulled my jacket off, feeling more comfortable in the dark. Before I could tackle the issue of the single queen bed, she slipped to the other side of the room, tossed half of the duvet my way, and climbed underneath the rest of the blankets. Any random fear I might have harbored that all of this was an elaborate hoax faded. She didn't want me in her bed.

That had certainly happened before.

While she settled in, I toed off my shoes and pulled my phone from my pocket. Serafina settled onto her side with her back to me, her wild curls spilling across her pillow in kinky lines. I lay on my back and stared at the ceiling, my thoughts a jumbled mess. Whatever I thought would happen tonight, this wasn't it.

But this might be better.

"Benjamin?"

"Yeah?"

"Thank you for being my friend."

I swallowed and searched for a response, but she didn't seem to need one. Instead, she snuggled deeper into the covers and, with a careful breath, yawned. A little mewl escaped her at the end of the yawn, then quieted.

She hadn't gone into any details, but her brother must have cracked her pretty good—probably with a solid kick—to leave an injury like that. Not to mention the bruise on her face. What would that be like, to be a woman and hit around by your brother? A lover was one thing. A family member, another. How long had this been happening? Why didn't her parents do something about it sooner?

When my entire body tensed, I had to push those thoughts away. Thinking about what Sera endured wasn't going to help me sleep.

Even though I could reach out and touch her back, she still felt miles away. Twice I opened my mouth to say something, and twice I closed it again. What was there to say? Not much longer after she settled in, her breathing softened into the steady, even cadence of sleep.

I stayed awake, my thoughts spinning.

Chapter Seven

SERAFINA

When my eyes opened the next morning, an immediate groan followed. I lay on my back and tried to roll over, but a sharp protest stopped me. Lightning-hot pain spread through my body and ended on my spine. Several seconds passed before it came back under control and I could breathe again.

Breathe, Serafina, I murmured. *Breathe . . . slowly.*

My eyes popped back open when several thoughts crashed into me at once.

Talmage.

Hotel.

Benjamin.

With heavy morning breath, my head spun over to see an empty bed and ruffled covers next to me. Not sure whether I was relieved, or annoyed, to find him gone, I sank further into the bed. Then I pulled my hair over my face to hide from the world and groaned. Benjamin Mercedy had stayed the night.

What was I thinking?

Of course, I hadn't been thinking when I asked him to stay. I'd been scared. Traumatized. The brother I'd always known had been replaced with someone that could have killed me. I already knew that I felt safe around Benjamin, so when he showed up looking so concerned and awkward, I'd broken.

Like a cracked porcelain doll.

With a grunt, I shoved out of bed, braced myself against the pain, and took stock of my body. The headache had mostly gone away, but now I felt sore all over. My cheek was swollen, so my eye didn't open all the way. I forced myself to shuffle to the window and open the drapes. A gray sky waited outside, plunking raindrops down the window. I peered out on a quiet parking lot, only a hint of the main road visible. My brain was a mess of thoughts I didn't try to unravel.

If not here, then where was Benjamin? No note. No text. Just disappeared.

Probably better that way.

A hot shower woke me the rest of the way, easing some of my tension and tightness. I popped some more over-the-counter pain relievers once I'd changed into a pair of yoga pants, a t-shirt, and a light blue jacket.

My phone chimed with a text as I ruffled my hair out over my shoulders to dry.

Mom: We should be able to fly out Saturday. I'll keep you posted. Any word?

Serafina: None so far.

Mom: You doing okay?

Serafina: I slept surprisingly well. Thanks. Love you.

Mom and Dad were flying out as soon as Dad could clear his surgery schedule, which could be a few days. Talmage might only be in the county jail for a day or two, if even that. No doubt Amber would sign him out. He certainly hadn't called me, which was for the best. My mind spun with the implications of everything that happened yesterday. Talmage had been scary, but he wasn't like that all the time.

When he was Talmage.

Part of me wanted to see him now that time had passed, but the other part of me recoiled at the same thought.

He was my brother, though, not my lover. I couldn't just get rid of him or change history or my genetics, and maybe I wouldn't want to. A deep part of me loved Talmage, but a more real part of me feared him now. Because, in some way, this guy *wasn't* Talmage.

Noooope, I wasn't ready to see him again.

Not yet.

Since I wouldn't work until next week, that left me with five days to find a new place to stay, all while avoiding an inevitable confrontation with Talmage at some point in the future. More than likely, he'd avoid me until our parents came. Then we'd meet again and hash out what *moving forward* looked like.

Without me living at his place.

And maybe without me living in Pineville anymore. That thought didn't sit well either. A mountain summer is exactly what I wanted. Besides, this could be the impetus to change that Talmage needed. With help, he could move forward. With me in a safe environment, Talmage's recovery was worth working for.

While standing at the coffee maker, I slowly combed through my tangled mess of hair with great wincing and muttered curses. Clumps of hair were still tender from being dragged across a room. Once done, I piled all the curls on top of my head, secured them with a few clips, and left them to dry into their own riotous mess.

A gentle tap came on the door, startling me.

I padded over, peered out the window, and recoiled in surprise a second time. Benjamin stood outside. His coat covered his head to protect him from the rain. Quickly, I whipped the lock off and pulled the door open. He glanced up, looked me over in a fast glance, and followed my silent hand wave to step inside. Oh yeah. Wild, weird hair. Swollen face. No make-up. Cozy, fat-day clothes.

Winner day for Serafina over here.

When he walked past me, arms full of what appeared to be breakfast, he smelled like rain.

"Hey," he said, eyeing me as I closed the door behind him. "Feeling better?"

"A bit sore, but better. Thank you. Did you stay all night?"

He nodded.

I tried to infuse all the gratitude in the words that I could manage. "Thank you. It was . . . I needed a friend."

He seemed prone to ignoring praise, so he grunted and distracted me by setting a brown paper bag and a coffee cup carrier on the small table on the other side of the room.

"I brought you some breakfast. And I wasn't sure about your coffee, but I guessed you liked it with more cream and sugar than the average human."

"Wise man."

He passed me a to-go cup and I had a tentative sip. Warm, not too hot, and perfectly sweetened. He was one macaron away from being my favorite person. Two styrofoam containers came out of the bag next. The smell of eggs, bacon, and butter followed.

"Wow. Thanks."

He handed me a fork. "Seemed like it was my turn to repay the favor."

We settled at the table and started to eat. Unlike last night, this silence wasn't burdened. Chewing was fine if I took it slow, although my cheeks ached with the movement. Before I asked how he slept, he broke the quiet. "Can I take you somewhere after we eat breakfast?"

I'll follow you anywhere, I thought, but asked, "Where?"

Warm coffee flooded my tongue while he poked an over-medium fried egg piled onto a piece of wheat toast and met my gaze.

"My brother's coffee shop."

"The Frolicking Moose?"

"Yeah."

"Why there?"

He leaned back in his chair, like a panther. For all his relaxed state, he still looked ready to spring. "I want to show you something."

"At the coffee shop?" I clarified again.

He nodded.

Nothing waited here but a quiet, rainy hotel room, and going anywhere with Benjamin sounded like my favorite day.

"Sure," I said. "Sounds like an adventure."

* * *

The Frolicking Moose was an adorable little coffee shop at the center of Pineville. I'd only been in a few times since they'd renovated from top to bottom. A tragic fire from faulty wiring nearly burned the whole place down. Most people now went through the drive-through, but they'd recently opened back up. Rumors that they might start hosting parties in their expanded back room had started to swirl through town.

A good party always had my attention.

A girl named Christabel stood behind the counter of the Frolicking Moose, right next to Ellie, Maverick's adopted daughter. Christabel's gentle auburn hair was cropped short in an adorable pixie cut. Her face lit up as we walked in.

"Heya!"

Ellie gave Benjamin a nod in greeting, then her eyes fell to mine. Her gaze wasn't unfriendly but was too intense to be welcoming. While I wouldn't characterize her as a sad person, she certainly had a sense of solemnity about her.

A binder lay open in front of them, and based on Christabel's glazed look and the assortment of things that cluttered the counter, I'd guess Ellie was training her.

"Mav said we should expect you." Ellie tossed a ring of keys his way. Her gaze lingered on my cheek before it darted back to my eyes. A strange curiosity lived there. I met her stare but ignored the question.

Ben caught the keys easily.

"Thanks, Elle."

Christabel waved as Benjamin walked through a doorway to the right. It led down a short hall with what appeared to be a storage closet on the left and an office on the right—all newly paneled and fresh with the smell of stain. At the end of the hallway was a wrought-iron spiral staircase. Ben put a hand on the railing and started to climb.

My curiosity got the better of me as I followed him. Once we made it to the top of the stairs, he sidestepped and motioned me forward.

"This is the new Frolicking Moose loft."

Carefully, I ventured into an open floor plan that took up the entirety of the upper floor, which had been turned into a studio apartment. With the expansion below, they had a perfectly-sized place here. It wasn't overly large, but not too small either.

Windows streamed warm sunlight, while a candle that smelled like cotton lit the far side of the room. A gentle breeze stirred gauzy curtains. There were a few antique-looking pieces of furniture stationed throughout, with some books and blankets strategically placed here and there. In all, it looked like a catalog photo.

"The furniture is Bethany's thing," he said with a hint of amusement. "She's a realtor and loves to stage places. They're prepping this to put on the market to rent, which is why she has it all dolled up. She swears the candle increases offers."

I laughed, charmed. "I wouldn't doubt it for a second."

"Anyway," his expression sobered, "I was thinking about where you'd be able to stay in Pineville after what happened with your brother. I wondered if you'd want to see it. I asked Maverick and he said he'd hold off on listing if you wanted to apply to rent."

My gaze widened. "Seriously?"

He nodded. "You still have to apply. They'll run your credit and do your background check and all that, but he's willing to give you first dibs. He's . . . fond of you."

The words came out like they almost choked him, but I let that go for now. There would be time for analysis later.

"That's very kind."

"It's a six-month lease unless you'd want longer, with a down payment and all that stuff, but it's brand new with the reconstruction. Plus, it's safe."

I strolled around the edge of the room to touch the bookshelf, peruse the titles that I'd never heard of. Reading wasn't really my thing. I tried to picture myself here. My life had been nomadic for the last several years. I'd graduated with my associate's degree at twenty after doing advanced high school classes, tromped over to Europe for three months, and hadn't settled anywhere for longer than nine months ever since. Waitressing jobs, virtual assistant work, even cleaning horse stalls helped me bounce around the world on my whim.

Which meant that six months sounded just about right.

I owned no furniture to move in here, except for the few things that I still had at Talmage's. That could be remedied easily enough.

"Thank you." I turned to face him. "That was . . . incredibly sweet of you."

He ignored that, too. "I don't know what your financial

position looks like, either. Mav didn't tell me how much they'll charge on rent, but . . ."

He trailed off and I felt a big *something* coming. I paused near a thin, silver refrigerator that purred quietly in the corner. Next to it was a small range, a sink with porcelain spigots, and a cupboard with a few glass cups.

"But?" I asked.

He shifted his weight. "I . . . I wanted to see if we could help each other out?"

"How so?"

"Ava."

The name came out of his mouth like a rolling stone. I'd used it yesterday as if I had the right. He hadn't stopped me, but I had sensed some discomfort on his part.

"Ava?" I asked.

"Would you be interested in helping me take care of her?"

Until that moment, I hadn't realized there had been a slow-growing hope in my heart. A traitorous thought that built slowly, like an expanding balloon. One that was inflated by the idea that maybe there was something in that grinchy heart that felt for me.

But maybe it had just been about Ava.

For a moment, I stared at him in shock, doubly taken aback by the fact that he likely had never asked such a thing before.

"What do you mean?" I finally asked.

He rubbed the back of his neck in a half-grimace. "She gets out of school at 2:30, and the bus drops her off at Bethany and Maverick's house. Most of the time, she's fine there. Bethany is either home with Shane or sometimes Ellie is there. They're sort of her family now. Maybe more than me," he tacked on as an afterthought, but couldn't hide the wound-edness in his tone. "But Bethany is often showing listings and Maverick is doing renovations and Ellie is eighteen and running the coffee shop until her first semester of college starts at the end of the summer. They're busy. While they love Ava, I think she . . . she needs more stability. More . . . attention."

He turned to pace now, his tense body swallowing all the open space.

"When Bethany can watch her at night, she drops Ava off at the gym after they've finished dinner. Then Ava just stays with me at the MMA Center until way too late. She's never home and her life is disorganized, at best. She needs better. She *deserves* better. And she talked about you the whole way to Maverick's and you're . . . bright and happy and she needs the steady influence and attention of a woman like you in her life."

A thousand questions flooded my mind all at once. Where was her mother? Would she be in the picture? What grade was Ava in? But all those I set aside for the bigger picture that really mattered.

"What would helping look like?"

He paused, as if startled I'd even entertain the idea, and said, "Ideally, depending on your schedule or interest, you pick her up from school Monday through Friday. Take her home and do girl stuff or homework, I don't know. Then have her in bed at 8:00. I'm changing things at work so I'm not the one closing and I can be home by 8:30, but that's just too late for her. I'll pay $20 an hour."

Six-years-old likely meant first grade, and that schedule meant at least six-and-a-half-hours a day with her. My mind spun as I thought out the proposal. It would fit with my job and that kind of pay would probably cover a loft like this, although I didn't know for certain. I had no car, but maybe he'd be fine with us walking everywhere.

Above all the other questions was an undeniable urge to say *yes*. I forced myself to stop and figure out why. Was it an urge to be part of his world? To keep him close? To feel safe? For a few moments, I considered all of those, but realized none fit.

No, it was about that lonely little girl drowning in her father's world.

I still didn't know so much about Ava—about *them*—but I knew that I would agree. Not only would the work be fun and take my mind off the current affairs of my family, but it would give me a reason to stay here for a few more months. Besides, there was still a glimmer of hope for Talmage, and until that was completely stomped out by his own decisions, I wanted to stay.

So I swallowed and said, "Okay."

Several moments passed before Benjamin seemed to comprehend my agreement. He blinked twice, opened his mouth, and finally managed to say, "Okay?"

"Yes. Ava is a lovely girl and I'd love to spend more time with her. And help you however I can. Single parenting must be difficult on many levels."

Relief flooded him so intensely it altered his appearance. The coiled panther looked more like a sleepy bear now. He struggled to find more words, and I left him to it. Finally, he said, "Thank you. I can't thank you enough."

I waved that off. "It's my pleasure. Ava is wonderful."

"Can you start today?"

The plea didn't entirely surprise me. This man was nothing if not desperate, and I realized that he'd spent the whole morning with me, but likely had clients at the MMA Center right now. Clients that paid a *lot* of money to train with him. Besides, he may have just found me a place to stay, so there wasn't as much to occupy my time today anyway. I wasn't the type to sit around and mope. Being with Ava would be a good distraction until my parents arrived.

"Yes, that'll be fine."

For a second, he regarded my face. "Are you sure?" Then I realized that the bruises on my face may be a bit off putting for Ava.

"Oh," I said, "yes, I'll be fine. I'll . . . explain this to her."

"Right. Okay. I'll call her teacher and tell her to let Ava know." He dug into his pockets and pulled out a set of car keys. "This is for my SUV. You can use it to pick her up from the bus stop. When you start back to work, I'll drop the keys off at the Diner in the morning."

"What about you?" I asked, accepting the keys, still warm from his pocket.

He shrugged. "I'll just jog home."

I had no idea where he lived, but it could be several miles away. Then again, he probably didn't mind that sort of thing, and winter was in the taillights now. There had been something relaxing about my bike ride back to Talmage's at the end of the day. The thought of driving that massive SUV around gave me a little thrill *and* jolt of terror. How the crap was I going to climb up there with this rib?

"Okay."

Seconds later, he was on his phone, which buzzed in his hands. He dismissed incoming text messages to type something out, then my phone jangled in my back pocket. I pulled it out to see an address from him.

"My home." A look of something like vulnerability crossed his face then. "With the passcode to get inside. I trust you."

Those three words were as loaded as any I'd ever heard. Had something happened in the past with his home so he didn't trust people? At this point, all my shock points were taken up, and the questions cluttered my mind until I couldn't have asked even if I wanted.

"Great."

"Her school information is there as well. You'll have to pick her up from the bus stop that I texted you, but after that, you can figure out what's easiest, whether you pick her up or she can even get off the bus in town, if you want. Whatever you need. We just need to tell her and the bus driver."

His shoulders sagged slightly as he met my gaze again.

"Thank you, Serafina. I'm sorry, but I need to dash to work. Do you have any questions?"

A million, but I kept them pooled in my head for now. No doubt, most of them would work out over time.

"I'm good. I'll see you tonight?"

For the first time, a full smile found his face, no doubt driven by a sense of relief. "Tonight," he echoed, and my stomach turned to jelly. Like it or not, Benjamin and I were tied together now, at least for the foreseeable future.

How bad could that be?

* * *

That afternoon, Ava stared at me through wide eyes, a backpack slung over her shoulders that seemed to take up her whole torso. Female superheroes decorated it with bright colors and fierce expressions. She dropped it off her shoulders and dragged it by a single strap as she approached. It splashed through a mud puddle, but she didn't seem to mind.

"*You* are picking me up now?" she asked.

The rain had retreated, leaving a thick skein of moisture over the reservoir and a freshly-washed smell on the world. Overhead, a bright cerulean sky unfurled. I couldn't help but notice a gaggle of other girls peeling off another direction, talking together as if Ava didn't exist. Ava didn't seem to pay them any attention either.

Did she have friends?

"Yep!" I forced brightness in my tone, although I couldn't tell whether she was excited by the prospect or annoyed.

"What happened to your face?"

"Had a little accident," I said blithely. "Hardly hurts at all, except my rib is sore, so we'll need to be careful. Ready to go home?"

She trudged forward a few more steps, then chirped,

"Great!" and skipped over. Her backpack banged on the ground behind her. Without another word, she yanked open the SUV back door, which she could barely reach, and clambered inside.

A feeling of mental paralysis overcame me as I carefully eased into the driver's seat. The SUV seemed to swallow me whole and felt like driving a tank. It was tricked out with futuristic lighting and all the LED screens. Trying to figure out such a monster had almost made me late to the bus stop.

"What's your name again?" Ava asked from the back seat as she peered out the window.

Her blind trust took me by surprise. She didn't even know my name, but she climbed into a car with me? Not just any car, her Dad's car, but still . . . we'd have to have some talks about strangers.

"Serafina."

"Oh, now I remember. My Dad told me that. So did my teacher."

"Your teacher?"

She nodded. "Mm-hmm. Daddy called my teacher and she told me to watch for his car at the bus stop because someone *really* fun named Serafina would pick me up at the bus stop today. I'm glad it was you. I remember you. Do you have more brownies?"

Point for Benjamin—he'd thought this through to an impressive degree. For all his weird self-deprecatory comments earlier, he seemed to be doing a great job.

"Maybe I do have more brownies," I drawled. "First, let's get you home. Then we can go from there."

Her bright expression faded. "Do we have to go to the gym tonight?"

"Nope."

"Really?"

The happiness in her cry cut at me. "Really. You and me, tonight, babe."

"Awesome!"

The happy peal of her voice made me smile. Except . . . what was I supposed to do with her once we got to their house? Providing dinner was one thing. Six-and-a-half-hours of entertainment was something else entirely.

Filling out an application to rent the Frolicking Moose had taken up most of my morning, not to mention updating Dad on the current condition of my ribs, and Mom on her countless questions about Benjamin coming over. Although I hadn't done much today, I already felt tired.

With a sigh, I shook that off. Now wasn't the time. Now it was Ava-time. Step one: I'd see Benjamin's house and what I had to work with. I had a feeling that the father-run home would dictate what happened next.

Chapter Eight

BENJAMIN

With a sense of great trepidation, I slowed my run and turned onto my long, dirt-road driveway.

The house I'd bought when we moved to Pineville was just over a mile from the MMA Center, but the roads turned to dirt not far off of Main Street, and a long driveway separated the house from a road that wound back into the mountains. No one wandered this way, which almost negated my need for a security system, but I kept it anyway for Ava's sake. Some of the weirdos I'd encountered during my years in the MMA limelight had no sense of boundaries. I might be out of the spotlight, but reminders that I hadn't been forgotten popped up here and there.

The run felt good at the end of a long day, allowing me to loosen up. A sense of relief came with knowing Serafina would have Ava all afternoon. She'd texted me to confirm a safe pick up, complete with a picture of Ava smiling in the backseat. I couldn't stop turning my thoughts in that direction.

Had I sprung this on Serafina too soon?

Was this the right move?

Was this better, or worse, than having Ava at the MMA Center?

Serafina would provide Ava some much-needed girl time, not to mention an earlier bedtime, as well as more of a home life. But she'd be away from me. Not that hiding under the desk really equated to quality daughter-father time. Still, I wasn't sure that would make things better.

Parenting caused the worst kind of life-questioning.

Shoving that aside, I wiped the sweat off my brow and headed through the side door of my three-car garage. The SUV was parked on the far right, and still-unpacked boxes lingered in the garage months after the moving company had put them there. I ignored them and hurried inside, eager to see how the day had gone.

Once I stepped inside the back door, I stopped to listen. Not a sound met my ears. The back door opened right into our dining area, which led to the kitchen. Beyond a few walls were the living room, bathroom, pantry, and my master bedroom on the far side. Upstairs, Ava reigned.

A lone light in the kitchen illuminated the island in the middle, which was full of food pulled from the cupboards. Beyond that came the soft glow of a lamp in the living room.

Weird.

"Serafina?" I said quietly as I advanced into the house. No sign of her in the kitchen, but the dishes from breakfast and too many dinners had been cleaned up. A rosy light came from upstairs, where Ava's door was cracked open only an inch or two. Her night light. She must be in bed already.

"Sera?"

A shuffle of noise caught my attention from the couch. Serafina looked up, her eyes unmistakably bleary, from where she sat and stared at a photo. The bright frame glowed an obnoxious neon pink whenever the lights around the edge were turned on.

Inside that frame was a picture of Sadie and Ava the week before Sadie died.

My stomach dropped.

"Hey," I said.

Serafina didn't even smile at me, which made me feel cold all over. Exhaustion was bright on her face as she set the frame down. Yep. I'd sprung this on her too fast and too soon after a traumatic incident. She motioned to the couch next to her, lips rolled together. I sat on the edge of the cushion, careful to keep some distance between us.

"Everything okay?" I asked.

"Ava was fine. She's been asleep since 7:30."

7:30? I rarely even had dinner for her by then. "Was she tired?"

"Very."

Not much relief followed, considering Sera's voice was monotone, drawn, and there was something like uncertainty in her gaze right now.

"Thank you," I said and cleared my throat.

Sera winced as she leaned back against the couch, one knee tucked underneath her. Even though she was clearly worn out, she didn't haul out of here the way I would have. Instead, she hugged a pillow, folded her arms around it, and said, "Tell me what happened to Sadie."

All words left me.

I stared at her, speechless. First, how did she know Sadie's name? Ava must have told her. Second, this was the last question I expected. Maybe *where are the graham crackers?* Or *when will the laundry be done so Ava has clean clothes?* But not this.

She didn't look away. If anything, her gaze became more intense. I'd expected a lecture, maybe, like Ava's teacher. A review of how to parent from people that never had to bear the responsibility of a little life on their shoulders alone. So a question about Sadie?

I'd rather the lecture.

Serafina straightened. "I'd love some sort of explanation. You didn't tell me that your six-year-old lost her mother a year ago. That she hates school, doesn't want to do anything but watch that stupid tablet, and hasn't once done a chore in her life. She's also so far behind in school that I'm surprised they haven't dropped her a grade. There's no fresh food in the house, the laundry hasn't been done in so long I couldn't find clean pajamas for her, and I'm pretty sure you have a mice problem. Three of them ran in front of me today." She shuddered, then muttered with a vengeance. "Imma kill the little buggers tomorrow."

Frustration drove her tone, and I realized too late that it must have been a *really* hard day. Ava must have pushed her buttons and tried to watch the tablet incessantly or whined about not liking the food. All the food on the counter . . . had that been Serafina scavenging for dinner? I hadn't even left money for food. Had the laundry situation gotten so bad? Yeah, it definitely had.

I reached back, my hand on my neck, but before I could explain, she held up a hand. Then she drew in a deep breath, let it out, and met my gaze.

"I'm sorry."

I blinked, startled for the tenth time tonight. Wait, what?

"I'm sorry," she said again, and met my gaze. "That was . . . pretty harsh. I believe you're doing the best you can and it must be really hard as a single parent, but . . . I just felt a bit duped. Like there was a bigger mess dropped on my lap than I expected, but no boundaries set and no help given. Ava is amazing, but she needs more help than I thought. Did you know she barely knows her letters?"

"Her teacher and I have spoken about it."

She softened, then grimaced as she adjusted her position. Her arm braced against her ribs almost like an instinct now. "I just . . . I'm tired. It's been a long, somewhat unexpected day and

I'm sorry I took it out on you. I'm worried about Ava and my ability to help her, that's all."

True remorse filled her tone. I couldn't even doubt her sincerity, even though I normally did for almost-strangers. Were we strangers? How could we not be friends at this point? I cleared my throat again, only feeling marginally better for her apology. Her observations were warranted and spot on.

"This is my fault," I said. "All of it. The food, the laundry. The house. I'm a mess, Sera. I work so much that I crash on the weekend instead of cleaning the house. Both of us are . . . sort of walking disasters and it's not Ava's fault. She's a product of her ridiculous parents. If you wanted to leave, I wouldn't blame you. You're under no obligation and I'll write you a check for today's work right now."

She studied me for a moment, and I could tell she'd already considered that. Maybe she had been considering it for the last hour and a half that Ava had been sleeping. Panic filled me at the thought of her going, and it wasn't entirely tied to Ava.

"Tell me about Sadie?" she asked and it sounded like acquiescence. Like a willingness to move forward or get more information.

Whatever it was, it wasn't *no*.

I ran a hand through my hair, a bitter taste in my mouth. The last thing I wanted to discuss was Sadie, but it had to happen. Serafina deserved it. But the thought of Sadie's ugly shadow reaching Sera made me internally recoil.

How did she always manage to haunt me?

"Sadie was a fan of mine," I said, punching a fist into my other hand with a soft, quiet rhythm. My teeth clacked together while I tried to think about how to lay this story out. "She worked at the gym where I did most of my training and followed my career as it moved up and up and up. We would talk whenever I saw her and, eventually, I asked her out."

My chest ached just thinking about the early days with Sadie.

The good days, when we were just two people that liked to be around each other. Before the shadow of reality extended over even the best of memories.

"It was great at first. Young love. My career grew and she was at my side. Then it got . . . rocky. We fought. She grew jealous of other fans. Accused me of cheating on her all the time. Sadie was something of a party girl and loved the spotlight. It's like she craved attention. She was obsessed with the magazine features, social media, you name it. She ran most of my PR for a while, and that was a mistake I didn't realize I'd made at first."

Serafina hadn't moved from her position on the couch, but I didn't sense any tension from her, so I kept going.

"We were constantly breaking up, then coming back together. She couldn't control her jealousy and I stayed with her because she kept most of the other people off my back. Sadie, for all her faults, was key to my career growing the way it did. As a PR manager, she did her job very well. People had a way of just . . . doing what she wanted. Myself included. Then she let me know she was pregnant, and she broke up with me. For the last time."

Sera's eyes widened. Her lips rounded in silent shock. A bitter laugh bubbled out of my chest.

"Yeah. She left. At first, I thought it was one of her manipulations, but I soon realized it was real. I kept up with her as best I could. Paid child support. Saw Ava every chance I had, but Sadie never made it easy. She'd go missing for weeks and visit her family without telling me. She'd send me pictures and then just stop. Tell me lies about what the pediatrician was saying." I ran a hand through my hair. "It was a disaster. Then last summer Sadie was at a party with some friends. She must have been horribly drunk, somehow got ahold of her car keys, and tried to drive home. She crashed, then died the next day."

A warm hand settled on my wrist. I looked up to see Sera with a mixture of concern and compassion on her face. Did I look wrecked? I felt it. Those hours with Ava, at Sadie's bedside in the hospital, filtered back through my mind. Ava had been limp against my body, crying so hard in my arms that she'd thrown up, as Sadie slipped away.

"I don't mourn Sadie much," I admitted, and felt like a cold bastard for the harshness of the truth. "Maybe what we could have been, or her presence in Ava's life, but Sadie spent too long getting in between me and Ava for me to be sad she's gone. Sadie was determined to make me as miserable as possible."

"She sounds like a lovely person," Serafina murmured wryly, and something in her response crashed the tension in the air.

"She tried," I said, "but she hated me too much. Ava came to live with me last summer after it happened, which is when I came to stay with Mav. I needed his help. I'm not sure what life was like for Ava with Sadie. She refuses to talk about her Mom. But I don't think it was great. She's behind in school, seemed to spend way too much time on her tablet, and is wary of me."

"Think she dragged Ava with her to her parties?"

"Probably." He nodded. "Social events, social ladders, publicity. It was her love. Her god. She wanted more and more and more and I just wanted to get away from it. To get *Ava* away from it."

A dozen thoughts seemed to stream through Serafina's eyes, like a parade of sorrows, while she took all that in. My stomach still felt like a knot, but I couldn't deny there was also some relief. Sadie was out there now. I didn't have to live under her weight and the worry of what Sera would say when she found out.

Now Sera could stay or go.

"Okay," Sera whispered.

My brows rose.

"Okay," she said again, eyes on mine this time. "Thank you. That helps. The context will help."

"You're really going to stay?"

Sera softened. "Of course, Benjamin." She stood up slowly, and I wondered if her wince was from more than her ribs. She'd been so vague when I asked her about what happened with her brother. Had he hurt her somewhere else?

I scrambled to my feet.

"Thank you," I said. "I can't tell you how much it means. This will be better for her. So much better."

As always, she waved it off, downplaying my gratitude. She padded over to the front door, where a pile of shoes in various stages of muddy disaster were piled. Then she slipped into a pair of flip-flops on the edge and eyed it, like a monster she'd tackle the next day.

"I'll drive you home," I said. "Ava sleeps like the dead, and it's just a mile away."

She opened her mouth to protest, then nodded. "Thanks."

The ride to her hotel room was quiet as I dropped her off. She slid carefully out of the car, poorly attempted to hide a wince, then turned back to face me again. "Leave me some money for grocery shopping tomorrow?" she asked.

"Sure."

With a tired smile, she shut the door and disappeared. I waited until she made it back inside her room, then sent a cold glare to a man as he watched her go. The man held up two hands and stumbled away, singing under his breath. For several long moments, I sat there, lost in thought.

Then I turned back to home, Serafina cluttering my mind.

Chapter Nine

SERAFINA

That night, I stared at the dark shadows on the hotel ceiling and wished Benjamin was still there. Then I banished that thought.

For today, I'd had enough of Benjamin. The distance was good, even though I thought I could still smell him. He filled my head and took up space, even when I didn't want him to. Being in his house, privy to his past, only made it worse.

Although I'd seen him for no more than an hour all day, he lingered in the shadows of the day. The quiet corners of a house that was so forgotten that it would have felt sterile if there wasn't a dirty haze over it. The protein powder next to a fridge stocked with milk and oranges and not much else. Even the piles of laundry smelled a little bit like him. It felt a little like he'd followed me around all day, but hadn't said a word.

Weary didn't do justice to the state of my mind, but my exhaustion had advanced beyond sleep. Now I just felt wired, trapped in thoughts of Talmage, Ava, and Benjamin. Why, out of the three of them, did I feel like Benjamin was the most broken?

Frustrated, I punched the pillow and gingerly turned onto

my other side. I was too emotionally involved in this already. I shouldn't have asked him to explain himself. Should have just cleaned his house, stocked his fridge, and given him the receipt to pay me back later. It's what Mom would have done, and in these kinds of things, she always did the right thing.

But I'd asked.

And he'd answered.

He could have let it go. Refused to tell me the history between Sadie and Ava. But there had been enough concern and desperation in his eyes that he gave it all up. Now, both of us were mired deeper into this pool of . . . whatever it was. Deep enough that I wouldn't escape now. Not yet, anyway.

I could help with Ava, organize his life, and get his house clean. Eventually, he'd pull back together. That would give Talmage time to work through whatever he had going on, and then I could move onto my next adventure.

Because the whole nanny-turned-girlfriend thing had never sounded right to me. Wouldn't be right for Ava. Benjamin would get mixed up in his feelings of gratitude and affection for me being a positive influence over his daughter, think it meant something about the two of us, and we'd plunge into a relationship that would be a bad idea. Most of my relationships had been bad ideas born on infatuation, which only made a nomadic life easier. I almost always had something to leave behind, which motivated me to keep moving on. Nothing had ever inspired me to stay.

This time, however, I wouldn't recover so easily, so it would be better to just not go there at all.

With a sigh, I made the decision. I'd support Benjamin, love Ava, and do everything I could for them while I tried to help Talmage, soak up my new mountain adventure, and prepare for the next thing.

That's all this would ever be.

* * *

The next day, Maverick sent me an email to let me know they'd received my application and were processing it. *Expect to hear back in 48 hours,* he said. *I have no doubt you'll receive a confirmation. :)*

Which meant I had one goal in mind: stock Benjamin's house full of food while I waited.

That afternoon, I pinched $200 in cash in half and shoved it into my pocket while a squeaky-wheeled cart slipped into the Pineville Market. Warm sunshine heated my back with a gentle persuasion as Ava and I headed inside.

"The money your dad gave us," I said to an attentive Ava, "is going to feed you and your father for the next ten days. But I'm going to need your expert input. Are you willing to help me figure out some healthy, delicious meals that you want to eat?"

She cut me a suspicious glance. "You're not planning more sandwiches are you?"

"Don't insult me."

"Peas?"

"Not if you don't like them."

"Beans?"

"Maybe in a casserole with a lot of cheese?"

Relieved, she grinned. "Okay."

Once inside the store, I stopped to gaze around. I'd spent thirty minutes on the phone with Mom trying to get meal and snack ideas. Despite what Benjamin likely thought of my culinary skills, I'd almost exhausted my repertoire of family meals already.

"I'm thinking yummy stuff," I said as I grabbed a cart. "Liked sweet potatoes or salad that tastes like tacos or apples with peanut butter?"

Her eyes popped open wide. "Yes!" she cried, "I love apples with peanut butter!"

"Then let's go," I cried. "I'll even show you how to make a flower out of apple slices and peanut butter. You're gonna love it. Also, don't let me forget mouse traps. Those buggers gotta go."

Ava skipped along next to me. Like her father, she often communicated through throaty noises, whether they were grunts or squeaks of approval. Sometimes, she hummed. For the most part, she trotted along and tried to stuff the cart full of a constant stream of dessert. I appreciated her efforts and felt the same way, but turned her down more often than not.

And Ava was full of words.

"Then," she cried as I put a few groceries on the belt, "Mrs. Morgan said that I did a really good job with my letters and I got Star Student of the Week!"

A bag of pasta rustled in my hand as I whistled my congratulations. The cashier glanced up to me, looked to Ava, and back to me. Unabashed curiosity crept into her stare as she slowly started to scan each item. I tried to ignore it as some weird fluke—maybe I had food in my teeth or something—but the way her gaze darted between me and Ava had my hackles up.

Want to take a picture? I wanted to ask.

Once I finished unloading the groceries and pushed the cart forward with Ava standing on the side, the woman cleared her throat.

"So," she drawled. "You're that waitress from the Diner?"

"Yes."

She made a sound as she swiped green onions across the scanner. "And you're taking care of this adorable girl? I saw you drive up in his SUV. I admit, I was quite surprised. He's so . . . careful. So quiet."

His SUV rang through my mind. Were we talking about Benjamin because they were buddies? The feeling of having missed a step overcame me. Was there something odd about this situation or was that just me?

"You're a lovely girl, you know," the woman crooned to Ava.

Ava lifted one eyebrow. She carried many of her father's traits, but right then, I appreciated her skepticism the most.

"We're here to get groceries," I said. "That's all."

Delight illuminated the older woman's expression. "Indeed," she murmured over a carton of eggs, then leaned forward. "Is Benjamin Mercedy on the dating market again then? Or have you taken him off of it? How long have you been with him? A man like him with a waitress?" She shivered, as if with delight. "It's just too *good*. Patrice will never believe this!"

My hands clenched around the cart. Dagny had always rolled her eyes about *small-town mountain life* and the gossip that often moved like wildfire. I'd always ignored it, assuming she was being dramatic, but the proof lay before me now. Meddling, bored ladies with nothing better to do.

The phrase *a man like him with a waitress* skimmed through my mind. The temptation to show her just what this waitress could do to her attitude was tempting, but I let it pass. Then again, I'd listened in to any gossip about Ben just like anyone else. Although I hadn't badgered information from anyone. He *was* the local celebrity. His very presence put Pineville on the map and probably increased tourism by about ten percent.

Now?

I wanted to take one of those stale grocery bags and drop it over her head.

"I wouldn't know," I said coolly. "Can we please continue with the groceries?"

The firm rebuttal in my tone only seemed to delight her more. Her lips curled into a thin, coy smile as she murmured, "I'm sure you wouldn't."

My hackles rose. Any moment now and I'd snarl like a dog. She continued, oblivious to my bright annoyance.

"He seems like a wonderful father. He must be very busy. Does he keep a long schedule? He lives in the neighborhood just behind here, I thought. Bought the old Timm's place, I believe."

I ignored her.

She didn't care.

"It's been lovely to have someone of his . . . popularity . . . in our town. I'm curious . . . how did you meet him? You must not have been dating long."

My face flushed. *Keep calm, Serafina,* I told myself. Only Ava's presence kept me from absolutely losing it.

Without missing a beat, the cashier dropped all pretense of checking us out. Her hands rested on the scanner when she looked to my cheek, studied Ava, and back to me. Concerned lines formed in her brow.

"Is he having a hard time, then?"

Ava looked at me, face creased with uncertainty. She'd stepped off the cart to move closer to my hip, and I didn't think she was aware of the gesture. I doubted she understood the insinuation this woman had made about her father, but Ava seemed to know this woman was no friend.

"Manager!" I called as loud as I could. One of my arms lifted into the air as I strengthened my voice. "Can I get a manager over here?"

The woman gasped. "Whatever is wrong?"

"Manager!" I shouted.

Several customers glanced our way. I waved and hoped that would flag someone. Anyone. I didn't want to abandon the last forty-five minutes of work here to buy from another place up the canyon, but I would. My pride—and Ava's and Benjamin's —was worth at least that much.

The woman fumbled over a response, but thankfully a middle-aged man quickly headed our way from behind a desk. His presence snapped her mouth shut right away and prevented her from saying another word. His expression was wary when he approached.

"Can I help?" he asked.

I pointed to the woman. "Your cashier has made insinuations about my life, and the life of this child, that are no business of hers. She's made me uncomfortable with her questions even though I asked her to stop. Can I get someone else to check us out, or shall I just leave all of this here? At this rate, I wouldn't be comfortable returning and you've just lost several hundreds of dollars a month in sales."

Gaping, the woman simply stared at me. I met her gaze with a level one of my own. *Take that you nosy old biddy*, I thought.

"Of course," the manager said. "Take a break," he added as a terse aside to the cashier. The woman's nostrils flared as she huffed, stepped back, and slowly wandered away, as if lost. By the time she'd disappeared into a back room, the manager had nearly finished with our groceries. We didn't speak a word as I handed him the cash, gathered the bags into the cart, and thanked him for his time.

Ava followed solemnly at my side as we walked out to the SUV, loaded it up with careful attention to my rib, and then climbed into the car. The entire ordeal exhausted me. Tension followed me like a shadow until I sat in the driver's seat, gripped the steering wheel in my hand, and let out a scream.

Then I realized I still had a six-year-old in the car.

To my surprise, she giggled.

"You okay, Sera?"

"Fine. Just . . . frustrated. Do you ever get frustrated?"

Ava peered out the window. "Yeah," she said quietly. "Sometimes kids at school are mean to me and I get frustrated then."

She plucked at the bottom of her shirt, in a gesture that must have somehow been soothing to her. My heart cracked a little.

"I'm sorry kids are mean to you."

She gave a little shrug. I loosened my grip on the steering wheel and sighed. "Sometimes, at the end of a bad day, you just need to scream."

A twitch of a smile appeared on her lips.

"What do you say about heading home, putting these groceries away, and getting you some apples and peanut butter in a flower?"

Her whoop of affirmation started us home and I instantly felt better. Something about Ava soothed my rattling bad days.

Chapter Ten

BENJAMIN

By the time I jogged home the next day, I couldn't help a twinge of stress.

Would Serafina have had another hard day? Would she be ready to walk out again? Although she'd seemed fine when I dropped the car keys off at her hotel room this morning, there was no telling what havoc Ava could do to a single woman without kids.

Not having Ava at the MMA Center was both a massive relief and a distraction. At least when Ava was there I could see her, talk to her. But my trainees were already more focused the last two days because *I* was more focused. I made progress on projects faster than I'd expected without worrying about dinner, or homework, or fending off calls from her teacher.

Maybe, with a few more days like this under my belt, I could wrap up a few things and make it home before Ava went to bed. A bedtime routine sounded like a great connecting point, even if we still had mornings.

When I slipped through the garage and into the back door, the smell of bacon and lemon filled the air. A quiet song played in the background, accompanied by a low hum that made me smile. The lights were mostly on, except those near the stairs. Ava's pink night light glowed from her door, which was open just a sliver.

I closed the door quietly. "Hello?"

"In here," Serafina called.

Shock rendered me speechless as I advanced into the room, warmed by the jog. Cool air blew from an overhead vent while I tried to comprehend what I saw. Serafina stood on a stepstool, her hair tied away from her face. She wore a black apron and had every single cupboard in my kitchen open. Pots, pans, dishes, cups, utensils, and more littered the counters. Not to mention clusters of food I'd never seen before, and a piece of paper with two lists scrawled on it.

"Hey," I drawled.

"Sorry for the mess." She reached in vain for something on a top shelf with her right arm and grimaced. "Just in the middle of something."

"Let me get that."

"Thanks. Still just a bit sore."

She stepped back with a little smile as I reached past her, pulling an old box of unused sprinkles from the back of a cupboard.

"Interesting," she murmured, head tilted as I passed them to her. With a lift of my hand, I gestured to all the things scattered around.

"What's going on?"

She bit her bottom lip and looked adorably sheepish. "Sorry, yeah. I just . . . got lost down a rabbit hole. Think you can ignore this for one night and morning? I'll have it all finished tomorrow."

"Sure. What are you doing?"

"Organizing."

She said it brightly as if it should have been so obvious. Clearly, she'd put the $200 that I'd left to good use because I definitely hadn't bought sweet potatoes or avocados. Before I could form an opinion on how I felt about the rampant chaos in the kitchen, she broke the silence.

"You didn't seem to have any sort of system in place. I found spices in three different places. The cups were by the pantry, but the plates by the fridge, so with your permission, I thought I'd consolidate."

She pulled her hands together in a gesture meant to show that things were a bit wild and she wanted them back to something more normal.

"I mean, it's cleaning," she continued with a flip of her hand, "so if you do care then I can put all the dust back."

"No, this sounds great, thank you."

She grinned and I realized she'd been a bit nervous about my response. "Awesome. How was your day?"

The question startled me. I didn't recover from it well, but she was kind enough to not point that out. It had been since, well, *never*, that I'd had someone to ask about my day. With a large family like mine, chaos had always abounded between me and my siblings. Sadie hadn't been the question-asking type, either.

"Uh . . . good," I finally said. "I'm a bit more efficient when Ava isn't with me, so thank you again for what you're doing. I miss her," I added, "but I'm getting more done."

"She misses you."

Sera said it with a straight face and all the sincerity I could have wanted, but I still found myself doubting it. "How can you tell?"

Her brow puckered. "She doesn't really talk about you that much, but she watches for you. It's like she expects you or wants you home but doesn't want to admit it."

I grunted. Certainly wasn't the same as Ava throwing herself into my arms, but it was something. And it sounded real. Sera hadn't made it up to make me feel better, which actually made me feel better. I'd much rather hard truth over contrived fluff, no matter how difficult the truth was to swallow.

And Ava watching for me? I'd take it as a good sign.

"Thanks," I said.

Sera turned around, untying her apron as she went. The movement drew my eyes to the small of her back, then lower. I looked away. Nope. Definitely couldn't start ogling my new friend. Nanny? What was she?

Nope. Not nanny. Wasn't going there, even if I didn't know why.

"Change from the $200 is on the table," she said as she folded the apron and put it on top of a stack of unused kitchen towels I had vague memories of buying months ago, and then being unable to find. In their absence, we'd been using bathroom towels.

"Ava fell asleep just before you got home. Her homework is in her backpack and she helped me make her lunch for tomorrow. Dinner is in the fridge."

"Wait, what?"

Her casual list, rattled off so easily, sent my mind reeling. She'd gone shopping, had change from it, helped Ava do her homework, started to organize my kitchen, put my daughter to bed, and made both lunch *and* dinner?

Serafina moved over to the table and slowly pulled a jacket on. Clearly, she still favored her ribs. The bruising on her face had receded slightly, but still appeared painful.

"Ava requested BLTs for dinner," she said, "which is funny because she's so anti-sandwich, but what do you do? I made a BLTA for you because you seem like the healthy kind that would want avocado to go with it. There's an extra that you can have tomorrow for lunch, if you do that kind of thing. And I put on my list to buy you some containers for leftovers because that will be a thing now. So maybe just leave that change from the groceries? I think there's enough to buy the containers."

My mind raced to catch up, but before I knew it, she had grabbed her ratty black backpack and moved toward the back door. Did she ever stop moving? I snagged the keys off the counter and followed behind.

"Thank you, Sera," I managed. "This is beyond what I ever expected. I sort of thought you'd just watch Ava and crash on the couch after she went to bed."

She smiled. "No problem."

Or maybe that's just what I would do, which made me feel like a bit of an underachiever. No wonder our life was disorganized chaos.

We fell into silence at first as I pulled out of the driveway. My mind spun with more than just surprise, and a little annoyance, that she so easily managed a world that I stumbled over every single day. As if Ava and food and the world of parenting should have been easy.

No, more frustrating than that was the delicious smell of her shampoo. Coconut, which had always been my weakness, and a hint of lime. When we pulled up to the hotel, which I still hated for her, she reached for the door handle, then stopped. Her words came haltingly at first.

"Do you have an issue with people gossiping about you?"

My entire body tightened, like I prepped to take a blow that never came. No amount of mental relaxation softened my muscles though. I strove for casual, but my question came out with a bitter edge.

"Why?" I asked.

Serafina's brow rose. She shrugged. "No big deal, just curious."

"It's a problem," I said quietly.

She frowned. "Well, that's stupid." Her gaze cut out to the parking lot. "Anyway, I'll see you tomorrow, Ben. Thanks again."

With that, she departed with a wave and a flounce of her

hair. I watched her all the way to her room, let out a long breath, and then muttered a curse.

Long after she was gone, the car still smelled like Serafina.

* * *

The next day, Serafina dropped into the MMA Center around 10:30. The smell of syrup and fried food drifted off of her. She wore her usual Diner outfit, jeans and a black t-shirt with a mostly-clean apron over the front. Her hair spilled out of her ponytail when she stepped inside. Her expression was bright, eyes crinkled with a smile as she greeted my receptionist. I'd just finished a phone consultation when she walked up with her usual winning smile.

"Hey," I said. "Everything okay?"

"Better than that." She slapped something onto the counter. When she moved her hand, a silver key lay there. My head lifted.

"The loft?" I asked.

A lopsided grin swept across her face and swiped my heart with it. For a breathless moment, I couldn't respond. Could barely take her in. I was caught up in a moment of pure Serafina, and my heart squeezed.

"Yes!" she cried, eyes dancing. "I got it. Probably thanks to you, so I wanted you to be the first to know."

Light suffused her whole face. She seemed so far away from the girl that, just days ago, had been beaten around by her brother. My whole body eased under her joy.

"Congrats. That's fantastic. When will you move in?"

Her expression sobered slightly. "Tomorrow. They said it'll be move-in ready then, which is perfect. I still have stuff at Talmage's house, but . . ."

"Want me to go get it?"

My tone came out harder than I meant. It was supposed to be plain and innocuous but came out far too forceful. A flicker of something, maybe confusion, registered in her face before her usual laissez-faire attitude swept it away.

"Nah, but thank you. My parents will be here on Saturday and they'll take me. Mom called this morning and said that Talmage has been checking in with them every night and feels pretty awful about it."

"He should," I said.

Again, too forcefully. She ignored that.

"Anyway, I'm feeling a lot better and even more boxed in, so I'm going back to work today and tomorrow before my parents get here Saturday."

My eyes naturally drifted to her cheek, which did look much better. The angry bruise had faded slightly, the edges more of a green than black now. It still set my teeth on edge to see it on her face, however.

"You're up for that?" I asked.

She flashed me her usual smile. "Of course. I'll just carry plates individually instead of trays. Should be fine." She winked. "I practiced. Do you mind if Ava gets off the bus at the grocery store and drinks a milkshake at the Diner while I finish my shift? Dagny covered for me the past couple of days so I wanted to help her out. The shift ends at 3:00."

"Of course."

My quick response sent another smile through her. "Thanks. I appreciate that."

I motioned to the phone. "I'll call her teacher now and let them know which bus stop to get off on."

"Oh, even better. Thank you."

"Sure. Anything else?"

She paused, and I wondered if she felt the same thing as me. The camaraderie of working together for something or someone. Doing it together instead of alone. Being able to help her make it work felt just as good to me. It was this sort of teamwork that felt like a combo coming together in all the right places. Sadie and I never had this, not for all the years we'd worked together.

"No, thanks. That's it. Have a good day!" She turned to go, then called over her shoulder, "Chicken cordon bleu and scalloped potatoes tonight, so save some appetite. It's a good one."

Before my mouth could so much as water, she flashed me a thumbs up and was already gone.

Chapter Eleven

SERAFINA

While I waited outside the Diner on what I hoped was a well-timed break, I tried to fight off the occasional surge of panic that the bus would forget to drop Ava off or she'd go to the wrong stop and be waiting for me somewhere dangerous. The cars that whizzed by on Main Street didn't make me feel any better. Finally, a bright yellow bus appeared on the road and rumbled my way.

"Sweet relief," I muttered as Ava hopped off the bus. A bunch of other kids streamed out after her near the corner by the grocery store. I stood just outside the Diner and waved. She glanced over, saw me, waved back, and jogged my way.

"This is so cool!" she said as she grabbed my hand. "I get to go to the Diner!"

"I'm glad you think so," I said. "Because everyone is really excited to meet you."

The dumpy old place was loud when I brought her inside and set her at a special spot at the counter, a place where old men gathered to yell at the news and eat over-hard eggs in a veiled escape from their wives.

Dagny beamed from behind the counter.

"H-hi," she cried. "I'm D-dagny. You must be our g-guest of honor."

Ava blinked. "I'm Ava. You talk funny."

"Ava," I said quickly, "that's not—"

Dagny cut me off. "It's f-fine. I do t-talk funny sometimes. It's called a st-tutter. I was born with it."

"Oh." Ava twirled on her stool, then her expression illuminated. "Can I have a chocolate milkshake?"

"Coming up!" Dagny said. "One d-delicious chocolate milkshake."

Ava bit her bottom lip and grinned. Dagny winked at me as I headed to one of my tables to close out their ticket. For the tenth time that day, Benjamin ran back through my mind, but I banished him. No, there was *no* reason to think about him. Or the way his eyes warmed when I'd gone to the MMA Center earlier. Or his easy help in making my schedule work. His lack of judgment for me coming back to work when another few days off may have been smarter.

"Sh-she's adorable," Dagny whispered to me in the back when I refilled a pop. "She has her father's i-intensity though."

"I'm realizing that," I quipped. With a quick peek to confirm that Ava was still distracted talking to Bert, who had somehow produced both a milkshake and a sticker book with glittering hearts out of nowhere. I turned back to Dagny.

Dagny's eyes widened. "H-how is it going? Are you and Ben a thing?"

"No! I'm just his . . . something."

"It's always the *something* they fall for. Y-you should know that b-by now."

"False."

"Not false. He t-trusts you with his d-d-daughter. That's so big for a scar-ry guy like him, I c-can't even."

Her words, though lightly spoken, struck something in me. Perhaps it was combined with my irritation after the grocery store incident, which I couldn't bring myself to tell Ben about and I secretly hoped Ava never mentioned again.

Yes, I wanted something between me and Ben, but Ava and her past were now a very real complication in the algebraic formula of this situation. In other words—no. I wouldn't be the nanny-turned-girlfriend.

That felt not right on *so* many levels.

"Look," I said and shot her a hard stare, "there was a time when Benjamin Mercedy could have owned my heartstrings and whipped them around like a child's toy. But . . . Ava deserves better than that. When he asked me to take care of her, I had to draw the line. Nothing will happen between me and Benjamin. I'll help him stabilize his life while I'm here, then when I leave, he'll be ready for the next step. That's it."

One of Dagny's fair eyebrows lifted. "Right," she drawled. "Y-you think it's going to b-be that easy?"

"No. It's going to suuuuuck." I groaned. "But it's the right thing, and it's for the best. That much I am certain of."

Dagny grinned, a slight, adorable gap between her front teeth giving her a charming grin. "All right," she drawled. "I c-can't wait to s-see this happen."

Sensing something in her voice, I asked, "What do you mean?"

Her smile broadened as she gestured toward the front, through the swinging door that had just opened toward me. A familiar bright pink cardigan and head of fluffy blonde hair stood outside, barely visible as the door swung open.

"Your parents just arrived and they're with Ava right now."

* * *

Dagny's smugness wasn't misplaced. My parents had a habit of finding little kids to sponsor as pseudo-grandchildren until my ovaries kicked into work, and said kids tended to fall in love with my parents. Some parents loved them, too. It's why Mom's daycare always had a waiting list. Her deepest joy was taking care of other people.

Twenty minutes later, I found myself shuffled outside, into the back of my parents' car next to Ava, while we sped toward Benjamin's house to grab Ava's swimsuit. Less than half an hour later, Ava splashed happily in the river that fed into the reservoir while my dad pretended to half drown in water barely to his knees. Ava saved him with a happy screech frequently.

"What a baby doll," Mom crooned.

I cast her a sidelong glance. We sat side-by-side on the bank, my toes stuck into the water that still held a spring chill. Although we had fluffy towels and blankets at the ready, Dad or Ava hadn't surrendered yet. I couldn't say that I was surprised. Mom had figured out what Ava wanted to do more than anything within minutes of arrival, then Dad set out to make that happen.

My childhood had been something of a dream. Which made the tragedy with Talmage all that much greater.

"She's pretty great," I said.

"Your father has wanted to be a grandpa for the last twenty years."

"Janeen," I drawled in a warning tone, "please don't—"

She held up two hands, bright pink nail polish flashing as she did. She'd swapped out a cardigan for a pair of knee-length shorts and a t-shirt that said, *I wear the name Mom like a crown.* The obnoxious flaunting of her stay-at-home-mom status hadn't ended with my high school graduation, apparently.

"I won't," she said. "I won't poke a single word in that direction so you can stop calling me by my first name, thank you very much. I was just making an observation about why he's so happy to jump in that ridiculously cold water with her."

Reluctantly I conceded. "They both look very happy."

Sunlight glinted off drops of water as Dad challenged Ava to a splashing fight. She had the same ferocity as her father, and it showed in her expression. With determination, she slapped those hands on top of the water while my father begged to surrender.

"So," I said when the silence stretched too far. "Have you seen Talmage yet?"

She cast a sidelong glance at me. "What do you think?"

"Yes."

"Yes. We stopped before we came to see you."

"I thought you weren't flying in until Saturday?"

"Dad found someone to cover his shift. He's trying to move out of the OR anyway. Getting too old for those long surgeries, he said. Couple of younger guys moving in who wanted the hours."

Not surprising. Dad's love of the OR had always been a running joke in our family. Somehow, he'd balanced his time away with the time he was home so that it never felt like he was gone all that much.

"And what did you think of Tal?"

"He's . . ." Her voice thickened. "Sicker than I thought. Looks awful."

"Yeah."

She sniffled and cleared her throat, then threw a bright wave when Ava looked back, giggling. I grinned at Ava.

"I think going to the pain clinic is a good idea," Mom said when her emotion cleared. "It's the next step. He's agreed to some counseling, too."

"An addiction group?"

Her lips tightened. "Hopefully," she said in a strained voice, "the counselor he agreed to can help him see the wisdom of that step."

What she didn't say fell through the cracks like grains of sand. Talmage was still in denial, then, even for my parents. Normally they could get through to him. Well, his path to better was progressing at any rate.

"He wants to go to lunch tomorrow," she said. "With you. We'll be there, of course. Thought maybe we could clear the air." She looked at me, and tears still sparkled in her eyes. Her hand settled on my bent knee. "It's totally up to you, baby girl. You don't have to see him if you don't want to."

"I'll see him."

She quirked a perfectly manicured eyebrow. "You sure?"

I nodded.

Several moments passed while she studied me, but I'd been sincere. I did want to see Talmage, particularly with them there to referee if needed. Part of me wanted to see him without the drug-induced rage. Another part of me just wanted to get it over with. Maybe have some validation that all of this had actually happened—as if my bruises and aching ribs didn't tell the story well enough.

A flash of Mr. Hyde Talmage flashed back through my mind, and a voice followed that asked *and what would your middle-aged parents be able to do against that angry force?*

Nothing.

But Benjamin would, and that thought came next with a little stir in my chest. As much as I hated thinking about it, it was absolutely true. Probably the only person that could keep me safe from Talmage was Benjamin. My thoughts filtered to Amber, who had effectively disappeared from my life since I left Talmage's house, then away again.

"I plan to stay here through the summer," I said to dismiss those thoughts. "I'll probably leave before the snow, so I'd like to smooth things over with Talmage. We're bound to run into each other here, and I'd like to be able to support him. Within reasonable, safe means."

Her hand tightened over my knee momentarily. "You're a good sister, but don't push your boundaries. Talmage has to earn your support."

I leaned my head on her shoulder and melted into her

warmth. Sunlight glinted off sparkling drops of water while Ava's giggle floated across the water, and the only thing that could have made the moment better was Benjamin.

Maybe Dagny was right.

Maybe I *couldn't* keep Benjamin at a distance.

Chapter Twelve

BENJAMIN

Ava didn't stop talking about Serafina's family the whole way up the canyon, from Pineville to Jackson City, the next day.

I didn't often leave the small mountain town to do more intensive shopping in Jackson City, but Serafina's invasion of my cupboards made my lack of food plainly embarrassing. Serafina had left me a detailed list—*plastic leftover containers* and *kid-friendly kitchen cups* and *hot pads for the oven*—included. Her requests had me lost in the Bed and Bath store for far too long. These were simple things, so why were there *so many* options?

"Then," Ava cried in a voice so animated I didn't have the heart to ask her to leave me in silence for just one minute, "when we were in the river, Gary threw me in. I wasn't even scared and I swam back to him and I'm a good swimmer, Dad. Janeen said so."

My stomach clenched thinking about her in the cold river water, but I let it pass. Apparently, I needed to get this girl out more. Her joy was evident. I'd wrongfully assumed she'd hate the cold water.

Star Dad, over here.

Gary, I assumed, was Serafina's father. My curiosity was

105

piqued. For having just met Ava, she'd had quite a fun time with him.

Once we finally finished the shopping, I avoided a group of people that looked at me with a familiar, questioning gaze. I could practically feel their question from here. *Is that Benjamin Mercedy?*

Ava skipped through the parking lot as we stepped into her favorite restaurant, an old-time place with wagon wheel chandeliers and flickering, fake candlelight. The waitresses wore 1850's style dresses with boots and sometimes a bonnet. They served kids drinks out of mason jars and a banjo played in the background. Before I could even get inside the restaurant, she'd dashed in ahead of me.

Seconds later, a happy scream followed.

"Sera! Gary!"

My daughter became a blur of hair as she darted across the restaurant and threw herself into the startled—but waiting— arms of Serafina. Sera grimaced as Ava plowed right into her injured rib, but she didn't push her away. She sat on the outside of a booth next to a woman I presumed to be her mother. A middle-aged man with graying hair and a lean build sat across from Sera. Gary, likely. And there, right next to Gary and luckily by the window so I didn't punch him out, was the bastard brother Talmage. Every muscle in my body clenched.

Sera recovered from her pain, gently pulled Ava into her arms with a bright smile, and a quick, "Hello! How are you today? I've missed you."

Ava chattered like a squirrel to both Serafina and her mother while I approached. A wary smile lived on Sera's face as I arrived. When her eyes darted to her brother for half of a second and then back to me, I knew why. I intentionally ignored him, but felt an edge of pleasure when he squirmed.

"Hey," Serafina said, and her bright smile was forced. She wore her hair down today in wild curls that, somehow, seemed more tamed than usual. Everything about her was easy and casual, from her jean shorts to her flip-flops and the sunglasses holding her hair back. Behind it, however, was a hint of something that seemed almost ready to break.

"I didn't know you were coming up to Jackson City," she said, adjusting Ava on her lap when Ava laughed at a figurine that Jeanette made out of a napkin. "We were just grabbing stuff for the loft."

I gave her a quick, warm smile. "There was a very specific list waiting for me."

True pleasure stole over her hesitation, and her grin widened. "You should get better help, then."

I smiled more broadly, surprised to be so happy to see her, and her grin slowly dropped. She blinked, then looked away. With an uplifted hand, she motioned to the man across from her.

"This is my father, Gary. Everyone, this is Benjamin. He's the guy that helped me find a place and he's the amazing Ava's father, as you know. This is my Mom and my brother," she added quickly.

Gary held out a hand, and I returned his firm handshake. He eyed me but I didn't sense any wariness in him. Talmage looked at his plate but mumbled something I ignored. He was a surprisingly thick guy. Broad shoulders, rough face. Thick hands. He looked like the cowboys and farmhands that roamed through Pineville in the summer. A few of them had come to me for classes, interested in heavyweight fighting. Looking at Talmage, I couldn't believe Sera had escaped.

"Much appreciated for helping my daughter," Gary said and pulled me from my thoughts.

"I'll always be here." My gaze lingered on Talmage and I couldn't help the hard edge in my tone. "If she ever needs anything at all."

Gary grinned at Ava when she tried to shoot the wrapper off

a straw, no doubt ignoring the sudden tension in the booth. Talmage still hadn't met my gaze, but I spared him the humiliation and ruffled Ava's hair.

"We happen to really like Sera," I added, but didn't know why the *we* in that phrase felt so important.

Serafina stiffened.

"Serafina's pretty awesome that way," Gary said with a wink at Janeen. "Like her Mom. Natural skill with kids. Looks like the two of you are here for lunch? Pull up a chair and you can join us."

Talmage tensed. The temptation to accept was almost too great to bear *just* to see him squirm a little bit more. Sera's eyes had widened with worry, however. Reading women wasn't my forte, but I could have sworn I saw a sense of pleading in there.

To spare her the stress of my antagonism toward her brother, I said, "No, thank you. That's a very kind offer but we don't want to interrupt any family time, and we're on a daddy-daughter date," I added when I saw the building reply in Janeen's kind eyes. "It was great to meet you. Ava, let's go."

Serafina reluctantly let Ava go, but there was a wash of relief in her parting smile. "Thanks for letting me see her," she said. "It was good to see you too. Good luck with that list."

When I put my hands on Ava's shoulders and steered her to another booth, I felt the burn of Serafina's gaze on my back. Maybe her brother would feel mine.

Chapter Thirteen

SERAFINA

Once Benjamin retreated to his own corner of the restaurant, thankfully out of sight because of the tall booths, I let out a long breath. Mom reached down and put a hand on my knee. Dad was talking to Talmage about one of his friends from home after he had fallen quiet.

"Wow." Mom's eyes were wide. She let out a low whistle. "Hello fighter, indeed. You didn't tell me he was such a hunk."

A weak smile was my only response at first. Thoughts of the way my stomach curled and my heart raced the moment I saw him swamped my mind. Rarely did I get to see Benjamin with Ava. His affection for her was obvious. And that smile? That honest, true, wide smile? The first I'd ever seen it, and that warmth couldn't be denied. Had the bottom dropped out from under me the moment that smile appeared? Because my heart had fallen and it still flopped around down there.

"Made me a bit breathless," Mom murmured. "Seems like a great father, too. Look how Ava has already gotten attached to you! They're both adorable." Mom set her jaw in her hand. "You've done good."

"Not helping," I sang.

She laughed. "I know! It's so fun to be a Mom."

Talmage, who remained mostly quiet during lunch, darted his gaze toward me again, then back to his plate. He tended to stare at the bruise, and I wondered if he remembered any of it. The brief thought that he didn't bring Amber registered in my mind, then I almost laughed. Amber would never slink out of her hole to come here.

We'd already been here almost an hour. Our plates were picked clean, but Dad had insisted on pie and Mom agreed. Me? I'd rather go back home. But the loft wasn't really home yet, was it? Benjamin's house rose through my mind. I pictured myself curling up on his couch, a blanket around me, and falling asleep without rib pain. Benjamin in the kitchen, or mowing the lawn, with Ava singing a dramatic cartoon song at the top of her voice.

Then I shoved that away.

Nope.

Wasn't home. But maybe I wanted it to be.

But why wouldn't it be? my traitorous heart whispered. Even if my mind refused to acknowledge it, my heart had seen the fire in Benjamin's eyes when he saw Talmage. Heard the coiled threat in his voice as he stared my brother down. My heart was the one that wanted to curl up inside Benjamin and never leave. Today's protective display only made it worse.

My declaration to stay distant and friendly felt pathetic against the waves of adoration and affection that crashed on me now.

Part of me hated seeing Benjamin react that way to my brother, even with justifiable cause. Hated to see Talmage reduced to the miserable state he was currently in. Hated the way I tried hard not to watch Talmage carefully. Remembered the rage that flashed in his gaze. The sound of his shouts. His hands shook as he sat at the table now. One of them was on the table in a fist so tight his knuckles had turned white.

They were two different men, Mr. Hyde Talmage and my

brother. The one here at the restaurant was pale, a shadow of the old Talmage. The skin slightly sallow. When someone spoke unexpectedly, he twitched. But he tried hard. When my parents picked me up after I'd checked out of the hotel, they had all my stuff from his house in their trunk. I silently appreciated not having to go back there. Talmage was sitting in the front with dad when I carefully maneuvered into the back.

He laid eyes on me and said, "Sera, I'm so sorry."

I'd nodded and said, "Let's get you better."

The stoic tears in his eyes had faded into silence while Mom and Dad picked up the chatter, and now we sat here in the slightly awkward booth and tried to act like everything was going to be all right. That was fine. I didn't want to harp on Talmage. Didn't want to shame him. Poke him. Prod him. At some point, we all had to move forward into something better.

But would it?

My parents were trying to help Talmage with his obvious pain medication addiction, but it had to be beyond that. His shady girlfriend, and the way he screamed at me, spoke to something else. Amber had brought more into his life than just pain meds. I had few doubts that Talmage had moved into different reprieves. This was so much bigger.

No, Talmage was moving into a different sphere. For some reason, I didn't think my parents saw that fully yet.

Maybe they didn't want to.

With those heavy thoughts, the waitress appeared with our pie. Dad dove in with gusto, and I poked at the piece of triple berry with ice cream that Mom and I had decided to share. She put on a good face, but only half of the pie ended up getting eaten and only one bite was mine. Talmage wolfed a piece of apple down, and said little.

Once back in the car, and while Mom and Dad chattered in the background, I stared at the canyon walls as he headed back to little Pineville.

I thought only of Benjamin and Ava.

* * *

Mom let out a long breath the next afternoon, then clapped her hands together. A little bit of packing dust cleared from her fingers and floated in the air before it slipped out the open window.

"It's lovely," she declared. "Empty, but . . . lovely."

I silently disagreed. The loft was open, spacious, and filled with sunshine. Sure, there wasn't much in the way of furniture. A simple twin bed, woven laundry basket, and closet where all my clothes hung, hidden by a gauzy drape. One couch filled up the center of the room, where a second-hand flatscreen was propped near the far wall. In between both of those was a braided rug I hadn't been able to turn down.

For six months, it would be just right.

Mom closed the fridge, now freshly stocked from her own credit card with my favorite foods. She'd meal prepped four different dinners for me and stashed them in the fridge, then organized my food pantry by color, size, and shape. She'd also purchased a large crockpot—bigger than I'd ever need—and dropped a roast into it that would have fed a family of four. Potatoes, onions, and carrots simmered away in a delicious au jus that had my stomach growling.

"A crockpot will be just what you need for those two cuties you work with," she'd said with a wink. "They're a lifesaver, my girl."

In a weird moment of realizing I had become my mother, I could finally see that she'd done to me what I did to Benjamin. I loved it.

Dad hooked an arm around me and gently pulled me into his side. The ache in my rib had been slowly subsiding with over-the-counter pain meds, but he still handled me with care. Pain from the bruise had started to fade, but the discoloration was still there.

"Love you, kiddo. Super proud of you and all you're doing. I'm sorry again about what happened with Talmage. We'll make sure it won't happen again. I think . . . I *hope* . . . he's on a better path now."

Get rid of Amber, I thought, *and he has a chance.*

I wrapped my arms around Dad's waist and drew in a deep breath. The smell of spicy aftershave brought floods of childhood memories with it. Safe places. Giggling summer nights. Long winter days playing Monopoly and drinking hot chocolate.

"Thanks, Dad. And thanks for helping me move in and gather some things."

He tutted under his breath. "Your wandering spirit is sure something. I can't imagine fitting everything that I own in a few bags."

I grinned. "It's the nomad's life."

"Will it be this way forever?"

"Unlikely. I just need to find a reason to stay somewhere, I guess, when there are so many things to see in the world."

He laughed, pressed a kiss to the top of my head, and pulled the keys to their rental car out of his pocket.

"Ready, honey?"

Mom cast one last look around, then reluctantly nodded. With teary eyes, she fluttered over and pulled me close. Her grip on my shoulder was so tight it would have hurt if I didn't crave it so much.

"I love you."

"I love you too, Mom."

With a sniffle, she pulled away, squeezed my hand, and followed Dad out the door. I waved from the window as they climbed into their car and slipped away, Mom blowing kisses the whole time.

For several long minutes after they left, I felt their absence like a missing limb. Maybe this room *was* too empty now. Too big. Too much for me alone. Maybe I should have taken the offer to move back home . . .

Maybe . . .

My phone buzzed against my pocket. I reached back and pulled it out to see a text from Benjamin.

Benjamin: Business as usual this week?

Serafina: Yes! Sounds good to me. I'll pick her up from the bus stop tomorrow.

Benjamin: Thank you.

My heart gave a little *thump*. I didn't want this exchange to end on a business-like, cordial thank you. Didn't want this end at all, in fact. Despite the rustle of movement, life, and the smell of coffee from below, I felt too alone and too afraid. Talmage had agreed to give me time and space, but nothing felt stable anymore. My frazzled state of mind wasn't entirely Talmage's fault, either.

Benjamin owned this one. With his serious expression that I wanted to crack into a smile. The solidness of his very personality, like an immovable rock.

I wanted to text him back and say, *can I bring you Sunday dinner?* and then stay and eat with them and really see what Benjamin was like behind-the-curtains. All the time we'd ever spent together had been around other people. Except for the night in the hotel room, when I'd fallen asleep minutes after he'd arrived, I'd never really gotten to speak with *him*.

But should I?

My resolve to keep it platonic for Ava's sake rang back through my head with dying power. Before I could fall into a worsening abyss of overanalysis and the guilt that might follow, my phone jangled in my hands.

Like a sign from the god of don't-do-this-you-might-regret-it and the other god of do-it-or-you'll-never-forgive-yourself.

Benjamin: Your parents must be heroes. Ava hasn't stopped talking about them since we saw you yesterday.
Serafina: They are. I adore them.
Benjamin: They seemed very nice.

Unable to resist the temptation, I typed my next message with my teeth sinking into my lip.

Serafina: Even Talmage? What did you think?

Several minutes passed before his reply followed.

Benjamin: Let's say that I hope Talmage and I never have occasion to meet under any circumstance that results from him hurting you.

Despite the fact that he spoke about my brother, a warm flutter moved in my stomach. Part of my love of living a nomadic life had been the way I could meet people through my waitressing jobs, and then spend my days off with myself. Traveling the world solo meant the quiet evenings were all mine to do with as I wanted.

Today, however, a quiet evening alone sounded exactly *opposite* from what I usually wanted. Giggling with Ava or just being in the same room as Benjamin, even if I never once had his attention, sounded far better.

What an entirely new feeling.

Before I lost my courage, I sent my next message and held my breath.

Serafina: You up for a home cooked Sunday meal? My mom made way too much pot roast and I'm willing to share.

His reply came immediately after.

Benjamin: Only if you bring yourself over with it and stay to eat. We just rented a new princess movie, so you can't get out of that.

I let out a little squeal.

Serafina: Princess movies are my jam! On my way.

Chapter Fourteen

BENJAMIN

"I come bearing gifts!" Serafina cried.

I opened the front door to find her carrying a massive crock pot, clad in fuzzy purple slippers that would have frightened a lesser man, and several bags over her arm. A pair of aviators hid her eyes from me, but didn't dim the immediate joy I felt seeing her again.

"You do way too much for us already."

"I love it!"

"Then welcome," I said, "and let me take that."

She gratefully handed the crock pot over, and the meaty, home-cooked-goodness smell of a pot roast bubbled out. What smelled better than slow cooked potatoes, carrots, onions, or meat on a Sunday afternoon? Absolutely nothing.

Except maybe the waft of coconut that came in with her.

In the kitchen, she unburdened herself of the bags, then extracted a new coloring book, a package of paints, a t-shirt with neon green glitter that said *rockstar,* and a giant roll of cookie dough from one.

"From my mother." She slid the glasses on top of her head. "She moonlights as the Easter bunny."

My eyes widened. "All of that is from your parents?"

"Yep."

"Wow. No wonder Ava loves them." That felt awkward the moment I said it, considering the fact that I had also met them. Was I supposed to love them also? "Meeting your parents was fun," I added, in case she noticed the stumble.

She illuminated like a Christmas tree.

"They are very fun. I'm glad you got to meet them. They were obviously in love with Ava." She gestured to the gifts. "So thank you for letting them spoil her."

"They were so . . ."

"Extra?"

"Bright." I cracked half a smile. "I was going to say bright. Happy. *Fun.* My parents were always so serious. The best word for Mom is stressed-out, and Dad . . ." I trailed off. "He was . . . sad."

Her expression fell. "I read about your Dad. I'm sorry."

My eyebrow quirked. Dad had committed suicide years ago after a tragic accident left him paralyzed from the waist down. He'd battled hard for years, but finally succumbed to the deep depression that consumed him after.

"Where did you read about him?" I asked.

Not a hint of abashedness showed on her face, even though I was ready to grill her on what *else* she read about me . . . and whether she believed it. The privacy invasion of the media in my life had been a blitz. Ironically, Sadie had sheltered me from much of it through her job, but once she left, it hit like a firehose. Even now, I still felt twitchy about people knowing anything about me that I hadn't told them personally.

Serafina waved a hand. "In a magazine or something sometime after the gym opened, I can't remember."

"It's been hard to work through it because my family isn't big on communicating. There certainly isn't the same sense of support that I saw from your parents, unless you talk about siblings. Maverick has always been in my corner."

She smiled. "I can tell. You two have always seemed close. I mean, you're not tattoo-level like I am with him, but he seems fond of you."

A lot of thoughts occurred to me then. About my brother, this conversation, and the thought that had been rotating around my head that told me so much of her brightness probably stemmed from such unconditional parental love. But the one that thought that rose above all centered on her lips.

With forced effort, I pulled the silverware tray out of the dishwasher and focused on that. Serafina grabbed the cookie dough and slipped over to the fridge, her obnoxious slippers wide enough to sweep the floor with.

"I promised Mom I'd let Ava eat some of the cookie dough if you're cool with that, before we make the cookies."

I shrugged. "Why even bother to bake them?"

"A man after my own heart."

Something in that phrase caught me. That was Serafina. Her tongue was fast, blithe, and never embarrassed. I couldn't fathom how she did it. Before I could make an awkward response like *marry me right now,* she peered around and asked, "Speaking of, where is Ava?"

"Outside with a sprinkler."

Her head turned to look that way, and I caught her profile. Lovely, sloping nose. Elegant neck. Wild, curly hair. Somehow, it just fit her. The urge to grab her wrist and slam her against my chest was almost overpowering, so I turned back to a stack of clean dishes that sat on the counter before I went full caveman.

"Your parents left?" I asked over my shoulder as I tucked some bowls away.

Serafina dropped onto a stool as the sound of a happy, girlish shriek came from outside. Ava darted by, skirting the edge of the sprinkler like she didn't want to get wet, even though that had been her exact request twenty minutes ago.

"Yeah." She propped her chin in a hand. "Their flight leaves this evening and they wanted to stop a few places before they went."

"Any word from Talmage?"

I managed to ask the question without adding *the bastard* at the end, the way I did in my head. Only her familial, genetic relationship with him and the pain in her eyes every time this topic came up stopped me. Still, I wasn't about to act like he didn't exist. Both of them needed to know I was tracking him.

"No." She tapped her other fingernails on the counter. "Which is probably just as well, for now. I texted him before I came over, but haven't heard back."

"If you ever need to go see him, let me know. I'd be happy to go with you if you needed or wanted someone else there."

The tension in her bled away. She smiled and it warmed her eyes.

"Thanks, Ben. Such a great friend."

I don't want to be your friend, I almost said.

I held her gaze, feeling like a sucker punch to the gut when she didn't look away. If gazes could ignite, my house would have been on fire. Despite the softness about her that always drew me in, I sensed an untamed wildfire beneath all that curly hair.

Seconds later, a dripping wet Ava stormed into the room.

"Sera!" she cried, then ran into Serafina's awaiting arms and clutched her legs tightly. Wet impressions remained behind, but Sera ignored them to wrap her arms around her. The moment broke. With a long exhale, I turned back to the dishwasher. Watching Serafina with my daughter gratified an instinct deep inside me.

"You are an expert sprinkler-runner," Serafina said, crouched down next to her. "I've been watching and I'm impressed."

"Thanks!" Ava's nose scrunched as she stopped jumping long enough to peer on the counter. "Did you bring dinner?"

"I did."

"Hooray!" Ava leaped again, whooping, and disappeared out the back door. Laughing, Serafina followed to the doorway. She stood there and watched for several minutes, her hip cocked to the side in an attractive curve as she occasionally called out a score from 1-10—it was almost always 15. I finished the dishes, feeling marginally better for having done some work in my own home, then followed over. I stood a few steps away, just to keep my hands where they belonged, and not on the small of her back. Or the curve of her ribs. The hollow of her neck.

The very soft pillow of her lips.

"Ben?"

Jerked from my thoughts, I looked up to see Sera watching me with an amused smile. "Did I lose you?" she asked.

"Sorry, what?"

She tilted her head outside in a motion that suggested she'd already said something while I mused about kissing her until she was weak in my arms.

"Ava. She doesn't have a lot of friends around here, does she?"

My gaze filtered through our backyard. There was no fence and only a small patch of grass that Ava ran through now. The property opened onto the curve of the river not too far away, and contained mostly scrub and bush. Along the river edge was a foot trail that runners and people who wanted to walk their dogs off leash would occasionally slip by. A few houses littered the road farther back into the canyon, but the trees hid them, and there were only two or three. Pineville was only a mile or so to the north, but the house had been built into a curve of the mountain so only one or two properties were visible from "town".

"Ava's never been very excited about other kids," I said with a frown, thinking back to the times when Sadie had still been alive and I visited Ava. "Even as a toddler."

"Was she not around them much?"

"It's hard to say."

Serafina's brow puckered as she seemed to think that over. "Dagny knows almost everyone here. I wonder if she could introduce me to some of the parents of the other girls. Maybe we can do some play dates or something."

"That sounds great."

She made a noise of agreement, but hadn't peeled her eyes away from Ava. Water flashed in the fading sunlight as it sank behind the mountain at our back. Now that I watched Ava, it did seem sad that she was out there by herself. But to reach out to other parents and schedule play dates? Never would have thought of that.

I ran a hand through my hair, shocked yet again by the vastness of this parenting job. No one trained me for this. How the hell was I supposed to know that Ava needed playdates with girls her age? Maybe it was obvious to everyone but me. To me, Ava was shy. Did that need to be fixed?

Serafina distracted me from my mental spiral when she put a hand on my arm. The heat of her fingertips brushed against the hair on my forearm, then was gone, a trail of fire in its wake.

"I'm starving," she said as she moved toward the pot roast. "Can we eat now?"

"Yes, please."

Anything to get my mind off you, I mentally pleaded, then whistled for Ava.

* * *

One hilarious dinner, two hungry girls, and three helpings of pot roast later, darkness had started to settle on the world outside. Twilight brought the quiet call of nesting birds, the scent of dry sage, and the gentle calm of the mountain air as it wafted inside. With a stomach full of delicious food, the promise of cookie dough later, and Serafina's rich coconut smell in my hair, I wanted to do this evening again.

And again.

And again.

Ava hopped into a quick bath while Serafina and I, without the need to converse, cleaned up dinner.

Now, the princess movie threw light on the dark room as the three of us finally settled on the couch. Serafina sat on the other side, one leg tucked under her the way she always had. Ava plopped herself in between us, a ratty old blanket in her hands. I took the other end of the extremely comfortable couch and tried to pretend I wasn't picturing *me* in the middle, with one girl snuggled up on either side.

Just before the movie started, Serafina whispered something in Ava's ear. She darted upstairs and returned seconds later with a brush and several hair ties. Without a word, Ava settled on the floor in front of Serafina. The movie started with the quiet purr of a brush through still-wet hair. Relief that I didn't have to be the one focusing on those braids followed a tight knot of affection.

This was so easy for Serafina.

So natural. I'd never seen anything so attractive in my life. I kept my focus on the movie so I didn't send too-hot looks to my daughter's . . . what? Friend? She certainly wasn't here to work tonight, so she wasn't a babysitter or nanny. Hardly an employee. Caretaker? That sounded too . . . old.

What would happen as Sera was seen with Ava? For the most part, the media left Ava alone. They'd come into the MMA Center to deal with me, but rarely was I pursued out of that anymore.

But if I dated someone, would that change?

While the movie played and my thoughts grew in intensity, I

found myself caught in a storm of potential web of social media articles and news displays that would plaster Sera's face all over the world. The potential headlines ran through my mind like a ticker-tape.

MMA Star Dates Nanny.

Ben Mercedy Steps Into a New Ring

Classic blunder. Could have seen that one coming miles away. And I already had seen it coming. In fact, I'd thought about a relationship with Serafina way too much the past couple of days.

So why did I invite her to stay and eat with us on our day off? Why did I feel like this house wasn't quite so empty when she was in it?

Nannies took care of the kids, not the dads. Serafina was definitely taking care of more than just Ava. She'd started to turn both of our lives into something not-so-overwhelming. Which meant she wasn't the nanny. More like my life manager. I almost snorted. That was probably exactly what I needed.

Until I felt the gentle brush of a stray toe and heard a quiet sigh, I hadn't realized how deep into my thoughts I'd spiraled. My gaze had remained on the TV, but hadn't comprehended a single image. At least thirty minutes had passed and I couldn't even remember the main character's name.

When I glanced over, my heart leapt into my throat.

Ava had fallen asleep sprawled on top of Serafina. Sera hadn't noticed yet, her bent elbow propped on the end of the couch and her head resting in it. She watched the screen with rapt attention. Her fingers toyed with a curl of Ava's hair where it looped at the end of her braid.

Serafina looked up to me as if she sensed my gaze, then at Ava, and her own smile stole across her face. The movie, and the presence of my daughter, saved me from grabbing Serafina's face and kissing her breathless. The main character fell off her horse and into a well. While she wept quietly at the bottom I whispered, "So what is it with princesses anyway?"

Serafina rolled her eyes, but she smiled too much for me to take her for face value. "It's . . . I don't know. For girls this age? It's just fun to imagine."

"The tiaras?"

"So important. Ava's six," she said quietly. "Things like that are just . . . *fun*."

"Fighting is fun."

"For her thirty-something father, yes. But she's a little girl."

"Please tell me there's something else besides princess movies Ava and I could do together."

Serafina quieted her laughter. Ava didn't even stir, but Serafina hadn't stopped playing with her hair yet. I wondered if Ava liked that kind of touch. Like me, she'd always been prickly about people in her personal bubble. All those boundaries seemed to have melted away the moment Serafina appeared in her life. Maybe Ava was just waiting for the right person.

Same, baby girl, I thought. At least my daughter and I had one thing in common. If there was anything I wanted to happen, it was Serafina's touch. Her hands on my skin. Her lips working against mine until both of us were out of air.

"So much you could do together," Sera finally said. "Make the cookies with her. Go shopping. Paint your toenails."

I held up two hands. "Whoa."

"For your daughter!" she whisper-cried. "C'mon. You don't have to show them off. Anyone would understand."

"My guys would destroy me."

Her eyes sparkled when she said, "It might be worth it to win over some affection? At the very least, let me buy her some new clothes."

"Hey! I just bought her those clothes."

She grimaced. "I know."

"They're girly and pink!"

She tilted her head back and forth, an uncertain grimace on her face. Appalled, I put a hand on my chest and pointed to Ava's pajamas.

"Pink," I said, as if that explained everything.

"Pink GI *Joes*." She shook her head, hair bouncing. "Sorry but she likes bunnies and kittens and tiaras and female superheroes. Plus, she doesn't like pink. She told me that yesterday. She prefers purple."

I blinked several times. Sure, I'd desperately bought most of her clothes when I realized, one day before school started, that she'd outgrown almost all the stuff we'd brought from Sadie's house. Just grabbed all the clothes in the right size—which had actually been the wrong one—when I was at the store. Ava had never seemed excited about her clothes, but what kid cared about clothes? When I was little, they were my ticket to getting outside and in the mud. Mom wouldn't let me play naked, though heaven knows I tried.

Serafina put a hand on my arm. "Don't beat yourself up. You're doing great, Ben. You clearly love her. She just . . . she's sort of hesitant about you and I haven't figured out why yet. But I will. I promise. In the meantime, some toenail polish, female superhero pajamas, and a tiara or two would go a long way."

My emotions must have been more transparent than I expected, because she'd driven right to the heart of my thoughts.

"Thanks," I said.

Ava let out a little sigh and wiggled her shoulders. While Sera turned off the princess movie with the remote, I wrapped my arms around Ava's shoulders and hefted her into my arms. She lay completely limp against me, her head on my shoulder, and I couldn't deny that feeling her weight gave me a father's reassurance. There was something about being able to carry her up the stairs and tuck her into bed that felt like a win. Maybe because my own father couldn't have. Maybe because I had her in my life, now. When Sadie was alive, this sort of simple routine had never been an option.

Which meant that Serafina had a point.

I was doing okay, and I did love Ava. Things as a single father were stressful and imperfect, but they'd been blind and terrifying when Sadie kept Ava from me. When she told lies that I knew were lies but couldn't prove. I'd much rather have stress and imperfection than what it had been.

As I slipped the covers over her and pressed a kiss to her forehead, I knew that I'd never change anything. Even if Ava continued to be weird with me, I'd love her. Even if she chose Serafina over me, I'd love her.

When I slipped out of Ava's room, Serafina still stood in the middle of the room, muttering something under her breath as she jabbed at the remote with her thumb.

"Stupid thing."

It might have been the positive parenting moment that I'd just had upstairs, or the power of the night with unfiltered Serafina and a happy Ava. Or it may have just been a gradual weakening of my guard that had finally given way. But I jogged down the stairs, strode over, and took the remote from her hands. Then I didn't give her hands back.

With one press, I had the TV off and the remote tossed on the couch. The only light in the room came from the slight glow of Ava's night light upstairs and the light from around the corner of the light over the stove. My palms held Sera's hands in mine, and I could feel her breath in the stillness that followed.

"Thanks," she whispered, but I couldn't remember why.

My hand lifted, brushing a stray hair away from her face. The tip of my finger traced the edge of her face. I felt like a totally different man. Distantly aware of every move I made, but watching as if I were someone else. As if I wasn't going against all wisdom. As if I wasn't planning on laying the deepest kiss on her lips that I could possibly imagine.

"Sera," I whispered.

Her breath hitched as I lowered my face until I was close enough to feel the burn of her heat. My hand settled on her neck, my thumb tracing her cheekbone. The bruise from her brother was a light shadow now.

Being this close to her had never felt *this* good in my dreams the past few nights, and I thought my dreams would never be as good as reality. When her hair rustled as she tilted her head back to look into my eyes, the sweet scent of coconut rose with it.

My other arm snaked around her back and pulled her into me. She sucked in a sharp breath as I gently pulled her chest into mine, careful of her rib. She hesitated, then set her hands on my shoulders. I could feel the imprint of each of her fingers burn into me.

"Tell me now if you want me to stop," I whispered thickly, "and I will let you go. But if you tell me otherwise, I want to do what I've been dying to do since you walked in the gym."

Her eyes were mere glimmers in the darkness as she studied me, and I wondered what she saw. Did she fear me like she feared her brother? Did she *want* me to ravish her with a kiss that would burn us both?

How could she not feel this power between us?

Words came to her lips, but never materialized. She seemed locked in a battle until her hand slipped across my collar bone and onto my neck. I shivered at the heat of her palm on my open skin.

Her hand came to my face next, the palm resting against my cheek. Starved for the touch, I closed my eyes and leaned into it. Her fingers curled slightly, accepting the desperate movement.

"Ben," she whispered. "I—"

The crushing sound of my phone broke the quiet house. I muttered a curse when the ringtone of the song *Let the Bodies Hit the Floor* peeled through the air. If it were any other caller, I could have ignored it.

But I couldn't. Not this one. This call was trouble.

I pressed my cheek to hers and drew in another tantalizing, torturous breath. The coconut twined through my nose until it hit my brain and I thought I'd lose it. My grip on her waist increased until I thought I'd drop her to the couch and kiss her there, but I pulled away. The moment shattered.

"I'm sorry," I whispered, my lips against her cheek. "I can't ignore that."

With a growl, I let her go, stalked to the other side of the room, and clicked the *accept* button just to get the stupid song to shut up. Then I snapped, "What?" into the phone.

"Benjamin," my sister-in-law Mallory drawled, but there was an edge of sharpness to her tone that didn't mean anything positive. "Always so good to hear your radiant voice. I call with news. Brace yourself. You aren't going to like it."

Chapter Fifteen

SERAFINA

When Benjamin shoved away from me and crossed the room like a wary panther, my mind scattered like a dozen whirling butterflies.

Geeeeez. What just happened?

My hands trembled as I lowered to the couch and pushed my hair out of my face. Had I dreamed all that? The look in his eyes as he crossed the room to me, grabbed my hands, and then my heart? Hadn't I dreamed of this moment every day of my life the past few days and maybe before that too?

Yes.

And it ended on a *phone call*.

Disbelief permeated my every thought, followed by an intense rage. Couldn't he just ignore the phone? Not that the sharp, grating tones of *Let The Bodies Hit the Floor* were exactly subtle.

Who had that kind of ringtone anyway?

I'd heard his ring before and it was the normal trill of a cell phone. If he'd programmed that song for someone in particular, maybe it meant something else. With a shake of my head, I stopped that train.

I should be grateful to whoever called.

Benjamin was, no doubt, feeling affection for me. I'd brought him a delicious dinner, gifts for his daughter, even *cookie dough* which would soften any mortal's heart, and snuggled up to his daughter. Of course he wanted to kiss me, the lonely old codger. Because of me, he didn't have to wrestle his daughter's braids in the morning. If he'd get out more, maybe he wouldn't be so desperate.

That didn't sound right, but in my half-delirious state, and with trails of fire in place of where his hands had been on my body, I went with it.

Desperate.

Yes.

He was just lonely and I was here. Is *this* why nannies ended up getting in trouble with the fathers of the children they took care of? The blurring of boundaries had powerful effects in a dark house after a satisfying day.

Except, no. I wasn't a nanny. No nanny came over on her day off, and certainly not to crackling tension like today had.

Or did they?

Frustrated now, I rubbed a hand over my face. Ben spoke in the background, and I was now *immensely* grateful for the caller. Not only had they given me a chance to pull back together, but to stop us moving this forward before I made one thing *very* clear: I wasn't a kiss-and-go person. If he wanted to kiss me, he had to commit to something more than a little extra action after the kid went to bed.

That was not me.

And, as I glanced at a picture of him and Ava on a carousel together, where both had the same pained smile that said they didn't want to pose for a picture, I knew that wasn't him either. The fact that I'd even had the thought made me feel a little guilty. He'd be offended if he knew I'd worried about that.

Just as I'd pulled my brain back together enough that I knew

I needed to get out of there, Benjamin ended the call. He stood there for a moment, staring at the very subtle glow of lights from downtown Pineville that came from his front windows. Something in his silhouette made me tense.

Uh oh.

"Benjamin?" I asked quietly.

He tossed his phone onto a nearby couch, then rubbed a hand across the back of his neck.

"Everything okay?"

"It's my mom," he said.

Carefully, I straightened up, worried he'd snap shut like a clam if I moved too quickly. "She okay?" I asked.

He shook his head. "Heart attack. She's in the ICU right now."

"Oh, no."

He turned to face me then, his mask a face of glass. I'd seen this Benjamin before, but it had been so lost in the recent warmth and amusement and affection that I'd forgotten just how distant he could be. The fact that he'd actually spoken about his mother today, and it hadn't been overly warm, clued me in that a disaster of a mess existed below that veneer. After losing his father, I imagined the prospect of being orphaned and going through all that again must be utterly terrifying.

"How can I help?" I asked.

He blinked several times, as if he'd just been dunked in cold water and couldn't reorient. I knew the feeling. The silence lasted for several beats before he said, "I need to go out there and see her. Need to call Mav. Bethany might be able to take Ava. If not, I could take her with me I guess . . ." He grimaced. "No, Ava's terrified of Mallory and Mom wasn't ever very . . . grandmotherly."

He trailed away, pacing now, but I doubted he realized it. I cleared my throat.

"I can stay with her."

He paused, looked at me, and shook his head. "I can't ask that of you."

"Why not?"

"It's too much."

"Are you mansplaining that to me?" I quipped, but there was an edge in it he seemed to respond to. He stared at me, eyes narrowed, as if sussing out whether I was lying. The thought of a few days with Ava wasn't that daunting. The only difference would be a few hours in the morning. I could work with Dagny to switch the hours before school around, then make it up to her later.

"No," he said. "I just . . . that's a lot to ask."

"It's not that much more than I do now," I pointed out. "Plus, it would be easier on Ava if I stay here with her. She'd be at home in her usual routine."

The first of his resistance seemed to crumble, so I pressed my point.

"And you can pay me for it, if that makes you feel better, but I don't need it. I'll happily do it for a friend. We're friends, Ben."

His expression tightened at the word *friend*. I feared for him and his family. Wanted him to jerk me back against his hard body and kiss me until both of us couldn't breathe. But the moment had broken, and I couldn't fight the feeling that he internally flailed around now.

His phone rang with a far gentler tune. The name *Maverick* flashed across the screen before he looked back to me with a vulnerable, frazzled uncertainty.

"You're sure?"

"Positive," I said easily. "Ava and I got this."

Chapter Sixteen

SERAFINA

The next day, Ava looked at me over a glass of milk and rolled her eyes. My phone vibrated for the third time in thirty seconds.

With a sigh, I picked it back up.

Benjamin: Final thing, I swear! I forgot she has a dentist appointment Wednesday after school.

"Is that my dad *again*?" she asked with teenager-like exasperation. I grinned and popped the last of a cookie in my mouth.

"You know it, sister."

My phone gave another little buzz.

Benjamin: The insurance cards are in the top drawer.

Serafina: We've got this. I already knew about the dentist and I was the one that put the cards there. Take care of yourself and your family. Ava and I are enjoying cookies before we launch into homework and laundry, then a walk at the river.

Benjamin: Thank you, Sera. Seriously.

I sent him a heart emoji. While Ava had a huge gulp of milk, I followed a whim and sent a quick text to my brother. My parents had only been gone a full day, but I'd want to engage with him eventually. Text seemed like the first step, and he hadn't replied yesterday.

Serafina: Hey bro, just checking in. Mom made her killer pot roast and I have leftovers with your name on them. Stop by the Diner tomorrow and I'll have them for you.

Once that was sent, I shoved the phone into my back pocket with the thought that maybe Talmage didn't want to talk with me.

Ava gave me an expectant stare as she chewed through the last of her second cookie. A sleepless night separated me from what happened with Benjamin, and now that Ava peered me right in the eyes, I gratefully shoved those thoughts away. It seemed far easier to face her knowing I hadn't kissed her father. Wanted to, but hadn't.

Still dreamed about it, though.

"What do you want to do next?" I asked.

She hesitated. "I get to choose?"

"You bet."

She grabbed a napkin and patted the milk off her lips while her gaze darted around the room. Nervously she asked, "Can we play with my dolls?"

"Sure."

"Really?"

"Of course."

Blinking, she just stared at me. One eyebrow rose. "You'll play with me?"

"I'm looking forward to it."

Her head tilted back slightly, as if she wasn't ready to believe that, but she eventually slid off the stool and headed toward the stairs. Her bedroom awaited at the top, a six-year-olds best disaster of toys, doll clothes, and discarded sandals strewn around the room. She glanced over her shoulder, as if to make sure I actually followed.

When I folded myself on the floor near her dollhouse, she sat on her knees next to me. With a hand halfway to her favorite doll, she stopped again.

"Are you going to get on your phone while I play?"

"Nope."

"Oh." Her body relaxed a little. "Okay, well, I'll be the purple one. You be the one with the green dress. Pretend that we're at a tea party and the queen is gonna come and we're wearing our best dresses."

I had to stifle twinges of both despair and love. First, she lived with an all-male father that couldn't comprehend this little-girl world. While he probably tried really hard, sitting down to play with dolls at a tea party had to be torturous. Secondly, I had a feeling that her Mom had left a cemetery of broken promises behind. Was Ava so suspicious of my plan to play with her because those promises had been made in the past, but never fulfilled?

Or fulfilled in front of a phone?

I brushed those thoughts aside to cast my voice in a high-pitched tone that made Ava giggle, and the happy sound sent tremors all the way to my toes.

When she laughed, she looked the most like her father.

Oh, yes. We'd be just fine.

* * *

That evening, after an hour of dolls, a walk around the river, and a quiet dinner, Ava lay sleeping in her room. I stared at Benjamin's bed as if it would swallow me whole.

The master bedroom filled up part of the main floor just beneath Ava. As long as I kept the door cracked open, I'd be able to hear her if she called out in the night. It was a sprawling room, with a large king-sized bed, a subdued headboard, and a foot-stool at the end that housed extra blankets. He had a walk-in closet with clothes on only one side. Everything was almost pristine except for a little dust here and there. But why? His house was an utter disaster without me, but this room almost sterile? He probably spent little time in here, and I wondered why. The decorations were as exciting as cardboard.

I walked past his bed and into an equally heartless bathroom. Tiled floors. Massive, jetted tub. Walk-in shower with glass panes and two sprays, one from overhead and one from the wall.

Yes, please.

The room smelled slightly spicy, like aftershave and men's deodorant mixed together. I peeked through his shower caddy, amused to find a bar of what appeared to be goat's milk soap that smelled like pine trees.

Fluffy towels lined two racks, and a separate room housed the toilet. The entire master bedroom and bathroom were bigger than the loft I rented.

A bit lost, I wandered back to his bedroom and stared at the bed. The duvet was a slate gray, with navy blue sheets and fluffy pillows I suspected he didn't even use. A nightstand with little more than lip balm and a book on fighting sat next to his bed. Benjamin's life was . . . barren. Almost sterile. Like he avoided home or something.

After I forced myself to change into my pajamas and turn out the lights, I lay my head on his pillow and drew in a deep breath.

Benjamin.

Like he surrounded me.

The luxury of sleeping in his very firm bed, without him, made me giggle a little bit. He'd offered it on his way out of the house, saying he'd changed the sheets, but I hadn't thought much of it until now. There were rooms that could be guest bedrooms, but he hadn't bothered to buy the necessary furniture for it.

A good friend would sleep on the couch, but I had long since ceased thinking of myself as just a friend. Neither of us had ever said the word *nanny*. Official Organizer? Mistress of the Mercedy Life? No, the moment on Sunday afternoon when I realized I wanted to be with him instead of alone at my new place, with a new world to explore, I knew this was different. That I'd given up on keeping things totally platonic.

No, I was more than that to Ben and Ava, but *what* that was, I wasn't sure yet.

With a quick flick of the lamp next to his bed, the room fell into darkness. I stared at the ceiling, wondering what Ben thought about before he went to sleep, when my phone illuminated with a new text message.

Benjamin: Things go okay?

Serafina: Beautifully. She's such an amazing kid, Ben. How are things there? Mom okay?

Benjamin: Can I call?

Serafina: Of course.

Seconds later, my phone sang. I accepted the call and said, "Hey."

"Hey." His voice was soft and weary-sounding. "Thanks. I hate texting."

I grinned even though he couldn't see it, and spiraled a piece of hair around my finger. He definitely hated texting. "I know. This is better because I like hearing your voice. So tell me what's happened today. What's going on there?"

"Mom is stable. Sometimes responsive but pretty out of it. They've already put a stent or something in. She needs hardware or . . . a pacer? I don't know. " He paused for a moment, as if totally overwhelmed. Then someone spoke in the background. A few breaths later he returned.

"Just a sec."

The distinct sound of rustling, doors opening, and then a ding followed.

"You still with me?" he asked.

"Always," I said softly, and hoped he didn't hear the double meaning in the words. It sounded like he was walking now.

"Sorry, I just had to get away from there for a while. My brother, his wife Mallory, Maverick, and a few other siblings are all in the waiting room at the same time and that's the worst idea ever. They're all so freaking intense it's like having a board meeting."

Tremors of frustration ran through his voice as he spoke. They came out in sharp bursts, like a staccato. The idea of several Benjamin's or Maverick's sent a little shudder through me. Maverick had always been so kind, but there was definitely something big about his size and quick mind. Benjamin, of course, carried himself like a panther, so he always looked like a prowling animal ready to pounce.

"No worries," I said. "Give it to me."

He paused. "Give it to me?"

My cheeks heated with the double entendre, and I decided to totally ignore the other connotations. I flapped a hand, as if he could see me, and said, "Yeah. Give it to me. Tell me all about it. Why are you frustrated? What are they saying? What flavor of ice cream would you rather be eating right now?"

"Ice cream?"

The perplexed tone made my eyes roll. Darling man-child, he had no idea how to just be a normal human. Clearly, I'd have to pare this down for him in a far more direct manner. Not for the first time, I wondered about his family dynamics. Did they not know how to talk about their bad days?

Now more than ever, Benjamin needed me. The idea should have scared me, but it didn't.

"This is an opportunity for you to tell me what's in your head, Ben. Tell me all the things, good and bad. And, you know, what ice cream you're craving. All bad days breed a need for ice cream."

"Oh."

"What thoughts are coming up for you after seeing everyone?"

"Are you my therapist now?"

An edge colored the human. Geez, but this man . . . Next he would tell me that he didn't eat ice cream unless it was made from something healthy, like coconut milk or something.

"No, because you couldn't afford me. Give it to me! What are you feeling?"

"Frustration."

"With?"

"Mom."

"Why?"

"Because she was four months late to her last cardiology appointment. They were going to do a stress test and could have caught this *before* she had a heart attack."

"Yikes."

"Yeah."

The image of him rubbing the back of his neck filtered through my mind. He sounded agitated. I'd bet all my savings he was pacing somewhere awkward, like a closed lobby, where people thought he might explode.

"And Mallory too?"

He groaned. "Don't get me started on her. She drives me nuts. In the weirdest way possible she's almost an exact replica of my Mom, except she was born in Sri Lanka and immigrated here as a baby. So she's somehow become the mouthpiece for my Mom's wishes in this family and everyone is arguing against what she thinks. But Mallory is taking them all down. Baxter, my brother, is just sitting there and letting it happen because he's totally whipped for her. I think Mallory is nervous, so she just takes charge."

No wonder Ava wasn't comfortable with her. Mallory sounded terrifying.

"And Mav?" I asked.

"He's the only thing keeping Mallory in check. He's the only one she really listens to." He sighed. "It has something to do with the fact that he saved her company. Anyway, the bottom line is that everyone is stressed and I don't want to be here."

The last part came out quietly and I felt a pang of compassion for him. Was there anything more stressful than broken family issues? No.

Could confirm.

"Sounds like a lot, Ben, and it doesn't help that your Mom's recovery is an unknown point amongst all this bickering. I'm sorry it's happening that way. Wish I could be there with you."

The last bit popped out before I could stop it, but when he said, "Me too," I couldn't bring myself to regret it. Underneath all those layers of lacking emotional intelligence was a frightened, vulnerable man.

So I snuggled deeper under the covers and said, "Ava had a wonderful day. Would you like to hear about that instead?"

"Absolutely."

For the next fifteen minutes, I filled him in on all the delightful things she did and said, including the weird moments with the dolls. He confirmed my suspicions when he said, "Sadie loved her, but didn't know how to parent her. A lot like me. I try to play dolls but it's so boring and mind numbing that I only last like ten minutes and get stupid bored and . . ." He sighed. "So that's probably my fault."

"Well, I'm getting paid for playing dolls and you aren't," I pointed out. "At the end of a long day, I'm sure there are other things you'd rather do."

"There are indeed," he murmured, in a warm sound that reminded me of a purr. Instantly, I was transported back to our almost-kiss. My breath caught and I must have taken too long to recover because he picked the conversation back up at that moment.

"Any word from your brother?"

I frowned. "No, but I did text him. Never heard back."

"Good."

"You sound tired," I said as I fought off a yawn. "Get some sleep? We can talk again tomorrow."

The response was a blatant invitation that made my stomach flutter a bit. If there was any other perfect moment for him to set a boundary and say *no*, this was the one. But his response was equally quick and sincere.

"You bet we will. Thanks, Sera. Talk to you then."

He clicked away as I whispered my goodbye. Seconds later, a final text message appeared. The perfect one to close out a day that didn't have him in it.

Benjamin: Thanks. Your voice was what I needed without realizing it. Be in touch soon.

With a sigh, I settled into a deep, restful sleep, the smell of Benjamin surrounding me.

* * *

"Where are we going?"

Ava asked the question the next day, her nose pressed to the window of the SUV. A frothing river passed to our right as we drove out of Pineville and up the canyon, to Jackson City. I flipped on the blinker.

"We are going girl shopping."

Ava's ears perked up. She immediately straightened. "What's girl shopping?"

"While doing your laundry this morning, I noticed that you wear the same five shirts and two pairs of pants. All of your shirts have bright turquoise, orange, purple, or yellow colors. You have a closetful of clothes that are pink but you don't seem to wear them much. So I thought you could use a little revamp."

Ava leaned back. "Yeah, those are my favorite colors." Her nose wrinkled. "Dad bought me a lot of pink."

"You don't like pink?"

She shrugged. "It's okay. I like dresses. With pockets! Dad didn't get me any dresses, and we haven't really been back to that store yet."

"Me too, sister. Dresses with pockets are the best. So we're going to buy you more clothes with your favorite colors *and* more dresses with pockets."

"Really?" she squeaked.

"Really."

With a squeal, she kicked the back of the front seat and clapped her hands with a happy chant. Before she'd settled back down, she asked, "Does Dad know?"

"No, but he won't care. He told me I could buy you some more clothes."

"He bought most of my clothes now."

"Yeah, he did pretty good. But I think you should pick them from now on, and he agreed. Whattaya think?"

"It sounds awesome!"

We belted out a few pop songs on the way up the canyon,

and I luxuriated in the brightness of unfiltered Ava. Rarely did I get her so full of life, and it seemed the prospect of a new adventure brightened her. Benjamin texted me sometime in our travel, so when I stopped at our first red light, I glanced at the phone.

Benjamin: Mom's up and out of ICU as of this morning. Mav and I plan to head back this evening.

Serafina: Good news! I work tonight, so Ava is going to stay with Bethany.

Benjamin: Thanks for arranging that.

Serafina: My pleasure. Fly safe! I'll see you soon?

Benjamin: I'll stop by to see you tonight.

My stomach gave a little flip. Technically, he could just go see his daughter at Maverick's and then I'd see him Monday morning. But maybe he needed to talk about something with Ava, or just wanted to touch base.

Because we were friends.

I ditched my phone when the light turned, and minutes later Ava and I stood in the middle of a girls section at my favorite clothing store. She stared, wide-eyed, at the glittering options.

"I can buy these?" she whispered.

With effort, I hid my suspicions and said easily, "Whatever you want. You choose. I'll control the budget, okay? You tell me what you like. Let's start there."

"Dad said I could?"

"He's happy for you to get something you want."

She nodded wordlessly, but I couldn't say that she was convinced. Why so reticent about Benjamin *allowing* her to get new clothes? It didn't add up to the dynamic I'd seen between them, but I kept my attention open. Slowly, Ava approached several different shirts. At first, she strolled past them.

When she reached out to touch a bright blue dress with lace trim, her fingers fell away just short of the material. Instead of throwing herself into the options, she just stared at them, a paralyzed expression on her face. I crouched next to her when tears sparkled in her eyes.

"Ava?"

"Mom said Dad wasn't nice," she whispered. A tear dropped down her cheek. Her lip trembled a little before she pressed on, her voice strained now. "She said I'd never be happy with him, and if he tried to take me away, I should never let him. I could . . . I could only be happy with her. She said he didn't like to spend money and I'd never feel happy at his house."

The sound of my heart cracking followed her little sob. I grabbed her shoulders so she faced me. Tears spilled down her cheeks in earnest as she cried, "Mom said Daddy would never love me!"

Unable to bear another moment, I crushed her to me. She sobbed into my shoulder. Big, heaving cries as she clung to me. Tears stung hot in my eyes, but I forced them back. This little girl who had lost so much . . . how had she even survived in the first place? I wanted to rake my nails across Sadie's face. What kind of person told a little girl such a thing? No wonder Ava had been so reserved around Benjamin.

When she'd cried the worst of it out, I pulled her away to look at me. Then I tucked a piece of hair behind her ear and said, "I love you, Ava. Do you know who else loves you? More than anything in this world?"

She shook her head, wiping a snotty nose off on the back of her sleeve.

"Your daddy. He loves you so much."

She hiccupped.

"Do you think what your Mom said is true? Do you think you'll always be unhappy with your Dad?"

Mute, she shook her head. Her cheeks were a tearstained red when I gently wiped them off with my thumb.

"I don't either," I whispered. "I think your Dad loves you more than anything, and he wants you to be happy. That's part of the reason we're getting you new, fun clothes. How does that feel?"

"Good," she mumbled.

"Are you happy with your Dad?"

She nodded reluctantly, her brow wrinkled. She let out a long breath, and in her silence, I thought I saw the answer.

"Are you afraid your Mom would be mad because you're happy with him?"

Her eyes swam again as she nodded. "I . . . I like it better with my Dad. Mom was gone. I didn't see her."

I pulled her in for another hug, and she came to me willingly. Her body shook through a few post tear hiccups, then calmed. When I pulled away, some of the composure had returned to her eyes.

"Better?" I asked.

With a trying smile, she wiped away the last of her tears. I pressed a kiss on top of her head, straightened, and took her hand.

"Great," I announced, "because it's time to get you some new dresses with pockets, my girl. Lead the way and show me anything that makes you happy."

Chapter Seventeen

BENJAMIN

Fresh, mountain air greeted me back to Pineville with the mellow rush of an almost-summer evening. Lights dotted Main Street from the buildings, illuminating the darkening avenue with a few open restaurants. Early season tourists spilled out of the buildings here and there. Stars popped out overhead.

But I ignored all of that.

Sleepless nights and jet lag aside, I had a mission. I'd dropped Maverick off at home, kissed my sleeping daughter's head after staring at her for a long time, then headed for the Diner. A check with Sera's name on it burned a hole in my pocket, but that was just an excuse to see her.

It had only been a few days—in hell, if you asked me—but I couldn't wait to catch up with Serafina. To really talk about Ava even though we'd texted or talked on the phone. Who was I kidding? I just wanted to *see* her.

Not to mention get an explanation for her evasive text last night that said *had a very interesting talk with Ava about Sadie today. Can't wait to tell you about it in person.* The in-person part of that had me a little concerned.

Anything with Sadie was problematic.

The Diner parking lot was full. With summer came tourists, and most restaurants extended their hours to accommodate the rush of foot traffic. When I slipped inside, people waited on benches in the main part of the parking lot, and music sang from speakers piped outside. Inside, Fight Night flickered across several television screens in a back room. Two lightweight guys grappled on the screen before the heavyweights would come through.

Normally, it would have sucked me right in. My trainees were probably here to watch it, somewhere in the chaos of people. A madhouse packed the back room of the Diner, accompanied by alternating screams, groans, or shouts depending on what kind of hit the champion took.

Tonight, I didn't care about fights, MMA, or rankings.

Once I stepped through the doors, my eyes scanned the area for Sera's wild hair and work jeans. She usually wore a navy t-shirt that said *The Diner* across the front, and *Bacon + You = True Love* on the back. Tonight took me several moments before I saw her slipping into the back room, mugs of frothing beer in her hands. Her hair was tied away from her face in a messy riot of curls on top of her head. She appeared frazzled, the color high on her cheeks. An apron tied around her waist gave away her curves, and I didn't like that. Not with a den of drunk men at her hands.

I tried to fight my tension as Dagny stepped forward and asked, "T-table for one?"

"No, thank you. I'm here to speak with Serafina?"

Dagny brightened. "Sure. Have a s-seat at the counter and I'll let her know you're h-here."

Instead of settling on the only open, frayed stool, I leaned on the counter and kept an eye on the shouting room of men. They packed in there so tight Sera could barely maneuver her way back out through the crowd. My hands fisted in front of me as I watched her try.

"Hey man," said a voice from my side. "How are you, brother?"

A hand clasped my shoulder, and I turned to see Hernandez standing next to me. Without his sheriff's uniform bulking his already strong shoulders out, I almost didn't recognize him. We'd done some training sessions together since I arrived, then he finagled a contract between us and the county to do more deputy MMA training with new deputies. I grinned when I saw him.

"Hey." We clasped hands and bumped chests. "How are you?"

"Can't complain." He shrugged, then gestured to the screens in the back. "Came to grab some dinner, but it's getting a bit rowdy back there. Thought I'd hang out a bit and just see what happened."

"Don't want to miss any action?"

He grinned, then muttered, "You know it. Crazy gringos."

His observation immediately put my attention onto the back room, and I turned just as Serafina began to worm her way back out, a tray of empty glasses in her arms. She looked up, saw me, and grinned.

That's when a nearby drunk idiot touched her back side.

He stood, shoving his body into her with a drunken cry. She lurched to the side with a gasp, glasses sliding off the tray as he brazenly reached for her chest. Glass shattered as the mugs fell to the ground.

And I moved.

Within seconds I'd crossed the floor. The next thing I knew, a groaning body lay under me and someone grabbed my shoulder, which was pulled back with a ready fist.

"Ben, get off him." Jayson spoke directly in my ear. The world had gone oddly silent. "Now."

In a flash, I took the new scene in. Eyes staring at me. Drunk guy on the floor. Beer pooling on the floor at my side. No blood.

No pain in my knuckles. I hadn't hit the bastard yet, but I was a second away from it. Both hands up in the air in surrender, I gained my feet and stepped back.

"You saw what he did?" I asked Hernandez.

"Every second. Now get out of here. Someone give me a phone. Let's get this guy in the drunk tank at county."

"Saw it, coach!" piped up one of my trainees from the other side of the room. A chorus of three other voices chimed in.

Duly exonerated, but thrumming with the urge to sock that guy, I spun around to find Serafina. She stood in the doorway, eyes wide, the empty tray clutched to her chest. I walked up to her, but stayed a few steps back. If I got too close, I'd pull her into a kiss that would stir all kinds of questions. People were already wondering what the hell I was doing anyway.

"You okay?" I asked.

She nodded, swallowing hard. "Fine."

"How much longer in your shift?"

"Thirty minutes."

"Go to it," I said. "I'll wait for you at the counter."

"But—" Her reply faltered until she finally nodded. "Okay, thanks."

We didn't speak again. She bustled around the Diner with a tired smile and busy strides. She kept me supplied with water and passed me a tray of fresh sliced veggies with whole wheat bread with a little smile, even though I hadn't asked. By the time her shift ended, the chaos in the backroom had died with the fight, and the last patrons swilled around.

Dagny approached her just after 10:00 and said, "I g-got this. I'll close. You g-go home."

"You sure?"

"Definitely."

"Thanks, Dag."

Moments later, Serafina reappeared from behind the swinging doors that led to the back. She had a jacket in her arms, her apron was gone. I stood, grateful to finally get her all to myself. Still wished I'd hit that guy though when I saw the uneasy expression on her face.

"You good?" I asked.

She nodded. I tilted my head to the door to indicate her to go first. She waved to someone and stepped outside, then immediately turned left. The Frolicking Moose was only a few parking lots over, hardly far enough to get the conversation in that I wanted. Deep in my bones, I desperately hoped she'd ask me inside. But seeing the tired lines on her face, wondered if that would be best if she didn't after all.

Frustration gripped me again, but I set it aside. Residual angst from seeing my family again, no doubt. No matter what I did, I couldn't relax. She broke the strained tension between us.

"I . . . That is . . . Thank you."

Serafina kept her gaze forward while she stammered out something. She'd pulled her jacket on, and I wondered if the cool breeze felt as good to her as it did to me.

"No problem."

We crossed the first parking lot with little more than the crunch of gravel at our feet. All the time I'd spent thinking about her while I was gone, and now that I had my chance to . . . what?

What did I want to do?

Stupid question. I knew *exactly* what I wanted to do, and it had everything to do with the unfinished business of a kiss that didn't happen. But whether she wanted it as well remained to be seen.

My tongue felt locked in the following uncertainty, so we remained in silence until the Frolicking Moose appeared. The shop interior was dim except for the blink of a red security light. Maverick and Bethany had created a separate entrance to the loft when they remodeled that prevented anyone from the coffee shop heading into the loft. Serafina angled us toward the back door that led to her staircase.

To my relief, Serafina saved me again.

"Come on." She tilted her head toward the back door. "Let's go upstairs. It's been a long night."

* * *

Wearily, Serafina climbed the spiral stairs, flicked on her lights, and tossed her jacket onto a peg on the wall. She motioned toward her couch with a wave and said, "I'm going to hop in a quick shower so I don't smell like fries and pickles. Then we can talk."

The sound of running water a few minutes later distracted me, and I tried to keep my thoughts off what lay behind closed doors. Instead, I paced off the extra energy from the night. Although I still wanted to hit that guy, Jayson had been right to pull me off. Tackling him in defense of Serafina was justifiable, but a hit could have gone a step further. That dirtbag might have come back at me with a lawsuit just to get at my money. It had certainly happened before.

My thoughts spiraled from there and back to Mom in the ICU. Her pale skin, pasty in the horrible light. Tubes running everywhere. Voice hoarse from breathing machines. Decidedly powerless, and all I'd ever known of Mom was a powerhouse. Seeing her that way sent a shock of mortality through me. The unease of immediate change in our world. Everything frightening seemed to happen in one terrifying moment.

Which only riled all the emotions caged up inside me.

Just when I thought I'd explode, a soft touch came on my arm. Then a warm hand. I spun to see Serafina just behind me. Her hair was still pulled out of her face, but all the makeup scrubbed off. Her cheeks were a light pink from the water, and I wanted to put a hand on them and draw her heat out. She wore a pair of baggy gray sweats and a worn I Heart NY t-shirt.

"Have a seat, Ben. You look like you're about to explode."

All the ire bled out of me with her touch, leaving something to simmer in the background. She settled onto a couch, her body canted toward me, and tossed a pillow out of her way. In response to her expectant look, I sank down not far from her. Still, we didn't touch.

"Give it to me," she commanded. "Say all the things after seeing your family and your Mom in a terrible situation."

She'd used those words before, but they still startled me now. Troubled, I just stared at her. I wanted to give it to her. To unload everything and let it out. But how was that fair to her? Besides, this wasn't how I worked through things. My emotions came out of my fists. Until I beat the rage out, the words wouldn't come.

"I need to beat the crap out of something first," I croaked instead.

She tilted her head to the side in an assessing gaze, then unfolded herself as gracefully as she'd sat down. Her hand opened to mine.

"Then let's go."

* * *

Twenty minutes later, I stood in front of my favorite bag.

Serafina sat on the mat near the wall, her knees tucked into her chest, and watched. Once the heavy metal music started to flow overhead, so did my fists. The bag didn't come to me with the same intensity as the fury inside. Bag work was more calculated than that. But something about the smash of my hands and the thud that rippled through my muscles after, calmed the storm.

Without a guy with pads calling out my throws, I settled for the methodical precisions of nailing every frustration with a punch, a kick, or a combo. In the steady hip movements and muscle control, I let it all go.

In the background waited Serafina.

By the time I finished, the music had cycled off. Sweat soaked my shoulders, and my hands trembled slightly in the gloves. I yanked them off with my teeth and threw them against the wall. Then I crossed the mat and sat next to her.

"Thanks."

She handed me a water bottle with a smile, seemingly unbothered by my sweaty shirt. "Anytime."

For several long minutes, we sat with our backs to the wall, then she turned to me with an expectant look and brow high. Time to *give it to her* then. I wiped the sweat off my face with the bottom of my t-shirt. Now it all made sense. The thoughts came into line easily, like soldiers.

"I didn't like seeing my Mom so helpless," I said, my jaw set. Serafina's head lifted to meet my gaze, but I kept my eyes on the clock on the far wall. "She looked small and powerless on that hospital bed and I hated it. I love her and want her to choose better for herself. Whenever my family gets together, we fight. We're all too opinionated, so I just shut the hell up and fade into the background, and I hate that too. So, seeing my family makes me tense."

I stopped to take a deep breath. Serafina hadn't said a word, but I felt her steady gaze. I kept going.

"I hate being away from Ava even for a few days because I don't know her mind, and I hate that too. I love her. I'm afraid something will happen if I'm not here to protect her. And I hated that that creep tried to grope you and I didn't get to break his teeth the way he deserved. That's why I looked like I'd burst."

She set a hand on my arm despite the damp sweat.

"Thank you for defending me," she said. "But mostly thank you for dealing with whatever was inside of you."

Only when I met her gaze did I realize that she might have been frightened of me. Had she sensed something in me that reminded her of Talmage? Did Talmage and I share a sense of rage that she recognized? She'd stopped wincing all the time from her broken rib, so I'd started to forget.

"Were you afraid of me?" I asked quietly.

Her shoulders slumped. "Not really." Her hair, which she'd let fall down, rustled with the movement of a quick shake. "I know you'd never hurt me, but I was concerned for your own sake. You seemed . . . agitated."

"I feel better now. Thank you."

Unable to stop myself, I reached over and touched her chin with my hand. Then I lifted it so I could stare into her eyes.

"You okay?"

She drew in a deep breath at my touch, then nodded. My gaze dropped to her lips, then back to her eyes. She put her hand over mine.

"Can I kiss you now?" I asked.

The words came out of me before I could stop them. Even after I heard them, I didn't want to take them back. Only a brief lull came between us before she leaned into my hand and whispered, "Yes."

In my imaginings, our first kiss would be hungry. A bit wild. A desperate reflection of the way I felt inside. But when I closed the distance between us, I stopped a breath before her lips. The heat of her breath, light with mint, slammed into me like a wall. I stayed there for a moment to soak in the sensation.

Then I gently pressed my lips to hers.

A low heat burned beneath my lips at first, accompanied by a sense of disbelief that I'd allowed myself to get pulled into her so quickly. Then she tilted her head, opening her mouth to me, and all my control vanished.

I gently grabbed her arms to pull her onto my lap. Her hands found my face and threaded through my hair as I pulled her close, banishing all space between us. She made a sound at the back of her throat, and I stopped. When we parted, she stared at me through passion-clouded eyes.

"You okay?" I whispered, panting.

She put both of her hands on my face, seeming unaware of how sweaty I'd become. Then she pressed her forehead to mine.

"Now I am," she whispered.

And I lost it again.

Chapter Eighteen

SERAFINA

The next day, I stared at my phone with a little frown.

Mom: Have you heard from Talmage? I haven't heard anything at all.

Serafina: No. He's been ignoring me. Want me to go check on him?

Mom: Would Ben go with you?

Serafina: Probably.

Mom: Then if it's not too much trouble, it would help me feel better.

Serafina: I'll ask tonight.

When I shoved it back in my pocket, the bells on the Diner door jangled. I stepped back into work with a smile, but it felt forced. I didn't want to be here right now. Normally, I loved waitressing. Today, I just wanted to be back in my loft and under my covers where I could analyze my first kiss with Benjamin in peace. Reminders of my brother certainly didn't help, nor did the perfectly cloudless, warm sky outside.

In the midst of refilling coffees and taking orders around a still-sleepy lunch crowd, Dagny arrived for her midday shift. I almost cried with relief when her bright, expressive face smiled at me.

"H-h-hey!" she cried. "How is the d-day?"

"Slow. Quiet. I'm slowly dying and need you to help me analyze something. You're so good at it."

A bright gleam claimed her expression as I followed her into the back. "I-I know, I hear it a-a-all the time. But uh oh," she sang. "D-did someone get a kiss?"

I slumped against the wall with a moan. "Yes!"

"A-a-and it was amazing?"

"*So* amazing."

"And you want more?"

"Yes!"

She grabbed an apron and tossed it over her head, then reached around to tie it in the back. A certain smug expression filled her face now. "I c-c-can't say I'm all that surprised with his ferocity last n-night. I would have kissed him t-too! A-a-and who kissed who f-f-first?'

"He *asked* to kiss me." I plastered a hand over my face and peered at her through my splayed fingers. "Like a romcom or something."

Dagny laughed. "H-h-how sad is your life, Sera?"

"I know!" I wailed.

"I mean, he j-just about killed a man for your honor last night," she drawled. "G-good thing Hernandez stopped him or it could have gotten b-bloody. Th-th-en he walks you h-home like a gentleman and then he *asks* t-to kiss you." She eyed me. "So what's wrong?"

"Nothing. Everything. I liked it way too much. He makes me feel safe."

"Again, this is awful."

I rolled my eyes. "What if it was a passionate fluke?"

"That streak of -p-p-protectiveness in him?" This time, *she* rolled her eyes. "Give me a break, Serafina. He may have been a g-gallant gentleman for any woman in that situation, b-b-but I doubt he would have been that pissed off. It looked like he b-barely held himself together. He c-cares about you."

That I couldn't deny. There was caring on both sides. His question last night, asked with such sweet vulnerability, whispered back through my mind. *"Are you frightened of me?"*

No, I had been anything but scared of him. At least, not like that. I'd felt emotional, maybe, because he'd just dropped in like an avenging god. Grateful, definitely. Maybe a little bit in awe of him, too. The only fear around Benjamin came from just how much I liked him.

While I'd dreamed of that kiss for a while, and it certainly hadn't disappointed, the aftermath felt more encompassing than I'd expected. He'd kissed me that time, then taken me home. We'd both been quiet, as if we were stunned. Now it had been hours since I'd seen him, we'd sent no text messages, and my mental state spiraled.

Did he regret it?

Would he kiss me tonight?

What now?

Where did we go from here? What *was* I to him?

Did one kiss create a circumstance to define what we were doing? He paid me to take care of his child, so I was a sort of employee, if I looked at it from that light. But that felt too awful. No, didn't like that. Maybe I wouldn't cash the check he gave me. Then it wouldn't feel so . . . weird.

Benjamin didn't strike me as a loose kisser, either. He certainly wasn't the type to go around kissing anyone. The man barely spoke outside of necessity. So the very fact that he kissed me meant something.

But what?

Could a kiss be a fluke?

Too late, I realized I'd sunk into a quagmire of thought when Dagny nudged me out of it. "You have people waiting," she said with a laugh. "G-go overanalyze while you're working. In the meantime, I d-don't feel bad for you."

She winked and sent me scuttling back into the Diner to greet some new patrons and take out a fresh plate of pancakes and bacon. My mind had settled enough even from Dagny and my minimal interaction that at least I didn't have to fake my cheer anymore.

A kiss *could* be a fluke, I decided.

If it was one, I'd ride it this fluke out for as long as it lasted or until it wasn't one anymore. Besides, I didn't think it *was* a fluke, I just didn't know what came next.

And there was never another chance for a first kiss.

* * *

The restless night after Benjamin kissed me caught up to me sooner than I'd expected. After work, Ava and I stopped by the library, then played at the park for almost two hours while a friend from school showed her how to swing from the monkey bars. Afterward, we ate dinner, created a chore chart, and she splashed through a warm bath.

At the end of the day, I gratefully collapsed on the couch.

While Ava hummed to herself in bed, a funny little habit she used to put herself to sleep, I curled up around a pillow with my eyes closed.

Just for a moment, I thought sleepily.

My thoughts ran naturally to Benjamin as I relaxed. Ava's humming slowed, then stopped. The house darkened as I replayed the kiss with warm purls of heat deep in my belly. Considered the empty state of my text messages, brother included. Then I tangled myself up slowly in sleep with the dusky night sky. With impressive strength, I resisted the urge to curl up in Benjamin's bed and remained on the couch in the languorous place between deep sleep and wakefulness.

After what felt like a long blink later, a whisper pulled me awake.

"Sera?"

The warmth of a hand gently squeezed my shoulder. My eyes fluttered open to see darkness, with Benjamin silhouetted by light from the kitchen. I blinked slowly.

"Hi," I murmured.

"You all right?"

He spoke in a low, quiet tone. His hand found my face and I leaned into it with a, "mm hmm," sound from my throat. He chuckled. His fingers pushed the hair off my face and trailed down my cheeks. I reluctantly shucked off the vestiges of sleep with the hope that he'd kiss me again.

"How was Ava?" he asked.

"So good." I yawned and curled an arm above my head to stretch it. "As always. She washed her hair tonight, by the way, and has a permission slip she needs you to sign for something next week. We got some new books at the library for her to practice reading more at night. Went well today."

His fingers danced up my arm and into my hair. Goosebumps followed them in a wave. I pulled myself closer with a little sigh.

"Good," he murmured huskily.

I turned to face him, my body tingling, but he had looked away. He sat there for several moments, his hand heavy on my ribcage. He stared at the wooden floor with a furrowed brow, as if lost in thought. When I sat up and put a hand on his arm, he turned to me. With a few blinks, heavy thoughts seemed to scatter, like clouds against a bright moon.

"You all right?" I asked.

"Thinking."

We danced a slow, careful dance right now. I could sense some hesitation in him, as if he wasn't sure how to re-approach after last night. But I saw the same tug in him that I felt. The undeniable pull to get us closer.

Despite his warm reception and gentle touches now, he seemed more like a curious, but wary, cat. As if he couldn't resist the lure of touch, but wasn't sure he knew what it meant. After spending all day considering it, I realized that he might be shy. Not about the kiss, but the emotional vulnerability with his Mom.

The man needed some firmer grounding right now.

"How was your day?" I asked.

Although tempted to let my hand drop, to guard against what could be a rejection from him now that he'd processed our kiss, I didn't. I left my fingers there to burn against his skin, and it took a considerable amount of courage not to slowly peel away.

His hand reached out and touched my face.

"I missed you," he said quietly.

I let out a long breath, and the whole day behind me felt silly in an instant. How had I even doubted? The passion in his gaze cut right to my heart. I reached up, touched his hand, and threaded my fingers through his.

"I missed you."

"I'm sorry I didn't text you," he said. "I suck at this. I . . . I was afraid that I came on too strong last night. That you'd start to get tired of me. Of us. So I wanted to give you space in case that was what you needed."

The fear in his voice softened everything inside me. My lips twitched a little as I said, "You're doing a lot of thinking for me."

He considered that, then sighed. "I didn't think of that."

"Benjamin?"

He'd moved closer, just enough that I could smell him again. Memories of his sheets, the scent of his pillow, washed over me like a warm wind. I swallowed, my eyes darting to his lips and then back. My stomach tightened with warmth and it took all I had not to utterly throw myself into his arms again.

"Yes?"

"Can I kiss you now?"

His lips moved into a smile. His hand slipped to my neck, where the tip of his thumb ran along my lower jaw. The touch of his palm felt hot against the back of my neck.

"I thought you'd never ask."

Like magnets, our lips found each other again. Tonight, though, the frantic buzz of energy had faded. Some sort of hunger always burned hot in Benjamin, but tonight it had been tamed. Whether it was his jog home, a long day at the gym, or distance from the experience with his Mom, I didn't know. But it translated to a calm touch for such a strong fighter of a man. His lips were so warm. His touch was so gentle. My heart flopped in my chest like a dying thing. And even though we hardly touched at all, my entire body felt like it was on fire.

When he pulled away, he didn't go far. His eyelashes batted open and gazed so deep into my soul I thought he knew everything. The intensity of our stare caught me up in it, and I couldn't have looked away if I wanted to.

"It was a rough day at work," he said. "Frustrating. Just . . . normal stuff, but still frustrating. Knowing that, at the end of it, I'd come home and you'd be here gave me such relief. I was worried that you would be distant or upset or frustrated. So I'm even more relieved to see none of that's true."

My fingers found a lock of his hair on his forehead and pushed the tumbling tendril away. I smiled softly.

"I'm here," I murmured. "Always for you."

Ben leaned back, grabbed a pillow, put it on his lap, and pulled me onto it. I lay across him and closed my eyes. He played with some of my curls with gentle fingers, the tips of his finger scraping my scalp in a soft way. His head was tipped back, his entire body relaxed. I wasn't sure whether playing with my hair was for his benefit, or mine.

"How was your day?" he asked with a wry smile and one hand on my hip. "Give it to me."

And so I did.

When I unloaded the day without the context of my spiraling thoughts, I realized that it really had been a good day. Easygoing, the way I liked it. At the end of my retelling, his fingers stopped. He stiffened suddenly.

"We didn't talk about how things went with Ava while I was gone. Wasn't there something you wanted to tell me about Sadie?"

Ah, tension. How quickly such a fickle mistress returned. Just Sadie's name garnered the same reaction in him. I sat up, shoving the hair out of my face. Wariness had replaced the hints of passion in his gaze.

"Right," I murmured. "I'd forgotten in all that mess last night. Ava talked about her mother and it . . . wasn't what I expected."

His throat bobbed as he swallowed. He looked ready to take a sucker punch. From what I knew of Sadie, I wasn't surprised. A lift of his eyebrows was my only encouragement to continue.

"It was at the store." I tugged on my own hair now, suddenly nervous. Would he be mad? What if I hadn't handled it the way he would have wished? Perhaps I should have said something different. I wasn't truly ready for this level of parenting. "She was weird about buying new clothes."

He frowned, as if he agreed, but said nothing, so I laid it out from start to finish. His expression didn't waver, except to go farther into his frown. I leaned against the back of the couch with one shoulder and stared at him in the shadows. His heavy brow fell on top of a stare that glowered at the coffee table.

"Sadie told her she'd never be happy here?" he asked quietly.

"Among other things. That's what Ava said, anyway. Sounded like Sadie just didn't want her to go to you. Maybe she knew that Ava would be happier with you, or something. She is happier here, with you. She told me that herself."

His nostrils flared as he shook his head, but he didn't seem to hear that most important part. For several moments more, he seemed to process what I'd told him, then stood up. When he paced, he looked like a caged panther again. Regret that I hadn't thought to tell him this last night, when he had something appropriate to punch, washed through me. This wasn't the sort of news that any father would be glad to hear, but Benjamin was already so insecure about his parenting.

"That's Sadie." He laughed, but it was mirthless and bitter. "If she wasn't with me, she didn't want me to win. She was competitive to the point of brutality. Even with her daughter."

I curled one leg into my chest and the other one underneath me while I attempted to put my thoughts together in a way that didn't make me sound like a shrew. "I'm sorry about Sadie. I . . . I'm sad that Ava had to lose her in such a permanent way, but I'm grateful she's with a more stable parent now."

He snorted and ran a hand through his hair. "Hardly stable."

"Ben, you're doing great."

"Sadie was . . . she took over everything. Sucked up all my energy. She took, and took, and took. Never gave back."

He finished his bold statement quietly, and something cold grew in me. Hadn't Ben expressed a similar sort of insecurity before?

You do way too much for us already, he'd said when I brought the pot roast.

His words rang hollow through my mind. A dramatic shift occurred in him now as he sat back down, but this time across from me. The warm, sweet Benjamin had disappeared entirely under the landslide of this stressed-out version. He didn't look at me as he immediately stood back up, and the dark feeling inside of me continued.

"Thank you." He oozed formality now, and I suddenly felt like the nanny. "Your response was perfect, and she talked about her clothes all morning. I'm beat from the day and I'm sure you are as well. Let's get you home while I . . . figure all this out."

My heart crinkled inside me with a cry. *No!* I wanted to say. *Don't put distance between us now. No walls. No fear. No self-berating.*

But the words stalled in my throat, because I saw the ugly brewing in his gaze. The rage at his deceased ex-wife. The frustration. Sadie had created unnecessary obstacles for the happiness of both father and daughter, and the legacy played out now in interesting ways. I wasn't someone that could help him pull those down yet. Not until he let me in. As far as I'd come with Benjamin, and I suspected there hadn't been any others after Sadie, there was still so far to go.

"Of course," I said instead. "Let me just grab my shoes."

Without a word, he filed into the garage and I followed, my heart heavy as a leaden weight inside me.

Chapter Nineteen

BENJAMIN

That night, I stared at my ceiling with an electric current of frustration that made it impossible to sleep. Sadie haunted my thoughts, staining the entire day with the same vile spirit she brought to my life even from the grave.

My fists clenched as I thought of what Sadie said to Ava. Ava, her daughter. My thoughts spiraled.

How was I supposed to fix this?

Would Ava ever trust me?

What did I even do with this kind of a problem?

Parenting was the hardest thing I'd ever done. Ava looked to me as the one that was supposed to know everything, but she'd freak out if she realized how little I knew what I was doing.

No, I had no idea.

And I'd been a total jerk to Serafina afterward. Distant. Stiff. Didn't speak on the way back to the Frolicking Moose, where she'd given me a warm, but nervous smile, then went inside without a word. And I'd let her go, like an idiot. Because... why?

Why would I do that?

I rubbed a hand across my chest. I didn't know why I did that. Sadie had her fingers in everything, and that was my fault because I let her take over places she shouldn't be able to go, but she still did. Most of the time, I could forget just how manipulative she'd been. But moments like this made it abundantly clear.

When it came to women, just like parenting, I had no idea what I was doing.

For the tenth time, I punched my pillow, flipped onto my stomach, and hoped that sleep would come. Tomorrow was another long day of training, and I owed Serafina something. An explanation about the sudden reluctance. The fear. The way my throat closed off when I thought of Serafina, because Sadie quickly followed.

I didn't have an explanation for my sudden panic, and one didn't seem to be coming anytime soon.

Chapter Twenty

SERAFINA

The phone rang empty in my ear yet again.

Annoyed, I slammed the old thing back on the Diner wall and folded my arms across my middle. Dagny sent me a questioning glance.

"My brother." I frowned. "He's not answering."

Dagny rolled her eyes. "G-good. D-d-don't go over there. I still haven't f-f-forgotten what he did to you, even if you have."

I ignored that. Mom's plea yesterday slipped back through my mind, followed by an uneasy feeling that all wasn't well with Tamage. The torn part of me resurrected. *He could have killed you,* said one side, but the other whispered, *he's your brother. If he can't rely on you, who can he rely on?*

The evening with Benjamin followed those thoughts with a rush of frustration. Telling Benjamin what had happened had definitely been the right thing to do, but I couldn't help my regret that he'd immediately shoved distance between us. I wasn't Sadie.

But did he know that?

Was I overreacting?

For the tenth time, I set it aside in my mind. Benjamin had

had a bad day, that was all. The fact that he hadn't texted me today was normal, except now it felt like a sign of doom. Ben had never been a big texter. Now, his communication while with his family seemed miraculous. Besides, I couldn't overthink my way into something that wasn't even real. He tended to do that enough for the both of us.

Dagny distracted me from my own mind when she frowned as she peered through the swinging doors.

"What's wrong?" I asked.

"N-nothing. J-just . . . Jayson is back."

"Hernandez?" I asked. So few people called him Jayson, it seemed strange to hear his real name from her.

She nodded and pressed her lips together.

"You don't want to serve him?"

"No."

She stated it simply, which wasn't unusual. Dagny had a rotating list of people she'd rather not serve, but I hadn't realized Hernandez made the cut.

"But . . . why? He's so sweet."

She scoffed, then grabbed two menus and slipped out. I watched her go in bemusement. Dagny had always been painfully shy, but I'd never met anyone so shy they didn't want to speak to Hernandez.

With a sigh, I sent my Mom a text.

Serafina: Sorry, Mom, didn't get over to T's last night. I'll try after work today.

Mom: No worries. Still no word from him. Do you have Amber's number?

The sight of Amber's name on my phone made me physically nauseous. Definitely didn't have her number, but realized too late maybe I should have had a way to run her down if I needed to.

Because, you know. Why not have your brother's dealer on speed dial?

Just in case.

Serafina: No, I never got her number.

Mom: Me either.

Serafina: I'm sure that's no accident.

Mom: Last I heard from him was a text a few days ago.
He said everything is fine.

Serafina: I'll report back soon.

Dagny returned and hooked a thumb to the Diner. "J-jayson wants to t-talk to you."

I peeked around her shoulder. Hernandez stood not far away, this time in his full deputy uniform. Instead of sitting at the counter, he stood not far away.

Here on official business?

My heart turned into a ball of ice as I followed her out. Only two patrons were in the Diner as I stepped out, Dagny a step behind me. She peeled away, but stayed close.

Jayson gave me a gentle half smile. "Hey Serafina, everything is fine. I'm not here to tell you about Talmage's death or anything."

Relief nearly swept me away. "Thank you," I said with a breathy sigh. "Can I get you something?"

"Coffee to go?"

"Sure."

"I do have some questions though." He followed on the

other side of the counter as I slipped over to the coffee machine and reached for a to-go cup.

"About Talmage?" I asked as I reached for the coffee. My stomach revolted again. Had Talmage gotten into something even worse already? Jayson just drummed his fingers on the counter with a poker face that probably got him on the force in the first place.

"He's dating Amber Wilson, right?"

"Reputedly."

He snorted. "Have you seen her around at all?"

His inquiring tone changed slightly. Probing, almost tentative. I didn't like that at all. The coffee felt warm on my fingertips as I poured it into his cup and reached for a lid.

"Amber and I aren't exactly the best of friends," I said as I set it down. "The only time I ever hear from her is when she's lurking around Talmage's house. Now that I live at the coffee shop, I haven't seen her once. Why?"

"Just looking into a few things."

"Have you seen Talmage?"

He shook his head. "Not recently."

"Me either." I chewed on my bottom lip. Perhaps I could solve two problems at once. The problem of Talmage's silence, and the awkwardness of asking Benjamin to go over with me while Ben was . . . floundering. "Would you . . . would you be willing to help me out?" I asked.

"With what?"

"I want to go to Talmage's and check on him, but I'm not sure it would be wise to do it alone. No one in my family has heard from him and I don't have a car that I could just drive by. I work non-stop so there's no time to ride my bike over there."

Jayson nodded once. "Let's call it a welfare check. When do you want to go?"

Overhead, the clock moved slowly toward noon. I reached

for my apron, then called to Dagny, "Can you cover for me while I take my lunch?"

She gave me a thumbs up. I reached for my apron strings and said to Jayson, "Right now?"

He swept up his cup. "Let's go."

* * *

Riding in Jayson's truck with him was intimidating at first. His canine, Odin, whined gently in the back as we pulled out of the Diner parking lot. Low-level radio chatter rang in the background, and equipment cluttered every available spot. As we started to drive, I didn't need to direct Jayson anywhere.

"Do you know where everyone lives?"

He grinned a quick smile. "Pretty much. Perks of small town deputy life."

I tucked my hands under my legs as we rode, feeling an acute sense of fear. Whether it was just nerves, or something more, I didn't feel right. A nagging something was eating at me, and I felt deep in my bones that it was about Talmage.

"So," Jayson drawled. "You and Benjamin, huh?"

Heat leapt to my cheeks. Stupid. Cheeks. They always gave me away. I didn't look at him, but wasn't about to deny it either.

"Yep."

Out of the corner of my eye, I caught his grin. "You got a good one. Tough one, but good."

Whether he meant *tough* in physical or emotional terms, I wasn't so sure anymore. For his steel-like exterior, Benjamin was a mess of a man. Tonight would give me a better idea of where things lie between us. He'd had some space and time to work through the Sadie revelation, which couldn't have been easy.

Now, I had to face my brother.

Or so I hoped.

Less than three minutes later, Jayson pulled to a gentle stop in the road just outside Talmage's place. My hands felt weak in my lap when I peered out on the unkempt lawn and weeds spiraling onto the grass from the field behind the house. A note fluttered on the door, and I wondered what it said. The inside was dark.

"This is it, right?" Jayson asked, but I could sense he already knew the answer. Of course he knew. Jayson had responded to my call the last time Talmage freaked out. But an awkward silence had started once we pulled up, and I realized he was waiting for me to make the next move. My ribs still ached from my last experience here every now and then. I put a hand on that spot from the memory and managed to nod.

"Yeah."

"You good, Sera?" he asked.

"Fine." I swallowed. "I just . . . I don't have a great feeling about this."

Jayson popped his door open. "How about I go in first? Unlikely he's going to try anything while I'm here."

That wasn't what worried me.

"I'll follow," I said.

Jayson's boots thudded lightly on the pavement as he walked around the car toward me. He spoke into a radio at his right shoulder. "Dispatch, we're going inside for a welfare check," and a monotone voice responded, "Dispatch copy."

Numb, my legs carried me up the path and onto the front porch, where dust collected on the furniture. Jayson rapped on the screen door, which bounced under his knuckles.

"Hey, Talmage," he called. "Hernandez here. Just checking on you, man. Your family is worried about you."

A creak followed, and then silence. Jayson glanced at me in question and I shrugged. When I peered past him, a sliver of light caught my attention.

"The door is open a little," I said. "Let's go in."

He pulled the screen and called inside, "Talmage? Oh, shit."

I peered around him and my entire body went cold. Talmage lay sprawled out on the ground like a starfish, face pressed into the carpet. Glass littered the ground, and a mark on the wall nearby looked like someone had thrown a cup against the wall and it shattered. The back door was open, admitting warm spring air through the house in a current.

Jayson was immediately on his radio, spouting out commands I could barely process. He held out an arm to keep me back as he walked up to Talmage, glass grinding under his boots. Dispatch said something back as he reached toward my brother.

"Talmage, buddy," Jayson called. "You with me still?"

My heart felt like a rock in my chest as Jayson reached for Talmage's neck. An interminable wait followed before Jayson turned to his radio and said, "Dispatch, I have a male, thirties, probable overdose, need priority EMS to my location."

He turned to me with a calm demeanor and said, "Stand back for just a bit, Serafina. Help is on the way."

Chapter Twenty-One

BENJAMIN

"What's wrong with you?"

Maverick cuffed me on the side of the head, or tried to, but I blocked him with my forearm, then glared. He glared back.

"Nothing," I growled.

The Diner sprawled around us with the quiet clink of glass and murmur of patrons. A game played in the background and the hiss and sizzle of what smelled like bacon drifted from the back. We sat at our usual booth across from Maverick. I felt surly as a bear after a sleepless night worrying about Ava, and Serafina, and the ghosts of women that couldn't stay in the afterlife. Maverick had ignored my annoyance that he wanted to lunch at the Diner today and insisted we come anyway. Still, I searched for Serafina, even as I feared finding her.

Dagny approached. "Where's Sera?" I asked her.

She gestured with a nod outside. "W-went somewhere with Jayson for her lunch break. He wanted t-t-to talk to her about something."

Maverick's eyebrow rose. My stomach turned cold.

"Hernandez, you mean?" I asked.

Dagny nodded, then turned to Mav. "Coffee?"

"Usual, please."

She disappeared before I could order water, but I knew she'd bring it. All of them knew everyone's drink preferences here. Small town life drove me nuts the way it pigeonholed people with familiarity.

What the hell, Hernandez? I thought, even as relief mingled with the suspicion. Serafina wasn't here now so I didn't have to awkwardly confront her about my coldness last night. A momentary reprieve until I figured my own mind out. But now I couldn't stop wondering where she went with Hernandez.

"You are a mess if you think she's doing anything like that with Hernandez," Mav muttered. "Serafina has the hots for you the likes of which I haven't seen since I found Bethany."

"I never said a word," I snapped.

Mav leaned back. "What. Happened."

This time, not even hammering my problems out with my fists had helped. I'd hit the bag for three hours between last night and this morning and Sadie still haunted me. This time, she brought Serafina with her. What did I say to Serafina after all this? What was the welling dread in my chest everytime I thought about her now?

"Sadie," I finally muttered.

Maverick grimaced. "Ah."

While I related Serafina's story, his expression only grew more grim. "I hate to speak ill of the dead, but man am I glad she's gone."

"I can't believe she did that."

"I can."

Dagny returned with our usual salad and sandwich combo, but my appetite fled. I poked around my salad and tried to summon excitement for it, but all I tasted was cardboard. With a sigh, I shoved it out of my way and put my head in my hands.

"You're wrecked, brother," Maverick said.

"I'm not."

"You're wrecked for Sera and you think she's going to turn into Sadie."

"You're making this crap up," I said with a surge of rage. "Serafina is no Sadie."

Unbothered by my glower, Mav simply picked up his sandwich. "I know that. Serafina knows that. Ava maybe even knows that. I don't think you know that."

His self-righteous smugness made me want to put a fist right into his teeth, but I schooled it back. I knew that Serafina wouldn't turn into Sadie. She didn't have it in her. But maybe I did.

The distant ring of a phone peeled through the air, and a cook in the back barked that they'd get it.

"Whatever," I muttered.

Maverick laughed, which only made me rage worse. Trust a brother to find something funny in this twisted situation.

"It's not just about Sera," I said. "What the hell am I supposed to say to Ava about this with Sadie?"

"Ask her about it like the human she is."

"She's six."

"She's smart. You need to address it."

I tilted my head back, gaze narrowed. "You have a two-year-old, what do you know?"

Mav laughed. "I've always known more than you, brother. Especially when it comes to people. Besides, it's what Bethany would do with Ellie after she first showed up, and that girl was a mess at a young age. Just like Ava. It works."

My phone buzzed on my thigh. Grateful for a distraction, I pulled it out. My gut clenched when Serafina's name flashed across the front. I opened it.

Serafina: Sorry to do this last minute, but can I have the afternoon off?

Seconds after I read it, a voice called from the back.

"Dagny, Fina's out for the rest of the day."

Dagny lifted a hand in acknowledgment as she pulled an order and hustled to another table. My brow creased.

"What's up now?" Mav asked.

"Serafina. She just asked for the day off."

"Why?"

"Don't know."

My fingers tapped out a quick reply.

Benjamin: Sure. Everything okay?

I waited five minutes, but no reply came. When Dagny slipped by, I called out to her and she sidled back over.

"Where did Sera and Hernandez go?" I asked.

She shrugged.

"Did you hear any of their conversation?"

"N-n-no. She g-got him something to drink, he a-asked some questions, and they l-l-left."

"Go after that girl, Ben," Mav said and tossed a sandwich crust back on his plate as Dagny walked away. "Go after her right now."

"I don't know where she is!"

"Find her."

I sent him an exasperated glare. "Find her? You want me to just stop training my new guy and go after her? Responsibility doesn't work like that, Mav. We aren't all our own bosses and can do whatever we want."

"Wrong." He tossed the crust at me and I chucked it back. "You *are* your own boss. You can leave anytime you want, you just won't. You choose not to."

"I'm earning money to raise my daughter with!"

He scoffed. "Please, Ben. Save that for Mom, or someone else that's willing to coddle you. You're avoiding your problems by staying at work. Just like right now. Something happened with Sadie, so now you're freaked about Sera and you're going to go back to work instead of find her. She's with the town deputy, you idiot, and she has a druggie brother. What kind of math do you think this adds up to?"

He held up both hands before I could articulate any sort of response.

"I'm just saying that something is wrong and she probably needed help."

That thought had already occurred to me, and I didn't like it. Didn't like it for so many, many reasons. The greatest of which was Hernandez was helping, not me. Why didn't she ask me? Because I'd been a cold idiot last night and she'd done nothing wrong.

Plus, I didn't want it to be right. It *couldn't* be right. I still hadn't figured out why I felt such need and terror over Serafina, and why Sadie hovered over me like an angry thing. While I craved Serafina, she terrified me at the same time.

"If you want to keep this one," Mav said, "go after her. Find her. Call Hernandez. Do whatever you have to to show up for her, Ben, the way she's shown up for you. That's how this love thing works. I know you didn't have anything real with Sadie so you're sort of a toddler with relationships, but you can have it now."

My phone rattled on the table. Sadie's school name popped up and sent a pang of anxiety through my chest. I answered it immediately.

"Yeah?"

A broken little voice, filled with tears, came through the line. "Daddy?"

"Yeah, honey. You okay?"

"I'm sick. Can you come and get me?"

"I'll be right there."

"Okay."

She hung up without another word. I looked to Mav with smug irony. "Pay for lunch, will you? My daughter is sick and needs me. *That* is how this love thing works."

* * *

Ava's face had finally relaxed out of the scrunched grimace that it had been for the last thirty minutes. I ran a hand over her head, slightly warm, and let it rest there. She opened her eyes to look at me, her lips turned down in a miserable expression. A bucket lay on the floor nearby, ready for her next round of retching.

"You okay?"

She nodded, but tears lingered in the corners of her eyes. "I don't like throwing up," she whispered.

My nose wrinkled. "It's the worst."

She nodded.

"Let me get you some more fizzy stuff, okay? Just sip it. It will help you feel better."

As I stood up, relieved that her stomach seemed to have finally calmed—she'd thrown up twice on the way home and five times since we got back—she tilted her head back on her pillow.

"Where's Sera?"

"She had to take the day off."

Her forehead scrunched. "Why?"

"I don't know."

Disappointed, she relaxed back against the pillow. Cartoon ponies quietly flickered across the television on the wall as I ruffled her hair and made my way back to the kitchen. Bethany had come from the Frolicking Moose with various drinks and home remedies after I desperately texted her for help. My thumb hovered over Serafina's name on my text message list, but skimmed past.

Hernandez. Her brother. It all ran through my head.

No, she had her own life. Just because I felt so deeply about her so quickly didn't mean she had to be available at my every beck and call. Besides, this very situation proved out a deep-rooted fear that haunted me ever since she first popped up: I couldn't be fair to her. I would be the Sadie in our relationship. The pull, pull, pull. The unfair drain on energy and resources. I wanted to help Serafina right now, but I couldn't. Ava had to come first.

Ava *always* came first.

Maybe this was a good experience. A reminder of the responsibilities in my life and where they fit before we dove too far into whatever magic had started to bloom. A shiver skimmed my body when I thought of Serafina's kiss.

I packed a few sippy cups with different drinks, grabbed a package of crackers, and set it all within arms reach of Ava. She had her arms around a ragged stuffed giraffe that she slept with every night and her eyes glued to the screen. While I collapsed onto the couch next to her, my thoughts spun to work. The new trainee. The paperwork for Stella to finalize some accounting.

Sadie.

Serafina.

Sadie.

Maverick's annoyance haunted me. *You're avoiding your problems by staying at work.* That didn't sit well. Maybe because it could be true. Not that it *was*, but it could be. Certainly, I avoided coming home because I hated this empty house with so many responsibilities. And today, I was not in the mood to figure out just how deep that went. Not with the heaping elephant of Sadie fat on my mind.

Instead, I put my hand on my daughter's leg. She glanced at me, then back to the screen. Just when I thought her contempt for me couldn't have gotten any worse, and Sadie's wishes for a damaged relationship between me and Ava would actualize, Ava shuffled. Seconds later, a bright purple pillow landed in my lap.

Ava sprawled on top of it, giraffe in her arms, and whispered, "Will you play with my hair, daddy? It makes me feel better."

"You bet," I said.

And somewhere, deep in my chest, my hidden heart finally cracked. Maybe she didn't hate me.

Maybe the two of us could do this.

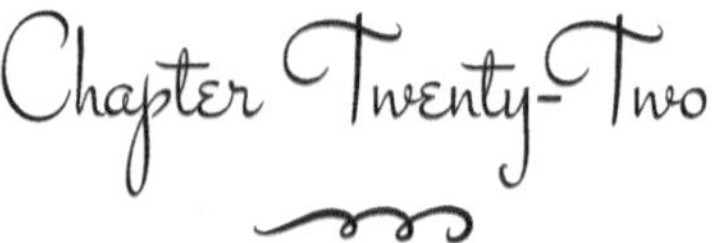

Chapter Twenty-Two

SERAFINA

The slow plod of Talmage's heartbeat rang in my ears as I sat next to his gurney, my head in my hands.

Nurses quietly bustled in and out as they administered fluids and medications meant to counteract whatever drugs they suspected he'd taken in. They'd already drawn labs, saying words like *toxicology* and *electrolytes* and I numbly relayed all the verbiage to my Dad over text. Mom would show up tonight after a red-eye flight into Jackson City, where the hospital awaited.

Talmage was conscious now, but his eyes were closed. Misery was etched onto his features. We hadn't spoken. There wasn't much to say. Amber hovered in my mind's eye, and I wondered what hole she'd skulked to while my brother lay dying. Had she thrown the shattered glass? Had he?

In the calm, my mind replayed through each moment again and again. Jayson's heroic actions and reassurance. The chatter of dispatch with updates. The sirens as they twirled down the road from the local volunteer fire department. I'd splattered myself against the wall to stay out of the way and prayed Talmage would wake back up. He woke up once they administered some medication all right, nearly a violent mess.

Then I rode in the ambulance with the volunteer driver and EMT all the way up the canyon, spitting out as much knowledge as I had about my brother for their paperwork. Then I said it all again in the ER.

And, in the back of my mind, I still thought of Amber.

Amber his dealer.

Amber, the woman that moonlighted in his life as a girl-friend, but only really cared about herself.

Amber who had stolen my brother.

This wasn't entirely her fault. Talmage was a grown man and made his own decisions. A hearty portion of my grief and rage pinned precisely on his responsible shoulders. If it wasn't Amber, maybe it would be someone else.

But maybe not.

If he hadn't met her, would he have started into street drugs? The question would forever remain unanswered, because Amber was a thorn in our side until Talmage let her go.

Talmage's phone, which I'd fished out of his jeans after they'd stripped him, put him into a gown, and let me into his ER space, lingered in my palm. It was a crappy old flip phone that I didn't know they even made these days. I remembered when he sent me a selfie from the new smartphone he'd bought last year, in which he glared and said via text *selfies are stupid* and then sent a GIF that made me laugh so hard I cried.

Had he sold it for drug money?

My heart turned back over as I looked at the text message thread between them.

Amber: come up with enough. I can bring it over but I'm not giving you more without cash

Talmage: can't sell the truck

Amber: or won't

Talmage: don't mess with me Amber. I need more
right now

Amber: i'll contact my guy and be over tonight

That last message came yesterday at 4:13. Presumably, Amber had showed up at some point after that. Whatever she'd given Talmage, he'd overdosed on. Did she stay? Did she realize what happened and bail so she wouldn't get into trouble? Most likely. She and I had a reckoning that brewed in our future.

My nostrils flared with rage at Amber, at Talmage, and life in general. The man on the cot was wasting away. His house had been unkempt and filthy, like he hadn't even tried in days. It made me want to take a shower. I didn't even know him anymore, and that was something I deeply mourned. How long would this spiral last?

And where did it end?

At a morgue, probably.

My eyes felt like sandpaper as I closed them and rubbed my forehead. We'd been in the ER for almost ten hours. Another deputy lingered just outside his room, waiting for medical clearance to take him to book at the county jail.

After that, I had no idea what came next. The note on Talmage's door had been obscure, something about money owed. Bills littered his counter, unopened. Would he default on his mortgage soon?

The time crept steadily toward midnight. Weary, I rubbed my forehead. Jayson and I had found Talmage sometime around 11:45 am. Mom's flight came in at 11:15 tonight. Or was it midnight? The world felt blurry. Ava popped into my head. Was Benjamin able to find someone else to take care of her? Did he take time off of work? Most likely, she just hung out with him at work again.

The thought made me unaccountably sad. Weirdness with Benjamin aside, I missed them both tonight. I should have explained to Benjamin what happened with Talmage, but it all occured so quickly. How did I text that sort of thing anyway? *Brother overdosed and might be dead. Can't come into work today.* I'd called work and texted him before the ambulance even showed up. Disappointment that he hadn't followed up or checked on me came next, but I brushed that aside.

Because what were we anyway?

Ghosts. That's what it felt like. We were surging toward something, and now he seemed to have pulled back. Then again, maybe he thought the same about me and these were just miserable circumstances.

Plus, I hadn't exactly responded to his last text.

Tonight, I was too emotionally exhausted and numb to reach out. Sleep was the next best step. Knowing Benjamin, it didn't mean anything that I didn't hear from him except he didn't want to deal with text messages. Or maybe he was avoiding me now that Sadie had reared her ugly head again. Every nerve end in my body felt frazzled, and I just wanted to curl up at home and sleep.

Tomorrow, I promised myself. I'd have a very frank, honest conversation with him then. We'd lay it out and get this awkward space behind us.

The drapes parted with the hiss of metal on metal and drew me from my thoughts. I braced myself for the nurse, but a weary face and bright eyes met me instead.

"Sera baby?"

Tears filled my eyes as Mom stepped into the room and threw her arms around me. I melted into her with relief, grateful to turn this disaster over to her more capable hands.

"Mom," I whispered. "I'm so glad you came."

I kept my eyes closed, but could feel her scrutiny of Talmage over my shoulder. She'd hold strong right now, but later, when Dad showed up, she'd break down. It was her way. And tonight, I was so grateful for that strength.

Chapter Twenty-Three

BENJAMIN

Pins and needles had taken over my body in a ruthless assault. When the welling nausea attacked again, I leaned over the toilet and vomited. Once my stomach emptied for the tenth time, I sank to the floor and pressed my face to the cold tile.

I wanted to die.

In the doorway, Ava pranced closer on her tiptoes. Her snarled hair fell in her face, and her pajamas were rumpled. Through the haze of illness, I could at least tell that she was walking on her own this morning.

"You're sick too, Daddy?"

"Yeah," I croaked, then groaned.

"Want some fizzy stuff?"

"Sure."

I didn't, but it gave her something to do instead of staring at me, curled on the floor and ready to pass out. Several minutes passed. I may have started to fall asleep again because I jerked back to life when Ava set a cup on the floor next to me.

"Here Dad."

"Thanks. Why don't you go watch ponies?"

"Kay," she said softly, then padded away. She wouldn't be

able to go back to school today, even though she appeared mostly better, and I couldn't have driven to save my own life. Somehow, I managed to crawl back to my bed and grab my phone. Every part of my body felt weak as I unlocked the screen and pulled up my messages to send one to Serafina.

Benjamin: Sick today don't come over

Only a few seconds passed before a reply beeped through. Or maybe it was hours. The spans of darkness that happened in between everything made it impossible to know. My brain could barely hold onto my own name, I certainly wasn't tracking the passage of time.

Groggily, I forced myself to look at the new message.

Serafina: Oh no! I'll bring soup as soon as I'm off work. Need anything else?

Before I could respond, I fell back to sleep on the thought that Ava had it right. It would make me feel better to have someone playing with my hair right now.

Chapter Twenty-Four

SERAFINA

The enticing smell of coffee drifted into my nose as I climbed the spiral staircase to my loft after work. The whirring of machines and quiet murmur of voices was a distant sound as I shut the door and let out a long sigh.

The smell of chicken noodle soup and fresh cookies greeted me next. Mom stood in my small kitchenette with a black apron on. Several small boxes stood in old grocery bags, no doubt filled with fresh soup ready for Benjamin. As soon as Ben had texted, I'd forwarded it to her. She replied, *I was born ready for this.*

She glanced up with a smile.

"Hey. Just got everything ready for Ben and Ava. I found crayons with glitter in them for sweet Ava. Can you believe that? Where have *they* been all my life?"

"Thanks, Mom."

"You bet."

Her cheeks and eyes were slightly reddened and swollen, even though she didn't so much as sniffle now. Definitely had been crying. A bag of cookies lingered amongst all the goodies, and it smelled like another batch might be in the oven. Mom was stress baking. I leaned against the wall with a sigh. Only one person could cause that right now.

"News on T?" I asked quietly.

After she'd talked to the doctors last night, and briefly with Talmage, who said almost nothing, we'd come back to Pineville in her rental car and crashed. A measly four hours of sleep lay behind me, combined with a long day at work, but I was grateful for a routine to fall into.

A morose expression crossed her face. "I'm able to sign him out of jail in just a few hours. They took him back after the hospital cleared him."

"And then?"

"We have flights home this evening."

"He's going with you?"

She nodded. "Yeah. I'm getting him out of here. I spoke with him this morning. He's still not feeling great, but he's good enough to fly. Your father will pick us up at the airport."

"And then?"

"Rehab, I hope. That kind of depends on what he decides. There's only so much help we can give. He has to do the rest."

"Good. I'm relieved they'll let you take him."

"For now, yes."

"You seem . . . sad."

Tears sparkled in her eyes, but she blinked them back. "I am. I'm very sad. Talmage deserves better than the choices he's made. But I'm working through that. We'll bring him back in six weeks for his court date, but Dad is already looking at rehab centers, and T has agreed."

Relief expanded in my chest like a cloud.

"That's wonderful."

A watery smile came next. "It is. Let's hope that we can get him out of his situation, sell his house, and help him start over again."

There was such hope in her expression that I didn't have the heart to beg her to stay with me. To tell her that I needed her. She was such a light that I couldn't bear to have her leave. Not with things so uncertain around Benjamin and me. But I held back. No, Mom needed to conserve all her emotional energy to get back home with Talmage. I'd be fine here.

Now Talmage would be gone, and hopefully that rat Amber would disappear to destroy another hovel. My responsibility to my brother had been fulfilled, so I didn't have to stay. My thoughts ran to Benjamin. We desperately needed to talk and lay out where things sat so I didn't make assumptions and break my own heart before there was need. Ava and Benjamin were my only ties here now. I wanted them.

Did they still want me?

Although I didn't know for sure, the discussion about Sadie still hung over my head like a dark cloud. While I had no blame there, I had a feeling Ben was pulling away because of what happened. Sadie's ghost, or something. The same ghost that seemed to have him convinced he was a terrible father, when he wasn't. Had Sadie told him as much?

Until I spoke with him, I couldn't confirm any of my suspicions. Now that Mom had finished everything here with T, I could go over and check on Ben. I straightened up when my phone buzzed in my back pocket. My heart illuminated with a moment of hope, then fell when I didn't see his name.

Bethany: Serafina! Any chance you can stop by and check on Ava for me? I got tied up with something and can't get over there until tonight. She's home sick with Ben. He might be too.

Serafina: Already on my way with some soup! I got this, you take care of that.

Bethany: Text me updates. Thank you so much!

Mom pulled the apron off. "Well, at least we've started the process of getting T somewhere better. We'll see if it can stick."

"I'm happy for Talmage having a new start," I said with a trying smile. "And glad that we can get him into a better place."

It felt like a death knoll in something, but I wasn't sure what yet.

"You going to Ben's now?" She nudged the bags packed with containers. "Lots of goodies ready for them."

"Thanks, Mom. If Ben is saying he's sick, it's probably death-bed level serious."

Mom reached out and put a hand on my face. I leaned into her warm, comforting touch with a rush of gratitude and love. A loving touch that someone like Amber probably never had. A loving touch Talmage *did* have, but bad things happened to all people regardless. He had his own demons, apparently. I soaked it up, then gave her a huge hug and kiss.

"Thank you," I said, and she held me close for a long, restorative moment.

As soon as she pulled away, she shoved the food my way and reached for the car keys. "Let's go help them feel better. I'll drop you off. Ava needs a woman's touch now more than ever, I'm sure. Love you, honey. Be safe."

* * *

Bags rustled off my arms as I shuffled into Ben's house a few minutes later. Mom pulled away in the rental car with a wave and I responded just before I shut the back door behind me.

Now, the sound of a TV played in the background as Ava rushed over, still in pajamas that had been buttoned wrong and wild, tangled hair. She smiled and threw her arms around my legs.

"Serafina! I missed you."

"Hey girlfriend!" I set the bags aside and crouched next to

her to receive her hug. Her little body felt normal and her eyes were clear. "I missed you too! Sorry about yesterday. You're sick, huh?"

With a pathetic face, she nodded. "But I'm feeling better now."

"Are you hungry?"

Her eyes widened dramatically. I nudged her toward the table. "Go sit down. I brought hot chicken noodle soup and my Mom sent some cookies."

Ava obeyed while I did a quick scan of the house. Chaos abounded. Dishes on the counters, open cracker packages, five different types of drinks, and clothes on the floor near the washer. While I ladled some soup in a bowl for her, Ava hummed and shoved her gnarled hair out of her eyes every five seconds.

"Where's your dad?"

"In his room. He's sick too."

"Have you been throwing up?"

Her nose wrinkled. "Yeah. Dad too."

"Tummy still hurt?"

"A little."

She grabbed the spoon when I set it in front of her, but I held up a finger in warning. "Eat slowly," I said. "See how your tummy feels. Just a little at a time, okay? Then we're going to take a bath and brush your hair. That will help you feel lots better."

"'Kay," she said, and shoved a heaping spoonful in her mouth. I monitored the first few bites, my stomach in a knot for her. Everything seemed to stay down so far. Next, I had to find her father. Did I want to find Benjamin? His text at work today had been a relief, and a worry. Maybe he hadn't responded yesterday because they were sick.

I found him in his room, curled up around his covers like a peanut and pale as his sheets. He had a low fever when I pressed my hand to his face. He stirred with a moan, but didn't wake up. A wet rag and a giant bowl sat on this bedside table. The room smelled acrid, so I yanked open a window to bring cool, fresh air into the room. He didn't even wake up.

I stopped at his bedside. Even in sleep, he had a sort of power about him. His firm jaw. Thick neck. A lock of hair had fallen across his neck in an adorable little curl that I pushed to the side.

Affection welled up inside me, followed by a healthy rush of fear. Would he push me out of his life because of Sadie?

I banished the thought. It wasn't helping at all.

Over the next couple of hours, Ava and I made sense of the house again. She took a long warm bath, I brushed the snarls out of her hair and French braided it so it would be out of the way for a few days. Then we played a few games, made sure she was caught up on her homework, and she wearily went to bed early.

Darkness had fallen on the house by the time I checked on Ben again. He tossed and turned in his bed every now and then, and I'd thought I heard retching at some point, but he hadn't emerged from his room.

Just before full dark, I put the soup in a container, shoved it in the fridge, and left a note.

Hope you feel better soon. Soup in the fridge. I'll stop by to pick Ava up for school in the morning.

With regret, I left the house to walk home when all I wanted to do was stay.

* * *

A bowl of half-eaten soup, some cracker crumbs, and a glass of tea dirtied the counter when I showed up the next morning to take Ava to school. Benjamin's door was closed, so I didn't venture into his room. Just quietly helped Ava get ready, grab a quick breakfast, then left out the back door. Thankfully, Dagny covered my early shift by herself at the Diner. I returned to work and felt like everything inside me waited on tenterhooks.

Would Benjamin be okay?

Would he text me?

My phone remained obnoxiously silent. I'd sent a message to Benjamin this morning after I dropped Ava off, asking him if he felt better. No response so far.

"Uh oh," Dagny mumbled under her breath. "Here c-comes trouble."

My head lifted. A rush of nerves followed when a familiar head of greasy, mousy blonde hair stepped into the Diner. Amber looked skeletal this morning, her face thrown into gaunt shadows, particularly around her eyes. For a moment, all I could do was blink at her in shock. Why had she come *here*? I'd never seen her away from my brother's house.

"Call Hernandez quietly," I murmured to Dagny. "Just let him know she's here. He wanted to talk to her. I'll deal with her."

"G-got it."

Dagny disappeared into the back as I advanced into the Diner with a falsely warm smile. Amber folded her arms across her middle and glared at me. Her gaze darted around the half-full tables.

"Hey, Amber. Table for one?"

"Where's Tal?"

"He's gone."

She shifted uneasily. "He okay?"

"No."

"He must be alive," she snapped, a little too loudly, "or they wouldn't have released him from the hospital."

"Oh." I arched an eyebrow. "So you know that he needed a hospital stay?"

Her frown deepened, giving her an otherworldly, terrifying kind of look. The listless edge of her eyes was frightening enough. Taken with her contempt and desperation as a whole, I'd never met anyone that startled me this much. Not even when I'd backpacked through southeast Asia.

"When will he be back home?" she mumbled.

"Never."

Her gaze jumped to mine. She had the audacity to gasp. "What?"

"My mom is taking him back to live with them and go into rehab for whatever disgusting filth you've been giving him. As soon as he approves, the plan is to put his house up for sale to resolve his debts."

A derisive snort took over her face, twisting it grotesquely. "Of course. Mommy saves the day. Must be nice."

Frustration welled up within me, warring for compassion. She was such a pathetic little creature. At one time, she was probably normal. Lovely. Full of chance and a bright future. But life had beaten her down. Circumstances beyond her control had probably nudged her onto this path, and she'd chosen to stay and invite others to it. She probably didn't have family that could, or would, swoop in to help out, which made me sad for her.

But I wasn't about to let her near my brother again.

Whatever her path, she'd made choices too. Now, I just wanted to never see her again and wish her luck on her path.

"We could get help for you too, if you wanted it," I said quietly, although it was a promise I had no power to make.

Amber rolled her eyes. "Can I speak with him?" she asked. "I just . . . need to talk to him about something."

"Money he owes you?"

She fidgeted with the bottom of her shirt and didn't answer. I folded my arms across my chest.

"No, you can't see him again, but I'll let him know you asked."

Annoyance made her gaze hot. Her nostrils thinned.

"I cared about him." Her voice was a dark rasp, and I sensed sincerity behind the words. "It's . . . he's a nice guy. I don't want him to get hurt."

"Little late for that."

Her jaw tightened.

"I'm sorry, Amber." I softened my response. "But you'll never see him again, if I have anything to say about it. He's going to go get better and he won't be back. With any luck we can sell the house and he can start over at home."

"He owes me a lot of money," she hissed through clenched teeth, her gaze suddenly bright with something like rage. Any caring she'd had—or pretended to have—disappeared. "I can't just walk away without anything."

"Hernandez is looking for you," I said. "Dagny called to tell him that you're here. He has questions for you. So you can stay and wait for him to show up, or you can make yourself scarce. I'd prefer the latter."

Amber snarled at me and advanced a step. "You think you can sweep in and save Talmage? You think I won't have the last word? He is my boyfriend and I love him! He owes me money!"

Her love and his debt seemed inseparably connected in her mind, and maybe they were in a life like this. Her voice rose several pitches, drawing the gaze of everyone in the Diner. I held my ground, arms at my side, chin high.

"If you love him," I said, "then you'll let him go."

Dagny stepped out from the back, followed by our fry cook, a burly man with a baby face and jowls like a pitbull. Amber shrank back at the sight of him.

"Time to go," he growled.

With one last sneer at me, she turned and skulked away, disappearing around the back of the building. I drew in a deep breath, pivoted on my heel, and stepped into the back. Dagny stood at my side, a hand on my arm, as I cooled down in the aftermath of the visit.

"That w-was intense," Dagny said. "You did g-good."

"She . . . infuriates me and inspires pity all at the same time. I don't know whether I want to hug her or slap her."

"B-b-both, I bet."

My blood still streamed through my body with shock and tremors when, minutes later, Jayson stepped through the swinging doors and right into the back. His gaze swung over to us almost immediately. Next to me, Dagny stiffened. Her gaze darted away.

"Hey Sera, is Amber gone already?" he asked.

"Yeah." I nodded. "Sorry, she didn't stay long. She headed toward the back, around the right of the Diner."

He sighed. "Not your fault. I tried to get here as soon as I could."

Dagny's hand shrank away from mine as she stepped away and put her back to us, busying herself with ice and a cup, even though no new customers had come into the Diner. I pulled in a deep, calming breath.

"Let me know if you see her again?" Jayson asked as he edged backward. "I'm going to go drive around and see if I can find her."

"I will."

He disappeared through the doors, and Dagny relaxed. I eyed her, suspicious of the way she stared out the swinging doors with a sigh on the edge of her lips.

"Hernandez?" I asked her.

She opened her mouth to protest, then grimaced. "Th-that obvious?"

"Not to him."

"N-n-never to him. He has no idea that I exist."

"You serve him all the time. He knows you exist."

Her gaze tapered. "W-well, yes. He sees that I'm h-h-here, but I have a knac-ck for f-f-fading into the background." She smiled broadly. "It's the way I like it. W-w-with him . . . it's even b-better."

"Better that he doesn't know you crush hard?" I guessed, grateful to escape the thought of Amber for a while. Dagny grinned, but it was woeful.

"Yes." She shuddered. "I hope he n-n-never knows that. We're f-friends. I'd like it to s-stay that way."

Chapter Twenty-Five

BENJAMIN

I stared hard at Serafina's text message. Vomiting my brains out for hours made everything fuzzy, but the world was more clear now than it had been last time I was conscious.

Serafina: Ava is off to school just fine. Are you feeling any better today? You looked pretty wrecked yesterday.

Serafina had been here?

I rubbed my eyes with the heel of my hand and stumbled into the house. Vague memories of waking up to the sound of bustling, a woman's quiet voice, and Ava's high-pitched response, filtered through my mind. That had been Bethany, right? She'd planned on stopping back by after some showings.

Everything was clean, organized, and smelled faintly like bleach. I grabbed the note on the counter that I'd read last night before I attempted soup at 2:00 am. My assumption was that it had been from Bethany.

Apparently not.

I texted Sera back.

Benjamin: Much better. Thanks. Were you here yesterday?

Serafina: Yes. I came over after work and stayed until Ava fell asleep.

Benjamin: I'm sorry, I didn't know. Thought it was Bethany.

Serafina: You were pretty out of it.

Benjamin: Thank you for your help.

My eyes sprinted all over the house again. Maybe it was the weak feeling in my body. Maybe it was just the circumstances around me. Maybe it was the clarity of so much sleep, but I felt a welling of dread in my stomach.

Sick or not, I couldn't put off talking to Serafina anymore. We had to figure this out.

Benjamin: Can you come over later and talk?

Serafina: I'd like that.

An hour, one very long shower, fresh clothes, and a change of sheets later, I felt exhausted, but restored. After checking in with the MMA Center—which ran surprisingly smooth without me there to coordinate—and answering a few emails, I lay back on my couch and stared at the ceiling.

So many thoughts streamed through my head, the greatest of which was the most obvious: *I am not good for Serafina.*

The scales were balanced way out of her favor. First, she took care of us, just like yesterday. I never really got a chance to take care of her. Second, I'd kissed her like a dying man, but hadn't even taken her on a real date. She received the dredges of my time and attention, meanwhile poured her time and attention into me. When she didn't have to, she cared for both of us. The list of what she did for me extended into eternity when I considered that she cleaned my house, made me food, and cared for my daughter.

Just like I had with Sadie. Given my all, my everything, and to what?

Dredges.

Even after I'd been a cold and distant jerk that kissed her like he meant it, then didn't even text.

And what did I give to her?

Aside from a paycheck, which she hadn't even cashed yet, nothing. Clarity rose in my mind despite the haze of feeling sick. Wasn't I already just like Sadie? Sucking time and attention and not giving back? Ava was my first priority, which meant Serafina had to come second. Even third. Sadie had always been Sadie's first priority, and I had come in the dredges of her time after everything else. She kept me close enough to control, satisfied enough that I didn't rock the boat. Never the priority.

I couldn't do that to Sera.

My fists clenched. The knot of tension unfolded in my chest like cords of fire. It still burned, but now I knew what it was. We had to figure this out. I cared for Sera, probably even loved her, though I wasn't really sure what that looked like. Whatever this desire to protect and hold her meant, it was more than I'd ever felt for anyone before.

But how could my world ever be fair to her?

* * *

A timid knock came on the front door later that afternoon. Bethany had picked Ava up from the bus stop and taken her home while I disappeared into a second nap. It restored a bit more humanity to my life, and another bowl of soup sank into my belly and stayed there. When I opened the door, I wasn't sure what to expect.

Serafina stood on the porch with a crock of food in her hand. The sweet gesture knifed through me. Of course, she brought even more comfort and nourishment into my life. A car pulled away from the driveway, but I couldn't see who waited inside. Dagny had dropped her off, likely.

"This is kind of hot," she said, her gaze hidden behind aviators and her usual bouncing hair. "Can I go set it down?"

Too late, I realized I'd been awkwardly standing there, holding the door open. I startled and stepped back with a wave of my arm.

"Of course. Sorry."

An awkward tension followed us inside the house as I closed the door and she slipped into the kitchen. The warm smell of beef, potatoes, and fresh bread followed. My mouth watered. Had she brought homemade bread and beef stew? I sincerely hoped so, even while it frustrated me.

Why did she have to be so good?

Part of me hoped that she'd realized just how much she did in this situation. How little she gave received for what she gave. I wanted her to stand up for herself, the way that I never did to Sadie.

Instead of telling her all that, I followed her into the kitchen like a lost puppy.

Her flip flops slipped their way over the floor and her hair bounced behind her as she walked. The smell of coffee followed gently in her wake, as if the coffee shop permeated her life so deeply.

"It's beef stew," she said. Her voice had a higher pitch to it, like she was holding something back. She puttered her way around my kitchen expertly, probably because she'd organized most of it, and all without looking my way once. "There are some homemade rolls and I wasn't sure if you had butter so I—"

I trapped her wrist with my hand, stopping her. She paused but didn't look at me. Even without the full power of her eyes, I could see exhaustion in her. Fatigue drove the slow blinks of her eyes. The weariness in her low shoulders.

"Sera, we need to talk."

A thousand other words wanted to rush out of my mouth right then. *Stay with me. Marry me. Be mine forever.* No, I couldn't go down that path. I may have been a selfish bastard in the past, but I wouldn't be now. Not for Sera, because Sera mattered. I would not become Sadie to her. Suck the soul and life out of her, then leave her a bitter, hollow shell.

Something in her slumped shoulders told me things weren't good. Did she already know that something was wrong? I hadn't exactly been communicating, but I'd also wanted to die from vomiting my bowels out. I released her when her skin burned against mine.

She bit her bottom lip and said, "Sure."

Suddenly, I felt like I had too many hands and didn't know what to do with them. With a helpless gesture, I motioned to the couch. "Let's talk in here. I just had some of the other soup so I'll save this for later. Thank you again."

The formal tension between us could have thickened the air until I couldn't breathe. I pointedly ignored it and led the way. She shuffled behind, but her footsteps were uncertain. When I sat on the couch and angled toward her, forearms on my knees, she followed. Her aviators came off and tucked her hair around her face, revealing uncertain eyes.

I swallowed. All my planned words had suddenly fled and what came out was the result of pure fear.

"I don't think I'm good for you."

Her brow crinkled. While I tried to gather air back into my lungs to explain, her mouth dropped open.

"What?" she croaked.

Agitated already, I rubbed the back of my neck and leapt to my feet. She stayed on the couch, appearing small, her head tilted back to watch me pace.

"You do so much for us, Sera, and I don't really give you anything in return. I'm afraid that if we let things go any farther, you're just going to hate me in the end."

Saying the words felt like a cascade of relief. At the same time, my world seemed to have paused. Several moments passed again before she was able to pull words together. When she responded, it was a whisper.

"I could never hate you, Ben."

I scoffed. "You can, I promise. Sadie did, even though things were so good in the beginning. It seemed like the issues that destroyed most relationships could never touch us. But everything changed. We're not even, Serafina. You are beyond me. I . . . have Ava." My voice dropped. "I could never bring to this relationship the same things you do. Could never be as present for you as you are for me."

I ran a hand through my hair. This didn't feel as good or as right coming out as I wanted it to. The expected relief didn't follow again. Venting it was one thing. Living it was another thing entirely.

Why didn't she say anything?

She blinked several times. "Ben, I . . . ." She stood, and I stopped pacing. We stood three feet apart, but the heat from her gaze still slammed into me. She tilted her chin up slightly, her shoulders squared. Despite her defiant posture, her tone was gentle.

"Ben, I love you."

My soul shattered in a million pieces. *No,* I wanted to say. *I can't be too late. How could you love someone so broken?*

Like a sucker punch to the ribs, I sucked in a sharp breath.

She couldn't love me.

How could she love me?

"Exactly as you are, right now," she continued, brave despite what must have looked like fright on my face. "You give me *you* and that's all I want. You are enough, Benjamin Mercedey. For me. For Ava."

"You say that now, but what if that's not enough later?" I whispered. "When things are even harder. When we're deeper into this and our true colors come out and things aren't as exciting?"

A wounded look came to her face. I stepped forward, nearly toppled by the lightest scent of coconut shampoo as it slammed into me.

"Serafina, I haven't even taken you on a date. I've kissed you without even dating you." I swallowed hard. "There are things I want to do to you that . . ."

My fists clenched with a blaze of heat, and it took all my considerable control not to bound across the space and grab her. I wanted to lock her into my arms and never come back up for air.

Her eyes were so wide the edges were ringed in white.

"I don't know if I can earn the right to have you," I continued mercilessly. Because she had to know. "Two days ago, I wanted to help you after you sent me that text. Wanted to call you and find you and see if everything was okay. But Ava called right after. She was sick and needed me to pick her up from school. I couldn't be there for you. Not the way you're always here for us. This is what happened with Sadie. It was perfect in the beginning, but it changed. It devolved. Eventually, she became a monster that took, and took, and took. She would have owned my soul if I let her. Maybe she even did. I can't . . . I can't be that to you."

Her hand twitched at her side, but stayed there. For a long, long time, something swelled between us. I couldn't read her gaze. She appeared exhausted. There were bags under her eyes, and I realized that I didn't know what had been happening for her the last couple of days.

Perhaps this was more selfish than I'd thought.

Finally, she asked, "What do you propose, Ben? Is this you breaking—" Her brow furrowed into deeper confusion. "What does this mean?"

"I don't know."

Her nostrils flared. "You can have it or you can't, Ben," she said furiously. "You brought this up. *You* have decided for me that I won't benefit from an arrangement that previously made me very happy. You tell me what *you* want now."

The feeling of being a selfish jerk that I'd been trying to avoid all this time started to creep up. Had I completely misinterpreted all of this? How could she possibly find joy in a relationship that didn't offer something back?

I just didn't want to be Sadie.

Didn't want to destroy Sera the way Sadie destroyed me. Until I was in a position to do more for Sera, how could this ever be fair?

"I want you to be happy and safe," I finally said. "That's all I will ever want for you."

She sucked in a sharp breath and moved back a step. "No," she whispered, and moved back another. "That's a damn lie, Benjamin Mercedy. A lie you're telling yourself to feel better. You don't want that more than something else, because I *was* happy and safe. *You* made me feel safe. Being with you and Ava brought me joy. I understand that you're trying, in some convoluted way, to do what seems right in your head. But you're missing the point." She pressed a trembling hand to her chest. "I'm. Not. Sadie."

"I never thought you were," I said quickly. "You could never be Sadie. You're too good Sera. I am the Sadie in this situation."

She softened slightly. "But *you* aren't either," she added quietly. Her head tilted to the side with a sorrow that stunned me. "You're afraid, Ben. That's what's wrong here. This isn't about me—not really. This is about Sadie and her hold on you. Until you let her go, you're right. We aren't ready for each other. You can't give enough to me, Ben, simply because you don't even have enough for yourself. Sadie still does. You can't even let yourself see what a good dad you are. It's like she's still whispering in your ears, or something."

"Sera . . ."

But my response died. I didn't know what to say. Her jaw tightened when her gaze dropped to the ground. Another silence followed, as if she debated something, before she finally pulled in a deep breath. Her shoulders set. The abyss of fatigue in her expression made me want to reach for her, but I held back.

"I wasn't going to tell you," she said, "because you have a lot going on right now, but you should know that Talmage overdosed two days ago."

My jaw dropped. "What?"

"Jayson took me to Talmage's house on my lunch break yesterday and we found him. He's fine," she added, "for now. My mom signed him out of jail and he's agreed to try a rehab place back at home. They're already gone."

"Sera, I'm so sorry."

Tears glittered in her eyes. "I had planned to stay in Pineville because of you and Ava. Because I love you both. But if being apart is really what you want, I won't stay. So if this is the path you want, I need you to be sure. Once I leave, I won't be coming back."

A tear dripped down her cheek. Words failed me. With one last haunted gaze, she turned and walked out the front door. It closed quietly behind her, the *snick* of the lock like a bomb in the night.

I slowly lowered to the couch and hung my head in my hands.

Chapter Twenty-Six

SERAFINA

The quiet shuffle of the coffee shop below settled around me as I cried. Hot tears broke through my fingers and dropped onto my pillow. Not for the first time, I wished Mom back already. Wanted her to play with my hair the way Ben had only a few days ago. Reassure me that every darkness would eventually fade.

Now, I just felt stupid.

Crushed. Blind. Confused. Livid. The emotions knotted up in a giant tangle deep in my chest until I didn't know one from the other. In some more perverse ways, this ending came as a relief. A relief that whatever gorgeous thing Benjamin and I could have had ended, because I supposed I'd always thought it would. All of them did, eventually, because none of them ever inspired me to stay. Leaving had been easy after the initial drama of pain.

Yet . . . none had felt like this.

The others had the depth of onion skin compared to my time with Ben. Of all the boyfriends in all the countries and all the circumstances that I'd experienced, none of them saw me with the same intensity. None of them stoked a fire in my stomach just when they looked my way.

The fact that Benjamin saw the relationship so differently than me set all of this on a different axis. Should I have told him point-blank that, like my mom, I showed my love through giving? That food and care was a comfort, but really just a way to connect? To create stronger bonds? It fed my soul to be part of their lives.

To be part of *something*.

No, it wouldn't have mattered. Whatever fear he battled was deeper than me taking care of them. He'd already decided that things wouldn't work. The only person that could convince him that we'd work was him. His fear was Sadie-deep, and the only person to swim those waters was Ben.

Somehow, he'd managed to pull Sadie into what we had. That I could barely comprehend his reasons—as sincere as he seemed them to be—made it almost impossible to understand.

Two more tears slid free, scouring my already painful cheeks from the previous hour of crying. Did he deserve this kind of response? This level of pain? We'd only kissed a few times. And, as soul-turning as it had been, he was right. We really hadn't been on a date. Everything between us was the result of working together for Ava. Passionate exchanges. Him helping me navigate this strange world of Talmage's new addiction. Was my heart-break pre-emptive or excessive?

What did it matter? The pain was real. The loss was even more real.

The loft lay in almost-darkness when I wrapped myself up in a blanket and lowered onto the couch, eyes stinging and puffy. The cushions felt cool beneath my cheek, and a breeze wafted inside from an open window. Sounds of Pineville at night followed, and the sense of not being alone was oddly soothing.

Finally, my tears slowed.

Eventually, my thoughts cleared, then shuttered themselves into neat little lines.

There would be no getting through to Benjamin from my

end. Even if he came over tonight and said he wanted to try again, I'd send him away until he faced whatever Sadie demon still worked within him.

But I had my life to think about now.

This situation meant some potentially awkward moments after I took care of Ava, but if I played it right, Ben and I could almost avoid each other. As long as I knew when he would be home, I'd be ready to leave the moment he stepped inside. With summer here, I could easily walk back to the Frolicking Moose in the daylight, and Pineville wasn't that scary anyway. After a week or two, it would be tolerable, I was sure.

Knowing that there would be no more of his smell wrapped around me, however, gave me a physical pain. No more making myself at home in his space. No more feeling *safe*. The loss of such security crushed my very heart.

One week. I'd give Benjamin one more week to sort through the Sadie monster. If he still wasn't ready to face the truth, I would leave. If he didn't do that within the next week, would he do it at all? Seeing him at night when he returned from work would help me gage whether the budding relationship we had would live or die. If he worked out his Sadie issues, I'd know it by then.

And if not?

I'd stay long enough to find someone for Ava, then I'd move onto my next place. Tomorrow, I'd start to find backup locations for a mountain summer. There had to be thousands of other small mountain towns that could fill my desire for a summer in the sky.

Good plan, I thought, feeling marginally better. The plan behind me wasn't one I wanted, but I had no choice. It left me in a glum, morose mood, but that would eventually lift as the excitement of a new adventure followed.

I hoped.

My eyes fluttered shut. I tried to block out all sounds, afraid that if I listened too hard, I'd hear the crack of my own heart.

* * *

I woke up at 5:30, my neck tight and head swimming like a thick liquid filled it. Bleary-eyed, I struggled to the bathroom, splashed cold water on my face, and completely avoided the mirror.

A cup of coffee revived enough humanity that I was able to stumble into my jeans and t-shirt, slide on my tennis shoes, and shove a pair of reading glasses over my eyes to hide the evidence of tears. My hair went into a sloppy ponytail that sprouted curls like a chia pet down my back, but at least it was out of my face.

With every breath, I avoided thinking of Benjamin.

A brief review of last night after restless sleep didn't paint any prettier of a picture. Just thinking about what he said sent hot prickles back to my eyes. I pushed them back. Normally, I'd sleep off a spurt of heartbreak and be ready to plan the next stop in the morning. Today, I just felt groggy. Worse.

No, I could do this.

I'd go to work, pick up Ava, and live the same day I'd already lived many times. The end of the day, however, would be different this time. That was fine. I could figure this out. I'd done scarier things before.

When my phone buzzed, I snatched it off the floor so fast it flew out of my hands and I bobbled it for five seconds. Once it rested firmly in my clutches, Ben's name flashed across the screen. I had to stop and let out a long breath. My heart raced. A daydream of a text that said, *I'm sorry, come back. I thought about it all night and I totally screwed up,* slipped through my mind.

Finally, I rallied my courage and opened the stupid thing.

Benjamin: I realized while I was sick that I'm not as essential at work as I thought. I'm going to start leaving work at four, so Ava can come to the MMA Center after school and I'll take her home. Then I can spend more needed time with her. Hopefully this softens things for you a bit. I hope you're doing okay with everything. Let me know if I can help with Talmage.

Any hope in my chest withered and died.

He didn't need me.

And now he'd just taken Ava from me.

Like a machine, I grabbed my keys. My backpack. Parts of my heart died with every beat as I shut the door quietly behind me and slipped down the stairs.

Cool, morning air rushed across my face as I stepped outside and around the Frolicking Moose, headed toward the Diner. Cars slipped in and out of the drive-through of the Frolicking Moose while Ellie bustled around inside, surprisingly alert for such a starkly early hour. She gave me a quick wave through the windows as I passed the porch, her dark hair glossy in the growing daylight.

I stopped halfway across the parking lot and gazed across the street. The MMA Center cast light onto their parking lot in the still-quiet morning. A few early-morning bodies worked out at the equipment. I could just make out the figure of the woman I'd seen there before, running it instead of Ben.

My jaw tightened. *Then I can spend more needed time with her.* Yes, Benjamin absolutely needed to spend more time with Ava. Hadn't I encouraged him to do that? To leave work early and come be home with her? He was only doing what was absolutely necessary, particularly in light of what Ava had revealed about Sadie's underhanded tactics.

But he wasn't supposed to do it to the exclusion of me, I thought.

My fist tightened.

Well, that text certainly sealed the deal, didn't it? There

would be no ascertaining whether he was working through his issues now. No seeing him. I'd been shuttled out of his life without a chance to even say goodbye to Ava. He'd made it perfectly clear where we stood. I turned and stalked into the Frolicking Moose.

Ellie glanced up, one eyebrow lifted. She took me in with a quick glance. "You good?" she asked.

"No. Do you have a piece of paper?"

"Sure."

A plain white paper and pen found their way to the counter seconds later. She didn't ask questions as I scrawled across the front.

This is my official two weeks notice, given May 23rd. My last day of work will be June 6th.

Serafina Courdray

Ellie studied me as I shoved the pen back toward her. "Ben's an idiot, isn't he?" she asked.

"The biggest," I snapped.

Her cool gaze met mine. "Whatever he did to break your heart, I'm sorry."

Somehow, despite not knowing any details, there was real sorrow in her voice. Ellie, the sharpest, toughest girl I had ever met, spoke with experience in her moderated tone. In that moment, I felt a bond with her. A sense of broken-heart camaraderie. Tears filled my eyes, but I blinked them back.

"Me too," I whispered.

She tapped her teeth together, as if considering something. When the bell rang indicating a new customer in the drive-through, she ignored it to quietly say, "The first few months are the worst. Eventually, you learn how to live without them again, which brings its own sorrow. I hope healing for you is quick."

With that, she spun on her heels and headed to the window. I watched her go, my stomach in a knot, until I found the strength to turn away.

The fresh air jolted me back to reality again. Although rage still simmered in the background, and I deeply dreaded work today, Ellie was right. Her brief moment reminded me that I had approached all of this wrong. I had to think of getting through this differently.

Smaller.

Today, I just had to get through the day without crying on a customer. That would be my ultimate goal.

The first *everything* after a breakup was always the hardest. First day. First week. First laugh. First date. I just had to re-learn that I could still exist without them. Had to re-learn that the world moved on, and so could I. The first day of that months-long process was always the hardest.

Today. I just had to get today behind me.

The backlights to the counter were still off when I stepped inside the Diner, slapped my paper on the counter in front of Bert, and looked him straight in the eye. Dagny, only a few steps away, eyed the paper.

Then she gasped.

"Sorry, Bert," I said. "But it's time for me to leave."

BENJAMIN

The new take-care-of-Ava-without-Serafina plan seemed almost foolproof. Right now, it might be the only way I could take care of Sera, the way she always took care of us.

After school, Ava would get off the bus at the same stop by the grocery store, but instead of going to the Diner, she'd walk to the MMA Center. She'd hang out at the office with me for half an hour and do her homework while I finished up.

Then we'd leave at four every day to go home, do chores, play. I'd cook dinner. She could have bathtime, then go to bed after we read her books to practice. It's what we'd done before . . . sort of. If getting home at eight or nine at night constituted routine. The new plan offered everything she needed, and those needs were fulfilled by her actual parent. Routine. Parental guidance. Positive reinforcement.

Except I had no idea how to realistically make this happen.

First, I had no idea how to fix meals that she'd ravenously eat, the way she did for Serafina. Ava rarely liked what I had attempted in the past, and the fights it bred over dinner weren't worth the work. I'd have to look into a meal delivery service, which was unlikely in the mountains. Or, maybe, just learn simpler stuff. Spaghetti that didn't taste like watered-down tomato soup with firm noodles, for one.

Second, laundry, housework, oil changes, grocery shopping, and a dozen other adult things had to fit in this plan somewhere. I hated doing all of that, but a maid service felt too much like a privacy invasion. Plus, Ava had to learn to do chores, but someone also had to *teach* her, and that person had to be me. Serafina had created a chore chart somewhere, but I'd already lost it.

Third, my plan still didn't address the fact that Sadie had hated my guts and made it her life mission to turn Ava against me. Nothing but figuring out how to talk to Ava about her mother would fix that problem. That conversation? Ticking time bomb.

Finally, none of this involved Serafina. And that was a much bigger problem than I originally anticipated on every single level.

I frowned at my phone as I considered the text message I'd just sent her. Had she seen it? In hindsight, it sounded too abrupt. I'd just been spinning the idea out and wanted to give her an out. A reason to avoid the awkwardness of seeing me after last night, particularly with all Talmage had given her to worry about. She needed less on her plate, not more, and not dealing with a sassy first-grader would surely lighten her load.

Amidst all this was the undeniable truth that last night, she'd single-handedly given me the emotional smackdown of my life. Not even talking to my ailing mother, who had also called yesterday, had been so devastating. No one could wound me like Sera. Not even Sadie, which seemed like it meant something.

My thoughts spun back over Serafina's challenge regarding Sadie. The sorrow in her eyes hit me harder than anything else. Was she right about that? Of course she was probably right, because it hurt like a beast to think about and I'd been avoiding it all this time. Just like I avoided coming home.

Why did I do that?

And now that I had an opportunity to be home more, why did it tighten my throat?

With a ragged, sleep-deprived sigh, I ran a hand through my hair. A quiet voice appeared at my elbow, and I glanced over to see Ava standing there.

"I'm ready for school," she said, a new, bright teal lunchbox in hand. "Serafina is picking me up after school today, right? It's milkshake day and I'm so excited! Bert said I could try the birthday cake one with sprinkles in it!"

A groan escaped me and I slapped a hand against my face. I'd totally forgotten that I still had to talk to Ava about our new arrangement. And we needed to talk about her deceitful, deceased mother. Not to mention her reading schedule. Which, according to her teacher, had been improving since Serafina's work with her before bed. What books did they read anyway?

"Okay." I grabbed the SUV keys. "One thing at a time, Mercedy. Let's get this day over with."

Ava's nose scrunched. "Are you talking to yourself?"

I put a hand on her shoulder and wheeled her to the door. "It's a dad thing, just ignore me."

She giggled. "Sera does it too."

That certainly didn't help. While Ava buckled into the back seat, I backed the SUV out of the driveway with Serafina's voice ringing through my head.

If this is the path you want, I need you to be sure. Once I leave, I won't be coming back.

Asking her to come back solely for my own comfort was out of the question, but I couldn't say I hadn't considered it. I'd never ask her to return to our lives just to take care of us. If Serafina came back, it had to be for all the right reasons. The ones that, when I thought about it, Sadie seemed to block.

Unfortunately, I had no idea what the hell I wanted anymore.

* * *

My fingers drummed the counter later that afternoon as I strove to keep my tone moderated. Ava and I had just returned home and I'd already snapped at her. She'd given me attitude back and I'd just *barely* escaped a yelling match.

Off to a great start in our new world.

"Ava! Why is your backpack in the middle of the floor?" I cried.

Her voice was muffled as she called back.

"I don't know."

With a sharp intake of breath, I forced myself to cool down. A long day at the MMA Center didn't help this situation feel any easier. Every twenty seconds, all day long, I found myself staring at the Diner, praying for a glimpse of wild curly hair and bright eyes. No such luck occured, which left me in a truly foul mood.

"Come pick your mess up!" I called, then added tightly, "Please."

Ava flounced down the stairs with a hum, skipped to her backpack, and tossed it onto the peg near the back door. While I shuffled through the mail, she picked up her shoes and socks, set them on the mat at the door. A rice package that was supposed to be mixed with chicken bubbled on the stovetop. I'd forgotten lunch again, and felt ravenous now. It would be too salty for my usual taste, but the pre-cooked chicken that whirred in the microwave right now was too easy to ignore for dinner tonight. My head pulsed with a headache, anyway, and I still had hours to go in the day.

With no Serafina at the end of it.

My phone rang in my pocket when Ava faded out of the room again. Maverick. Awesome. The last person I wanted to talk to was my insufferable brother. I declined the call.

"Daddy!" Ava called from the other room. "I'm hungry! Can

I have an apple flower with peanut butter in the middle of it? The way Sera does it."

What was an apple flower?

"You can get an apple from the fridge," I replied and shoved the phone back into my pocket.

"I want it with petals on the plate!"

What on earth was she talking about? Apples didn't have petals.

"What?"

"The way *Sera* does it!" she shrieked, apparently at the end of her patience as well.

"Well, I'm not Sera," I snapped. "They taste exactly the same no matter how you eat it. If you want the apple, get it from the fridge."

My phone rang again. Agitated, I ripped it out of my pocket, answered it, and snapped, "What?"

"Well, good day to you, brother."

Maverick's rolling voice set my teeth together. I wanted to smack the smugness out of his tone. Instead, I shoved a hand through my hair.

"What do you want, Mav?"

"Just calling to ask what the hell happened."

My stomach clenched. "What do you mean?"

"Saw Sera at the Diner today. She looked like she'd been crying all night and Bert had her behind the counter instead of taking her usual tables. She wouldn't even look at me."

"Sounds tough," I muttered because I had no idea what else to say. Behind me, Ava muttered under her breath with mutinous rage as she grabbed an apple and stepped outside on the back porch.

"You're an asshole."

"You have no idea what's going on with Serafina," I shot back. "Why don't you reserve judgment until you have more information? Which, at this rate, will be never. I don't feel like talking to you, Mav."

"You broke it off."

"Not . . . exactly. You can't break what wasn't defined," I muttered.

"Bonehead point, bro. You need her, Ben. She's a freaking angel to put up with you, first of all, and you're not going to find that again. Secondly, you love her. Try to deny it, I dare you. Third, have you thought about that little girl that *also* adores Serafina?"

"Why did you call?" I asked through clenched teeth. "If this is the only reason, I'm hanging up."

"Serafina also said . . . nevermind. Listen, I had my reasons, but now I don't. Doesn't matter. Just forget about it."

"What the hell does that mean?"

"Nothing you need to hear anymore."

The *anymore* was overly emphasized and irritated me to the point of pain. Before I could respond, the call ended. I dropped the phone to the counter to resist throwing it across the room, then stalked to the washer. A moldy smell drifted out of the basin the moment I opened it. I swore under my breath. I'd forgotten to put the washed clothes in the dryer last night and they already smelled rank.

With a slam of my palm into the button, I restarted the load on a heavy rinse cycle and tossed some detergent in with it. Any attempts to piece together what Maverick meant were shoved aside. He could be cryptic on his own time.

Ava appeared at my side.

"Where's the rest of my snack?" she asked.

"The rest of it? Didn't you just eat an apple?"

"Sera always has an after school snack for me." She motioned to the counter. "She puts it right there. And it's more than just an apple, which tasted old so I threw it away."

"Then eat something else."

"The fridge is empty."

I blinked, mentally extricating myself from the laundry. She wasn't wrong. Of course, I hadn't gone grocery shopping on the way home. We'd been thirty minutes late leaving the MMA Center and I'd completely forgotten in the midst of Ava complaining about being there again.

"Dinner will be ready in twenty minutes." I crossed the room just in time for the rice to boil over, and barely slowed a swear word as I scrambled for a towel. "You'll be fine."

"Dad!" She groaned, one hand on her stomach. "I'm hungry now! The apple wasn't enough."

"Go play outside. It will distract you."

"No!"

Her sharp reprimand was punctuated by the stamp of a bare foot against the wooden floor. A familiar glower, a near-perfect mimicry of mine, folded her face into harsh lines. Her eyes were tapered in fury. Memories of Sadie flashed through my mind, setting me on edge.

"Excuse me?" I whispered.

"I'm hungry *now*."

"That doesn't mean you can speak to me like that."

If possible, her glare deepened. Her hands propped onto her hips, leaving her elbows out like chicken wings.

"Sera gives me a snack."

"Sera isn't here."

"Why not?" she whined. "I like Sera's food better!"

My jaw clenched shut as I closed my eyes, pulled in a long breath, and let it back out. Impatience warred with annoyance in my chest yet again. Sera wasn't here and wouldn't be here again today, probably. Ava acting just like Sadie sent a whirl of bad memories through me. Distantly, I knew my wrathful response had nothing to do with Ava, but her attitude didn't make it any easier.

"Sera isn't here today," I muttered. "You have to deal with me."

"Will she be here tomorrow?"

"No."

"When will she be back?"

Ava had tilted her head back, a nagging pitch in her tone that set my teeth on edge. It rang of her mother and ran along my nerves like a cheese grater. The truth wasn't any easier to set free.

"She may not come back. We're not sure."

Ava gasped, eyes wide. If possible, those eyes filled with water in a flash. Her voice wobbled and I groaned. Not tears. *Anything* but tears.

"What?" she whispered.

"I don't know yet," I said quickly. "I don't . . . we're not sure. We're working things out. But Sera has a life and she needs to get back to it."

Ava stepped back.

"You did this!" she cried. "This is all your fault! Mommy said you didn't want me to be happy, and now I'm not. You're taking Sera away too! Mommy was right."

Shock rendered me momentarily speechless. Taking her away? No, I desperately wanted her back.

"That's not true, Ava."

Tears filled her eyes. "I want Sera back. Please, daddy. Don't take Sera away too, you can't take her away too!"

Her voice became hysterical. Her eyes widened in panic as she shook her head back and forth, tears jarred out of her eyes and spilled onto her cheeks. She'd just rotated through four emotions within four minutes, and even I felt the backlash. All my ire fled in a flash as I knelt on the floor next to her and grabbed her hands.

"Please," she pleaded. "Please don't. Please!"

"Ava, what's wrong?"

To my shock, she collapsed in my arms. Deep sobs wracked

her body as I folded my arms around her. For several moments she cried. In the brief respite, I tried to pull my thoughts back together, but all I could think about was Sadie. About Ava's words. The terror in her eyes yet again.

Mommy said you didn't want me to be happy.

When her cries slowed, I put my hands gently on her shoulders and leaned back. "Ava, can we talk about this?"

Red-eyed, she passed an arm under her nose and reluctantly nodded. Afraid I'd lose her if I even breathed too much, I gently asked, "What did Mommy say about me?"

Her bottom lip jutted out a little. She fidgeted with the bottom of her shirt and whispered, "That you didn't want me to be happy. That you didn't love me."

My heart cracked a giant, ugly fissure down the middle of my chest that would have spilled the nastiest vitriol if I let it. Emotions like what swept through me then were too strong, too locked up, to be ignored. But I'd been trying, and now I was still lost in something that was powerful. Grief, probably. Terror. Despair.

Even though Serafina had warned me about what Ava told her, hearing it still shook me all the way to my core. The terror in Ava's eyes sealed the deal.

"Wow," I said.

We were a bigger mess than I thought.

There was no hesitation anymore. Hearing those words from Ava's mouth made it all too clear: Serafina had been absolutely right.

Sadie still had too much power over me. There was too much here to deal with alone, both for me and Ava. Ava watched me carefully. When she wore a wary expression like that, she looked just like me. Nervous for her answer, but needing to know exactly where we stood, I swallowed and asked, "Do you think that's true?"

She held her breath, frowned, and after a pause that felt like several eternities strung together, she finally shook her head. Relief I'd never known in my life poured through me.

"Why don't you think that's true?"

"Because you came back for me."

"To the hospital?"

She nodded.

The night I heard of Sadie's accident whipped through my mind. The moment Ava's nanny called me to tell me about Sadie's condition in the ICU, I'd asked Maverick to find me a flight while I packed my bags. Within eight hours, I held Ava in my arms at the hospital while she cried on me. Sadie passed an hour later. At the time, Avan and I didn't know each other well. Sadie had jealously guarded and kept Ava from me and from most of my attempts to be part of her life. But Ava knew me well enough that she came to me then. Clung to me. She seemed to understand that I was all she had left, for better or worse.

"Good," I whispered, and gave her arm a gentle squeeze. "Because it's just not true that I don't want you to be happy, or that I don't love you. You are the most lovable little girl in the world, and I love you more than anything, Ava. You are the most important thing to me. And I want you to be happy."

She sniffled. "Okay."

"That doesn't mean I'm perfect," I said wryly. "I'm going to mess up a lot, and sometimes you're going to be frustrated with me. Sometimes, I'll be frustrated with you, but it doesn't mean I don't love you. It means . . . that we have things to talk about. Okay?"

She nodded.

"So you might have to help me and be patient with me and I'll promise the same."

"Okay."

"I'm sorry your Mom told you that, and I hope you can let it go. Love you, little bit."

A hesitant smile appeared on her face. "Love you too,

Daddy." She stepped into my open arms and wrapped her little arms around my neck. For the first time in a while, something settled deep inside me.

While she skipped off to find something to do, I stared at the spot where she disappeared. At least we'd mostly cleared the air. I'd started the Sadie conversation and learned that we needed more help than I could give.

Now, I had to figure out something for this beating, broken piece of molten lava where my heart used to be.

My gaze darted around the house, which now smelled burnt and still looked disastrous. While I missed the little touches of Sera in my life, none of this stupid stuff mattered. My house could fall apart and Ava run around naked like a feral child for all that I cared. None of it meant a damn thing without Serafina here.

Yes, her help running the house made my life better, but that wasn't why I missed her. Ava and I had managed this chaos before, and we'd do it again. But when we'd managed it with Sera? It had been better.

I had been better.

Happier. Full of more joy. I looked forward to waking up. In fact, I looked forward to coming home, a place that was neither empty or pulling on all my time. A place that hadn't been safe until Serafina brought her sunshine into it.

The question was—had *she* been better? Happier? Full of more joy.

To her words, yes.

My eyes slammed shut on that thought. With a muttered explicative, I stood up. Dammit, but I had it all wrong. My fear of becoming like Sadie, or maybe just losing Sera because I even resembled Sadie, had overtaken me to the point I didn't even *ask* Sera her side of it. Didn't ask her if she wanted me, just assumed she'd hate me later and wanted to shut it down before it hurt any further.

Although I could hardly believe it myself, there had to be some redeeming aspect of me that brought her back. That initiated those heart-stopping kisses I couldn't stop thinking about. That gave her that broken-hearted stare that nearly broke my heart. That could possibly induce her to want to stay with me and Ava.

I straightened.

Maybe it was time to ask Serafina and find out the truth once and for all instead of deciding for her. Because my daughter had been fighting for her. Now it was my turn to fight in what was the most important fight of my life so far.

"Ava!" I called.

"Yeah?"

"C'mere. You and I need to do some work together."

Her head popped around the corner with a curious expression. "On what?"

I grinned.

"On getting Serafina back."

Chapter Twenty-Eight

SERAFINA

My throat tightened as I looked over the mess for the tenth time.

The loft looked like a tornado had ripped through it. Stuffing torn out of the couch. Clothes shredded and thrown on the floor. Plates smashed. Glasses flung across the wall, indenting the drywall. A giant spider web crack crossed the second-hand television set Mom had found.

I had no way to prove it, but everything inside me knew this had been Amber.

A deep, welling frustration lived in my center now. It drove my thoughts, pushing me to the point of fury, and then despair. Why did bad things happen in groups? Why couldn't heartbreak catch a break just once? What was that saying? Bad things come in threes?

Well, I was on seven, thanks.

You can stop now, universe, I thought.

The sound of feet on the stairs came behind me. I glanced back to see Maverick ascending, his large body at odds with the small, spiral steps. Bethany walked just behind him, swamped by his broad shoulders. They both wore grave expressions when I nudged the door to the loft wider for them to see it.

Bethany gasped. Maverick frowned.

"Hernandez said he's on his way," I said. "I'm so sorry. I feel like this is my fault somehow."

Bethany put a reassuring hand on my shoulder with a smile. "I'm just glad you're safe, Serafina. Things can be replaced. We have insurance for a reason. We tend to use it quite a bit these days," she added drily, with a smile aimed at Maverick.

Maverick's jaw remained tight as he stepped into the room. The troubled expression didn't clear from Bethany's face. She wore her hair down, but styled, elegantly at odds with her simple yoga pants and t-shirt today. Normally, I saw her as the high-end real estate agent, not this casual version.

Ellie already leaned against the doorway, her forehead grooved into a frown. She hadn't come inside, but she hadn't left me alone after I ran downstairs and asked her to call Maverick. Whoever had done this did it in the middle of the day, during the twenty minutes when Ellie was on a quick lunch break and the shop closed for a bit. They must have been watching and waiting, but Ellie hadn't seen anyone loitering.

For this level of destruction, they had been fast.

"Wow." Maverick whistled low as he stepped farther into the room. I'd already done a slow walk around. A gentle tour where I hadn't touched anything and attempted to comprehend exactly what happened. Thanks to all my travels, I didn't feel particularly attached to any sort of belonging. All of this furniture had been mostly new, not yet mine. The thought that I didn't care about the stuff crossed my mind. The invasion of privacy was disturbing, but not truly terrifying. The thought of this happening at Ben's house, however, made me sick to my stomach.

The message there was clear: this *wasn't* my home. Moving on was the right thing, no matter how painful.

Even if Ben's house felt more like home than here.

"Was anything taken?" Maverick asked.

"Not that I can tell. I don't keep any cash here, and my wallet was with me in my backpack, thank heavens. There really isn't much that I own, so I don't have a lot she could steal."

"She?" Bethany asked.

I pulled in a deep breath. "I think I know who did it," I admitted reluctantly, the pull and tug of guilt fresh with each word. "Amber, my brother's ex-girlfriend."

His drug dealer, I thought, but didn't add.

Maverick strode past the kitchen, glass grinding under his shoes. Bethany hung back, near us, as flashing blue and red lights came into the parking lot below. She let out a sigh of relief.

"Jayson is here," she murmured.

"Why do you think Amber did it?" Maverick asked as he surveyed some scratches on the cupboard doors.

"She's upset that we've taken my brother away. Says he owes her money. She probably came here looking for cash or something. Then trashed it to get her revenge. She and I haven't exactly gotten along," I said quietly.

Bethany squeezed my arm, and her lack of judgment was a deep balm on my heart. "There are security cameras outside," she said. "We'll get an eye on them soon. This may not even be her, but an isolated incident. It's not your fault."

"Thanks, Bethany."

The next hour came in a whirl. Ellie slipped back downstairs to run the shop, but Maverick and Ellie remained with me until Jayson had finished his report. By the time we'd cleaned up the glass on the floor and assessed the damages, with photos, for their insurance report, evening crept in.

Bethany paused in the doorway. "We need to go pick our son up," she said, "but I'm still worried about you. Are you going to be okay here tonight?"

Amber at large didn't reassure me, but I nodded anyway. None of the windows had broken, Maverick had done a quick lock replacement downstairs while I filled paperwork out, and the town lay quiet outside. At her core, Amber was a coward. I'd be shocked if she came back when I was here. That didn't give me comfort at all, of course, but I couldn't let Bethany know that.

"I'll be fine. I'll keep everything locked."

Her expression darkened further. "Maverick told me about you and Ben. I'm sorry. Men are total apes sometimes. I hope he comes around. This would have been the perfect time for him to step in."

I sucked in a breath, but could only manage a little smile. That thought had occurred to me several times in the last couple of hours.

Bethany squeezed my hand.

"If you want to give up the lease, I understand. Mav said you put in your two-week notice at the Diner. We can find someone to take it if you just need to get out of here. Broken hearts sometimes trump contracts. There's wiggle room in the lease if you find someone to take it."

"Thank you, I appreciate knowing that. And I might actually know someone that will take it."

"Oh?"

"Dagny. She mentioned it to me today. She's been living at home with her Mom to save money but would . . . she'd like an out."

Bethany illuminated. "I know Dagny. She just applied to work at the Frolicking Moose when Ellie leaves for college at the end of the summer. How perfect would that be? She's delightful. I'll drop by the Diner tomorrow and talk to her about both. Thanks Serafina. Just let us know what you decide and we'll support you however we can. And I'm sorry about all this."

She wrapped me in a quick hug, and the warmth of another pair of arms only made me miss Benjamin more. How could he ever think I didn't need him? The safety of his arms. The security of just standing next to him. Was there a way to quantify the power of security? No.

But was that all he meant to me?

The immediate response didn't even surprise me. No. Not by half. He could be a file clerk with the strength of a puppy and the joy they both brought to my life would be more than enough. The brightness. The sense of stability and being *needed*. They were the only two people I'd ever wanted to stay for. To wait on and see the world with them.

Apes, Bethany had said.

I concurred.

Chapter Twenty-Nine

BENJAMIN

Maverick: It is absolutely none of my business, but you need to get your ass over there right now.

Benjamin: Is she leaving?

Maverick: Just do it. Drop Ava off at our place. She can spend the night.

Benjamin: The night?

Maverick: Trust me.

My heart thudded in my chest as I steered the SUV back toward Pineville, the text conversation with Maverick still plodding through my mind. Ava and I had been busy at work with our plan to win Serafina back from my boneheaded ways for the last couple of hours, but we wouldn't be ready for another day or two. I'd intended on giving Serafina some space, but one look at Maverick's expression when I dropped Ava off and I knew something had gone terribly wrong. He hadn't said a word, but he hadn't needed to. I'd simply handed Ava's bag over, gave her a hug, and disappeared.

Twilight had long since settled, giving way to the dark shadows of night. Gentle illumination came from the top of the Frolicking Moose when I parked around the other side, in the empty lot for the salon. The less advance notice she had of my arrival, the less likely she'd ignore me.

I hoped.

Main Street lay oddly empty when I crossed around the front of the coffee shop, then headed to the back door. Her bike, which she hadn't ridden in a while, was chained to a wall still. A good sign, taken with the buttery lamplight from above.

Heart in my throat, I tried the door. It was locked. When I knocked, the door rattled a little. When a minute passed and she hadn't answered, I pulled out my phone and sent her a text.

Benjamin: It's me downstairs. Can we talk?

Thirty seconds later, shadows in the dark shop shifted near the stairs. Serafina appeared, her expression wary. She wore a pair of loose sweatpants, flip flops, and her hair lay in glossy, wet curls around her shoulders. Her makeup had been scrubbed off. Not even concealer could have hidden the weariness of her eyes. Were her cheeks red from tears or the shower?

She stared at me through the window, hand halfway to the doorknob. I held my breath. Never had I felt so unravelled. Years of my life and a child with Sadie had never made me feel this way. Like my fate, my life was wrapped up in another person that walked around with my heart in her hands. Like I'd never be complete without them.

Like everything revolved around that woman staring at me with her soul in her eyes.

Finally, she reached for the doorknob.

I let out the breath when she pulled the door open. She

leaned her face against it and quietly asked, "What did Maverick tell you?"

My brow furrowed. "Nothing." My expression tightened with deepening concern. "What is there to tell me?"

Her nostrils flared as she considered me, then she shuffled back and motioned up with a jerk of her head.

"Come inside."

The sound of the lock sliding home followed her closing the door. I waited until she started up the stairs first, and nearly choked on the coconut scent that followed her. My fingers itched to bury themselves in her hair. To take all of her in and kiss the pain out of her gaze.

The silence accompanied us to the top of the stairs. Once there, she stepped into her loft with a breath that sounded like a burdened sigh. I paused just off the stairs, the hair on the back of my neck standing up.

I hadn't seen the loft since before she moved in, but it didn't require any familiarity to know that someone had wreaked havoc on her space. The cushions had been ripped open, with stuffing spilled out. The shells lay empty now. Scratch marks in the paint that Maverick and I had painstakingly put on the walls. Broken television screen. A tied garbage bag sat near the door, stuffed full with what appeared to be clothes and the sharp edges of glass.

"What happened?" I asked.

Serafina folded her arms across her middle. "I think it was Amber, but we're not sure. Maverick gave the security footage to Jayson as part of the evidence gathering this afternoon. I haven't seen anything yet."

My jaw ticked. This afternoon. Was this before or after Maverick called me and chewed me out? I skimmed the room, relieved to not see any broken windows. Then I turned back to her.

"Are you okay?"

She nodded vaguely, then motioned to the couch. The cushions were all there, but the second one was limp and nearly empty. She sat on the far cushion, which appeared half-full of stuffing, and motioned me onto the good one on the opposite side. I didn't want to sit. I wanted to pace. To hit something.

Idiot. Idiot. Idiot.

"Sera," I whispered. "I'm sorry."

Her eyebrows rose in surprise. She had her bent leg tucked up against her chest as she studied me.

"Sorry?"

I waved a helpless hand. "I . . . I should have been here earlier."

She shrugged that off. Her eyes dropped from mine as she gazed around. "It's not a big deal. I . . . I'm not really attached to any of this stuff and I just need a few more days anyway."

My throat tightened. "What?"

"I, uh . . . I gave my two weeks notice today." She met my gaze, but there was an unsteadiness there that nearly robbed my courage. "Dagny thinks she wants the lease and Bethany is going to talk to her about it tomorrow. If Bert doesn't need me, I may be able to leave in a few days."

Leave. My mind could barely comprehend the word.

"Do you want to?"

She blinked. Her lips moved several times, but no sounds came out. "It's what's best," she finally said. She picked at something on her pant leg as a heavy silence followed. My thoughts whirled, knocked totally off balance.

What could I say now?

Did her plan negate everything I'd just concluded and decided and felt? If she would only be here a few more days, then maybe she wanted to go to . . . wherever she'd be next. Maybe she wanted out and couldn't wait to get away from Pineville. Would it be selfish of me to divulge the way I felt now?

Or worse to hold it back?

I'd certainly been guilty of making decisions on her behalf in the past, which landed us in this exact position. If I'd let her tell me what she felt, maybe she never would have given that two weeks notice.

"I wasn't going to leave," she said and broke apart my thoughts. "At least not yet. I told you I'd give you a week and . . ." She trailed away for a second, then picked it back up. "After I got your text this morning, I realized you didn't need me anymore. I was hurt. I felt . . . pushed out of your life. Out of *Ava's* life."

Her admittance felt like a crater in my chest. Gaping. Empty. Smoking. Filled with ash and brimstone and something ugly. The irony was darkly comical, but I could barely summon the strength to even breathe. I'd sent that text to help her, to give her some space. Clearly, I had no idea what happened in Serafina's mind.

The silence must have been longer than I thought. "Please," she whispered, her brow heavy. "Say something, Ben."

"Didn't need you?" I croaked. "Serafina . . . I love you."

She sucked in a sharp breath. The words rolled out of me now, pressured. Intense. Brought from the depths of the cavern inside me that she'd left behind. They'd never felt so right.

"Not just because you take care of us. But because you are light and goodness and warmth and concern and everything I've always wanted but never had. You're the other half, Sera. The only other half of our family. Not just me, but Ava too. She loves you. She fought for you. She was so angry at me today that I . . . I realized it was my turn to be a fighter too."

Tears filled her eyes when I reached across the space and grabbed her arm. She hiccuped, like she was trying to hide a sob.

"Sera, I love you."

"What about Sadie?" she whispered.

Sadie. My heart clenched, but I forced it to release. "I found a counselor just a few hours ago, one that can speak with me and

Ava apart, and then together. Ava agreed to go. We both need it. You're right. Sadie has some power over me still, and I've let her. I've been so afraid of becoming her that I've forgotten how to trust myself. And others," I tacked on.

My fingers slipped down her arm and wrapped around hers. She accepted them, threading hers through mine, and my heart soared with the hope it inspired. I wasn't out of the darkness yet, but one step closer.

"I came back to ask you what you wanted," I said. "Instead of trying to save you from me, I . . . realized it was your choice. That you deserve the chance to say something. So I want to ask you what you wa—"

"You." She nodded. "I want you and Ava and I want to stay and I want to try this out as someone that deeply cares about both of you, not as a nanny or paid employee or any of that. I want a chance, Ben."

My heart fluttered. "Us?" I whispered. "It can't be just me. You'll never get just me."

"Both of you," she said quietly.

Her fingers squeezed mine.

There were things to talk about. Long discussions to have that would seal this. Expectations. Alignment. We had issues to sort through and talk about, but none of that mattered. The eagerness in her voice. The bittersweet agony in her expression. *That* was all that mattered now.

I yanked her off the cushion and into my arms. Her warm body slammed into my chest, but before she could so much as grunt over it, I had my hands on her face. My fingers in her hair. My lips on hers. The smell of coconut filled my nostrils until I considered the fact that I might have died.

Serafina.

In my arms.

And that would never change.

Chapter Thirty

SERAFINA

Benjamin's lips on mine felt like coming home.

I lay on top of him until he broke the kiss. In a move so fast I didn't comprehend what happened until it was too late, he wrapped an arm around my waist and swept me down. A breath later, I lay on my back on the couch and stared up at him. His weight was heavy on top of me, but not crushing. Breathless, I reached up to touch his face.

"Ben?"

"I'm sorry, Serafina. I'm so sorry."

Tears spilled out of my eyes again. "Me too. I don't want to leave. And I'm scared. I think Amber did all this and I don't want to be alone and what if she—"

He silenced me with the gentlest of kisses. The ease of his lips against mine stole my breath again. His hand splayed across my cheeks and into my hair. He held me so close that I felt my heart slam against him. My fears quieted.

Benjamin had me now, and this security wasn't a dream.

"You're not staying here tonight," he growled. "It's not safe. You're coming home with me, where *I'll* keep you safe. And if you say no, then I'll sleep here. And if you say no to that, I'll sleep on the floor downstairs."

Laughing, I said, "I won't say no."

He smiled softly and tucked a piece of hair behind my ears. "Good. Because you belong with me, Sera. I still can't figure out what you see in me. Why you'd want to spend more time with me, but . . . I don't want to lose this. To lose you. So I'll trust it. I'll trust you."

With our eyes locked, I could see the vulnerability there. The lines of uncertainty that held up a man with deeper emotions than I ever realized.

"You make me feel safe, Ben," I murmured, my voice husky. My finger traced the edge of his lips. "Alive. You make me . . . you make me want to stay and I've never felt that before. You make me feel tangled up in something bigger and better than me. You give me a reason to wake up in the morning and giggle through the day and something to look forward to. You're my light."

He covered my lips with his, taking absolute possession of my soul. As if he scooped into my chest and cradled my heart in his hands. I felt utterly swept away. Lost in the winds of his feelings for me. My joints became liquid so that I sank into him, lost in the heat of his kiss and the touch of his hand.

He pulled away, closed his eyes, and pressed his forehead to mine.

"Come home with me, Sera? Let me keep you safe and we'll figure all of this out as it happens?"

I smiled, my lips a breath from his.

"You got it, Mercedy."

* * *

Benjamin reached for my hand as I slung my backpack over my shoulder and locked the loft door. He held my laundry basket full of dirty clothes and other necessities with his other arm. The shop lay in darkness as we left it behind and I followed him down the spiral stairs. He didn't let me go.

I didn't want him to.

Stars had broken out in the sky over the reservoir when we stepped into the parking lot. Water lapped at the reeds not far away, and the deep, mournful cry of a bird came from somewhere out on the water. The fresh air was cool and refreshing on my cheeks. Ben sent me a quick, secretive smile as he pulled me into his side and nudged me toward the front at the same time.

"I parked over there." He jerked his head to the right. "We just need to walk around."

"Afraid I'd lock you out?" I quipped with a grin.

He laughed. "Yes, actually. And perhaps that would have been deserved."

With a giggle, I caught up to his side, deliriously happy to be headed back home with him. Away from the loft and the loneliness I'd been ready to carry with me into the night. Back into Benjamin and Ava's life, where I belonged.

The scrape of a shoe on gravel stopped us a second later. Benjamin paused, eyes on two shadows leaning against the wall of the coffee shop. They were just out of reach from the streetlight, their faces obscured in the darkness. He dropped the laundry basket and gently nudged me behind him with a hand, his entire body tense now. He stood tall, with his legs slightly braced.

"Get back, Sera," he murmured.

The shadows changed as the two men straightened and slowly advanced. The one on the left was broad shouldered, meaty and thick. A dark scowl crossed his features that made my stomach sink. The other was scrawny, with twitchy hands and bulbous eyes that darted all over the place.

A cold feeling of fear swept through me when his froggy gaze landed on me.

"Ben?" I murmured.

"Call 911 and get someone over here."

Ben stood his ground in front of me, but his gaze darted quickly around. No others approached, and the lack of traffic on the street left a ringing silence in the air. Even the usual shouts from the bar down the road didn't reach here. If I screamed, would anybody hear?

"You have five seconds to turn around and leave," Ben said calmly to the approaching men, "before I kick your asses into the next town."

The bigger of the two snorted, but the smaller had the brains to look nervous. He looked beyond me, then back to Benjamin. *Where are you, Amber?* I thought, but saw no sign of her. This had her written all over it.

"I didn't sign up for this!" the smaller cried. "I'm not fighting Benjamin Mercedy."

The larger one shoved him. "Shut up. It's two against one. I could fart on him and this guy would collapse."

"Call 911," Ben said quietly again.

My heart stammered nervously as I reached for my phone, then something solid hit my arm with a breathtaking *crack*.

I shouted and stumbled to my knees, my phone clattering uselessly on the ground. Pain ricocheted through my right arm, all the way to my neck, like electric ropes. Heat I'd never known followed. White stars broke across my vision as a vague, guttural yell followed the pain. Ben shouted, disappeared, and a scuffle of shoes on pavement began.

I tried to shove to my feet, but another *whack* slammed into my right side. The blow came just below my ribs, into the fleshy part of my side. I doubled over with another cry of pain, my breath gone. The sound of fists hitting flesh followed and screeches followed as I tumbled to the ground. Whoever shouted, it wasn't Ben.

A third whack followed, but this one glanced off my thigh.

A bat.

Someone had just hit me with a bat.

"Give me your money!" Amber cried. She hovered just over me, feral animosity in her wild eyes. "Your brother owes me and I'm going to get my money."

Gasping, I tried to struggle off my back, but she shoved me with a foot. My teeth gritted as my right elbow slammed into the ground, and another round of fresh pain spiraled through my body. Nausea welled up in my stomach.

"Get it!" she screamed.

With a ringing sound in my eyes, I ripped the backpack strap off my left shoulder with that hand. My right arm, still pulsing, cradled uselessly against my stomach. I blinked to clear my vision. Benjamin stood before the larger of the two, arms high, body crouched. The man had a streak of blood from his nose across his cheek and a hideous glower darkening his expression. He seemed cautious now and unwilling to advance. The second already moaned on the ground, inert on his left side.

"Come on big guy," Ben muttered. "I'm not even winded yet."

"Where is your money?" Amber shouted and pulled my attention back. "Give it to me now."

"Here." Any attempt to be careful was lost. I extricated the backpack. My right arm jarred as I pulled the strap off. Another bolt of fire nearly took my breath away. "Take it. Call . . . them off."

The words wheezed out of me as my breath slowly returned. The dull, throbbing ache on my side was no match for my broken arm, but now it tingled. My brain desperately tried to focus, but I could barely see. Benjamin filled my mind, a mere dark blur moving in the background now.

Amber stepped out of the shadows of the building again, bat held high.

"The bag already!" she screamed.

With a grunt, I threw the backpack away from me with my

left arm. The desperate look in her eyes set my teeth on edge as she scrambled for the bag. Her hair spiraled around her in a crazy mass, her skin pale and splotchy. A thin tank top strap dropped down one bony, dirty shoulder.

"You took him from me!" she cried. "I loved him. I loved him!"

What drug was she on to cause such a freakish tirade? Her eyes were wide and dilated, like a frightened horse. She paced back and forth, the bat on her shoulder. She pointed it at me and let out a shrill scream as she reached for the bag. Behind us, Benjamin circled the bigger man. Every few steps, he'd lash out like a tiger, then retreat. The other guy could barely keep up. His confidence seemed to be waning, even as he attempted to advance with sheer brawn.

Amber snatched the bag when I heard the grunts of fighting resume. She skittered back the shadows. I fumbled for my phone on the ground nearby and tried to keep my eyes on her, but everything moved too strangely. The fighting darkness as Benjamin and the man grappled together in full fight mode. The long light of the street lamp so far away. My fingers seemed to take forever to dial 9-1-1.

Finally, a voice came over the earpiece.

"9-1-1, what's your emergency?"

"A-attacked," I cried. "We're being attacked in the parking lot of the Frolicking Moose. There are three—"

A leg connecting with my stomach sent me onto my back with a grunt. Only a second passed before I understood that Amber had kicked me. The blow had barely been enough to overturn me, but I lost my breath again. She stomped on my phone, then kicked it away while I gasped for air. After her well-placed kick, I just wanted to vomit.

With a cry, she held the bat over her head and brought it down. I rolled out of the way a second before it slammed into the pavement where my head had been, ricocheting away with the *thunk* of metal on pavement. Pain raced back through my arm, but I was too frightened to feel it now.

Amber was going to kill me.

With a growl, she advanced. I shoved back, gained my feet, and saw it coming for me again. My left hand reached up, caught the bat when the next swing headed for my ribs, and stopped her advance out of sheer instinct.

My wrist trembled with the force of the bat slamming into my palm. I didn't hear a crack, but tremor streaked all the way into my shoulder. I ignored the welling pain in my hand. The throb in my hip. Everything faded away as I wrapped my fingers around the bat and yanked.

Amber stumbled into my reach.

I stomped a foot onto her toes. She howled. I ripped the bat from her hands, drove my knee into her stomach, and shoved her to the ground. Then I flipped the bat with my left hand so I held it by the handle and pointed it to her face as she groaned.

"Don't. Move."

My breaths were desperate pants of pain. Darkness swam before my eyes as the distant whine of a siren came from the far edge of town. Benjamin ducked a flying fist, but his attention was fully on the larger guy.

Amber sputtered from the force of my knee in her stomach. She attempted to crawl, but I shoved her back down with the pressure of the tip of the bat in her ribs. She grimaced, coughing.

"You," I hissed, "will never ruin another life except your own after this. I hope you rot in prison for the rest of your life for what you've done to me and my brother."

Red-and-blue lights filled the parking lot as two sheriff's deputies skidded to a stop in the parking lot. Their bright beams shone light on Ben as he slammed his fist into the bigger man's jaw. The giant toppled like a house of cards. A familiar voice approached through the bright haze.

Dazed, I stared into them.

"Serafina! It's Hernandez. Step back."

Another deputy broke up the bright headlights as he headed for Benjamin. I stumbled as all the blood seemed to leave my head. Someone grabbed my left arm. The bat dropped from my hand. A voice said something, but it sounded like it came through water. Distant. Slow. I fell to my knee. The pain jarred my broken arm. My side. The throbbing in my left hand.

"Ben," I whispered as utter quiet descended on the world. Ben looked up and met my eyes right then. I comprehended a flash of fear in his gaze.

And then darkness.

Chapter Thirty-One

BENJAMIN

The anemic lights of the hospital parking lot set my body into a heavy clench hours later. It had been rough coming down after that fight. The twirling lights. The ambulance. The edge of hysteria. Even Maverick appearing and the cool weight of his hand on my shoulder as an anchor didn't do much to extricate myself from the sheer adrenaline coursing through my body.

Even now, I waited for dangers from the shadows. Felt the gut-deep fear for Serafina's safety yet again.

Serafina.

Maverick put a hand on my shoulder as I reached for the door handle and tried to shove out.

"Wait," he said. "Let me go in with you. The ten-second lead on me won't make a difference, and we don't know what we'll find in there. I want to be with you. Serafina was pretty hurt."

My nostrils flared as I nodded once. The gravity in his tone centered me after the drive up the canyon to here. The forty-five minutes that separated me from the most frightening thing that had ever happened in my life. From intense questioning from the cops. Watching Amber's glazed eyes glare at me as they pushed her into the back of the patrol car. Serafina's pale face whisked away, her arm broken and body battered.

A shudder slipped through me.

Maverick climbed out of the SUV as I shut my door. The feeling of hot beads running through my blood pushed me to get into that ER as soon as I could physically manage, but Maverick was right. I had to cool it. Wait.

I didn't know what they'd say.

Maverick kept a faster-than-usual clip while we crossed the dark, empty parking lot and made our way inside. The high of a fight still sang through my veins, keeping me on edge. The giant had gotten one hit on my jaw, just glancing my lower lip, which ached. No doubt it was swollen, but I'd had worse from training sessions with newbies. That guy had been nothing but a hopped up druggie looking for an outlet and a quick buck from Amber. Gravel had torn up my back from the ground, but otherwise, I was fine.

Serafina was another matter.

Someone at the front desk straightened up when we approached. Backlights were turned off, giving the ER a dark appearance as we strode up to the desk.

"Serafina Courdray," I said.

She opened her mouth, eyed my lip, then nodded and stood up. "They're expecting you. Follow me."

Relieved, we trailed behind her as she navigated back to a circular ER with a big desk in the middle. She caught a nurse's attention, motioned to us in silent question, and the nurse nodded.

"Here." The girl pointed to a glass sliding door in front of a closed curtain. A bright red 4 was painted on the front. Most of the lights were off inside. "You can go in."

When I hesitated, the girl paused.

"She okay?" I asked.

She drew in a deep breath. "She'll be okay, yeah."

No further details came, but I didn't need them right then anyway. Maverick jerked his head toward the room as the girl disappeared back to the front desk. "I'll wait here. Go see her."

I clapped him on the shoulder, then slipped inside. Monitors beeped quietly when I slid through the curtains. Serafina lay on a bed, her eyes closed. The pain had mostly cleared from her expression. Her right arm was bandaged from elbow to wrist in what appeared to be padded gauze and a wrap. A precursor to a cast. No other visible bruises, but Hernandez had relayed her other, less-obvious injuries from the bat. Blow to the side. Kicks to the stomach. Possible broken hand.

I stopped to take her in, then let out a long, pained breath. We were lucky to come out of that alive.

Moments from the parking lot passed back through my mind in snatches. The sound of her bone cracking under the bat. The advance of the men the moment Amber attacked. The helpless feeling of not being able to protect Serafina washed back through me until I forced it to slow. They'd rushed me the moment Amber had her revenge. Coordinated attack. The first had fallen quickly, but the second had been brutish and heavy enough to keep me busy.

Didn't matter now. Sera was alive.

She made it.

Somehow.

Or as far as I could tell.

I advanced another step so I could put my hands on her. In the aftermath, I felt shaky. Exhausted. Now that I saw her breathing, I wanted to collapse, even though I was still ready to beat the—

"Ben?"

Those familiar eyes blinked at me, groggy from pain meds, I hoped. I lowered into the bed next to her.

"Hey."

Tears filled her eyes when I put a gentle hand on her face. She leaned into my touch with wide eyes.

"You're okay?" she whispered.

"Fine. Nothing but a training match. You?"

She swallowed. "Broken arm. They want to keep me tonight to watch for internal bleeding. Amber got me on my side with the bat." She tilted her head to the right, then grimaced. My nostrils flared from a poor attempt to control my emotions as I peeled back the flimsy gown they'd wrapped her in. Dark blue mottling had started to form along the creamy skin of her stomach, not far below her ribs.

She watched me carefully when I tucked it back down.

"Where else?" I croaked.

"My thigh, but it's just a bruise. There's a hairline crack in one of the bones of my hand, but it'll heal on its own. She got me in the stomach with a kick, but no lasting issues there. That's it."

I snorted. *That's it.* As if I didn't want to murder someone over it.

As if she sensed the stirring darkness in me, her hand reached up to touch my face. Tubes and tape and monitors strapped all over her arm didn't deter her. "Please," she murmured as her thumb gently touched the swollen lower edge of my lip. "Say something."

"I hate this for you," I whispered.

A tear dropped down her cheek. "Me too," she murmured.

I covered her hand with mine.

"They would have killed me if you weren't there," she whispered. "Thank you for saving my life."

"She almost did kill you."

"Almost," she repeated quietly, "isn't accomplished. You saved my life." She glanced beyond me, then back. "Can you stay with me? Please don't . . . don't leave me?"

"Never," I murmured.

Relief turned her expression to something more relaxed.

Carefully, I lay next to her on the bed. She grimaced as she repositioned, then settled back against me. Her head rested in the crook of my neck when she turned onto her left side, cuddled in my arms, and sighed. Her eyes fluttered closed. Her heart rate slowed on the monitor behind us.

I stared at the ceiling while the hospital moved around our little room, and let the relief follow. Feeling her body pressed against mine was the reassurance that I needed. All the rest of the tension fled for now.

Sera was mine.

That's all that mattered.

Epilogue

SERAFINA

Collective whispers came from behind a closed door when I slipped out of Benjamin's SUV the next day. Walking felt good, but my head was still a little groggy from the pain meds. The quiet drive from the hospital back to Pineville had given me a moment to collect my thoughts. Benjamin hadn't let go of me, or left my side, since he arrived in the ER.

Now, he opened my door and helped me out. I gave him a little smile, and he pulled me into his side with a soft kiss to my forehead.

"Let's get you home," he murmured.

Home.

That was exactly where he'd brought me.

Hernandez had texted Benjamin updates early this morning. *Amber has pending charges and is awaiting trial on several counts,* he said. *Won't be getting out for a long, long time.* The smallest of the two thugs at her side had gone missing when the copes arrived, and Benjamin insisted I stay at his place until he was found.

I didn't dispute that.

Benjamin's hand paused on the doorknob seconds before it would open. He glanced down at me with a little amusement.

"You like surprises, right?"

I grinned. "Definitely."

"Good."

He pushed the door open and tears filled my eyes. Mom, Dad, Dagny, and Ava stood there around a monstrous bouquet of balloons that would have been obnoxious if they didn't spell out WE LOVE YOU. Shiny red heart balloons surrounded the letters, and a dozen pictures that Ava had clearly colored lay scattered across the table. Macarons of various colors scattered a plate topped by a chocolate cake.

Mom had been stress baking again.

Mom stood next to Dad, tears in her eyes that she smiled through when she saw me. Dad let out a relieved breath.

"Welcome home, Sera!" Ava cried with a happy squeal, then threw a fistful of confetti. "We wanted to throw you a party! And we bought lots of things for you!" She darted forward, grabbing the arm that wasn't broken, and tugged me into the room. "Come on! First, Dad called a lady and now we gotta go talk to her about our problems. He said that would help us get you back, and we both really wanted you back. *Then* he wanted us to buy these, but your Mom and Dad had to help us out while you were getting better in the hospital."

I staggered behind her quick steps and faster chatter until we skidded to a stop at the empty spare bedroom. This time, it wasn't empty. A new queen-sized bed stood in the middle of the room, fresh sheets stretched across the top. The far wall had a map of the world splayed across it, plastered there recently, if the hammer and nails on the top of the bed meant anything.

While Ava skipped around the room, chattering about how they put the bed together and a bad word that my Dad said when the mattress fell on top of his hand, another warm body moved up behind me. I leaned back to feel Benjamin back there. He put an arm around me and pulled me close.

"The bedroom is so you know you always have a place with us," he murmured against my ear, his breath warm. "But I don't intend for you to sleep here long."

"No?"

He brushed a few tendrils of hair away from my neck, the tips of his fingers gentle on the hollow between my shoulders and neck.

"No. Once I can take you on a proper date or two, talk to your Dad, officially meet your brother, and convince Ava to help me, I'll pop a ring onto your hand and we'll move you into the room you *really* belong in. Mine."

My heart soared at the definitive tone in his words. The intensity of the passion that clouded his tone. He meant every word. They'd given me a place to stay. He'd given me his *home*.

And I'd never wanted anything more.

My mom bustled in the background, chatting with Dagny. "I heard at the grocery store that the Frolicking Moose hired you?" Mom said. "Does that mean you're quitting the Diner?"

Dagny laughed. "G-g-good news travels f-fast around here. Y-yes. I'm s-s-starting next month, when E-e-ellie leaves for s-state university. I-I hate waitressing. The c-c-offee shop will be much easier."

Dad shuffled around, eyeballing each nook and cranny of the house, a screwdriver in hand, as he sought some way to be helpful and productive. Warmth and love and light permeated the house as Ava skipped past us, headed for Dad. Benjamin gave me a deliciously warm smile, planted a gentle kiss on my lips, then braided our fingers together and gently tugged me back toward my family.

Together.

Shy Girl

SNEAK PEEK INTO THE 5TH BOOK

Dagny: Jayson brought another date into the coffee shop tonight.

The text flew out of my fingers the moment I could send it without looking like a crazy stalker woman. Some magic in my phone sent it across space and over to my best friend, Serafina.

Her reply came seconds later.

Serafina: WHAT?!

A smile slipped across my face at her immediate—and appropriately shocked—response, but I stifled it. A quick glance to the other side of the Frolicking Moose Coffee Shop confirmed that Jayson Hernandez still sat at the same table where he always sat. This week, he spoke to a lovely woman with dark eyes and delicate hands that belonged in a diamond commercial.

Dagny: Third date, three weeks in a row, with a different woman. Comes every Friday night like clockwork.

Dots appeared on the screen to indicate her reply. So that I didn't look like too much of a slacker, I reached for a rag to wipe down the counter for the third time and prayed no one came through the drive-through.

This was prime-level girlfriend gossip material, here.

Serafina: Coffee as a first date makes sense.

Dagny: You think he's a serial dater?

Serafina: I could see it. He's always been a bit non-committal in the dating world. Do you think he's a player?

Her question swirled around my mind as I stole another glance at Hernandez. Truly, neither of us knew him all *that* well —despite the fact that I went to high school with him and reverentially adored him from the sidelines of my life for almost ten years. Freshman Dagny had serious feelings for Hernandez, the beloved Senior.

Was he a player? No. He *could* be, with those thick shoulders, razor-sharp instincts, and a confidence that carried him places. His way-too-long eyelashes and quick smile certainly didn't help matters.

But he wasn't a player.

Dagny: Doubt it.

Serafina: I feel like we'd know if he was trying to date, so what is going on and why hasn't he asked you out?

A laugh almost bubbled out of me. I shook my head as I replied.

Dagny: How would you *know* if he was trying to date?! That makes NO sense.

Serafina: Mountain life rarely does, I've found. Maybe the girls he brings are friends?

Dagny: Maybe? They aren't from here.

Serafina: The mountains aren't THAT big. None of them are familiar to you?

Dagny: None.

Serafina: I accept this romantic mystery and commit myself to figuring it out.

There was a sense of warmth and friendliness in all the women he visited with, but they didn't strike me as *friends*. Most of them dressed like they had someplace to go—form-fitting pencil skirts. Collared white shirts. Gleaming black hair. Sparkling earrings. If it was a date, why a coffee shop while wearing such glamor? Hernandez was always casual in a tee and jeans. One time he showed up in his deputy uniform. One time in mud-splattered pants and work boots, like he'd been out on his family farm.

Generally I had a good read on people, but in this situation I felt turned upside down. Nothing was clear except the facts.

Jayson Hernandez showed up every Friday at the same time, purchased the same drink, sat in the same seat, and met a different girl. The ritualistic aspect of the mystery killed me. The girls changed every week, arrived in separate cars, departed with a kiss on the cheek after approximately an hour, and nothing else.

Serafina: Is he in his deputy uniform?

Dagny: Not tonight.

Serafina: That's better. You'll drool over him less. He's suuuuuper hawt in the uniform.

In that, she certainly wasn't wrong, but it was time to change the subject. Watching Jayson on a date with another woman was hard enough. Analyzing only led to the same question we had every time: why not me?

Dagny: Are you still madly in love with Benjamin?

Serafina: SO madly.

Dagny: Your life is a fairytale.

Serafina: So is yours. You're just still in the scrubbing floors phase of your Cinderella story. Will you send me a pic of Hernandez and this girl? I need to size her up.

Dagny: That is SO creepy. No.

Serafina: Fiiiiiine. Next Friday, I'll just drop in and we can text each other the way she rates. You know, like he always rates his food? It will be hysterical.

Dagny: Done!

Serafina: How is school going?

Dagny: Almost done with this semester. On track to graduate in December. It's so—

"Hot boyfriend?"

The unexpected voice startled me out of a reply and I fumbled to avoid dropping my phone. With my luck, the whole screen would shatter. Thankfully, I caught it a second before disaster struck in a not-so-graceful fumble that sent a lock of hair into my eyes. Because, of course.

Why not make it impossible for him to see me as anything but an awkward barista? Like I was still fifteen years old, gawping at him from where I hid in the library.

I looked up into a familiar pair of dark eyes. Jayson Hernandez stood there in a button up white shirt with the front untucked, a pair of jeans that fit him a little too perfectly, and the same work boots I saw most weeks. Such a casual outfit belied his natural intensity. When his angular face wasn't caught in a thoughtful expression, it looked like he half-smiled most of the day. Plus, his shorter hair was slightly curled at the ends, and I wanted to run my fingers through the adorable locks.

He blinked, which brought me back to reality.

I'd die of mortification if he saw an entire text message thread about him on my phone, so I clicked my phone off and shoved it in my back pocket.

"N-no." I forced a smile. "N-n-not exactly."

He grinned and set an empty coffee mug on the counter between us. Of the hundreds of mugs on the wall that customers could choose from to drink their coffee in, he'd chosen the one with the Mexican flag. His date had chosen a water bottle, and she tucked it into her purse before surreptitiously fixing her hair in the window reflection.

So what did they talk about over water and coffee? They'd been here almost an hour. No signs of awkwardness between them. Not even indifference or attraction. Just . . . a friendly, neutral air.

Curiouser.

"Thanks again, Dagny." He held up a thumb. "Five stars. Perfect coffee, as always."

I nodded instead of speaking, less out of shock at his proximity—which sometimes happened when I could smell him—and more out of a trained habit not to speak unless I absolutely had to.

He turned to leave with another quick wave and the girl followed.

Once they faded into the darkening parking lot, I let out a gut-deep breath, bent in half, and pressed my forehead to the cool metal of the counter. The chilly feeling against my skin had an oddly grounding response, like a ripple through my body.

No was the only reply I could come up with?

C'mon, Dagny, I silently chided. *You can do better.*

Actually, I probably couldn't. Squeaking any sound out was a win most days. A thousand other words ran through my mind now that he wasn't melting me with his eyes, but I dismissed them. *No* was innocuous, acknowledging, and friendly. He'd clearly asked the girl here on a date. The last thing I needed to do was step in and try to flirt. That always led to a disaster.

How did people flirt anyway?

Besides, my crush on Hernandez had lasted long enough. Years, in fact. It began in high school, when I existed in the shadows and he lived in the limelight. Hernandez had been a senior my freshman year of high school. He lettered in baseball, had a reputation as a kind but disinterested jock, and held a place high on the Honor roll.

He and a group of three other friends had been known for living life on the edge with stupid stunts, and they chronicled all of it through the legendary C-tape. In fact, the ancient C-tape had once circulated past my eyes, and I'd gaped in shock that it had been real. The only way I'd been able to watch it was with an ancient VCR in the library. I'd walked by the back storage room while Jayson and a few other baseball team players laughed over one of the Merry Idiots skateboarding behind a truck while holding a rope.

The C-tape was the only physical proof of some of their idiotic ideas. Skiing down a church with a steep slope. Jumping off 100-foot cliffs. Skateboarding down steep, paved roads on longboards. They even put a ramp on the roof of the local bank and tried to snowboard off of it and onto a jump at the end.

Meanwhile, I'd been known for . . .

. . . nothing.

Certainly *not* my stutter, nor my mom's reputation for crazy, both things for which I'd worked very hard to avoid repute. Anonymity was just what I'd wanted.

When the bell on the Frolicking Moose tinkled, I tucked those thoughts into the back of my mind, straightened up too fast, and my head whirled for a second. Once the dizzy feeling cleared, my gaze focused on a middle-aged woman as she advanced into the coffee shop. Her trembling hand wrapped around a small, black object that was pointed at me.

A mixture of uncertainty, confusion, and terror filled me like a flood of cold water. Was she carrying . . . was that . . . no. While my thoughts attempted to recover themselves, she'd crossed the room and stood a few steps away from the counter.

I blinked.

Yep.

Definitely a real gun.

A designer purse that gleamed with red sequins and gold trim hung from her other arm. Short heels cracked as they walked across the floor, as shiny and red as her purse. Her hair was tied away from her face in a once-elegant chignon that lost itself to tendrils around her face. My gaze darted up to cold, bloodshot eyes and my whirling thoughts fell utterly silent.

"Let's make this easy," she said breathlessly. "All I want is whatever cash you have in the register and a quiet exchange. Then I'll leave you alone."

For a split second, I thought of saying *no*. What would my boss, Maverick, say? Shouldn't I put up some kind of fight? But the urge passed out of me in a moment. No, I wasn't about to go down for a coffee shop. Instead, I stared at the empty, round barrel that faced my direction and swallowed.

"O-o-okay."

Her nostrils flared. The skin around her knuckles was white when she dropped the sequined purse on the counter with her other arm.

"Put it in there."

I reached for the cash register's *no sale* button and pressed it. The drawer chugged out with a high-pitched *ching* and I wondered if I could buy time. To do what? Fight her? Not happening. I hesitated as I looked at the empty slots in the drawer.

She straightened to peer inside the register, then frowned.

"That's it?" she hissed.

My hands began to shake as I calmly reached for what few bills lay inside. $1 bills, two $10, and three $20 came out. I piled them together.

"Q-q-q-qu-i-i-iet n-n-night," I managed to say. Under duress, my stutter became worse than ever. I didn't have the ability to tell her Maverick cleared the till and took the money to the bank earlier today.

Her upper lip curled in disgust.

"Oh r-r-really?" she muttered in a grating, high-pitched voice meant to mock me. "Well that's not enough!"

Her rising shout brought the rest of her hair tumbling around her shoulders. She lifted the gun a little higher so it felt like it pointed right between my eyes. I gulped, able to see the gaunt lines of her face now. At first glance, she appeared to be a striking woman. Now, the truth was so obvious. Too thin. Cracked lips. As if she tried to hold onto a former, healthy, more vibrant version of herself.

A drug addict, maybe?

"Where's the rest?" she demanded.

"C-c-credit," I said. "M-m-most people p-p-pay with cards."

She scowled, then nodded to the purse with a quick jerk of her head. "Put it in." I obeyed, then she motioned to the drawer again. "The coins too."

I scrambled to get the coins out. They felt slippery, as if coated in butter. The promise of the gun sent my mind into a tailspin as I tried to collect the change. I just wanted her to leave. Didn't want this to be real, or my final end. Getting shot in a coffee shop? How could *that* be my life? No, I wasn't this kind of person. I lived a quiet, gentle life. I would not be part of some drug addict's desperate attempt for money.

Just as I gathered the last of the quarters, the door cracked open behind her. The woman's head whipped around in time to see Jayson re-enter. My heart lurched into my throat during the second that it took him to process the scene. Just as the woman canted her hips to swing the gun around to him, my hand shot out. The edge of my palm smacked her wrist and she let out a little cry.

Then she disappeared beneath a hulking blur of white and brown.

The clatter of a gun falling to the floor and a shout of pain followed. Two seconds of silence passed before I managed to ask, "J-j-jayson?"

"Fine," he called. "Call 9-1-1. Tell them what's happening."

I reached for the phone in my back pocket and, after three attempts to type in my passcode, I finally got it right. My fingers trembled as I dialed 9-1-1, then waited while the phone rang dully. Another voice came on the line.

"9-1-1. What's your emergency?"

For a moment, it felt as if my tongue was glued to the top of my mouth. My lips would no sooner form the words *I need help* than my body could fly. The operator spoke again, her voice pressured.

"Hello?"

Panic and frustration made my mind fuzzy until I forced myself to calm down.

There is no pressure for me to speak.

A third attempt yielded no result, which only compounded my desperation. I knew what I wanted to say, I just couldn't get the words out. Not even a squeak or a sound.

"Hello?"

Finally, like a dam giving way, the words exited my throat. "N-n-need h-h-help," I cried. "F-frolicking M-m-moose. G-gun!"

The operator rushed to respond, but I ignored her to scramble around the counter. Jayson lay on top of the woman, the gun barely out of reach. I hurried over and kicked it out of the way as he struggled to get a flailing arm under his control. Once she was fully subdued, and screaming like a wild thing into the tile, he glanced up at me.

"You good?"

I nodded.

"Help coming?" he asked, his face a mask of concentration as he held her pinned to the floor.

I nodded.

"Good work, Dag."

His praise came seconds after the first siren screamed down the street toward us. Red and blue lights whirled outside, seconds away as they barreled down the Main Street in the quiet mountain town of Pineville.

"Wh-what can I d-do?"

"Nothing." He sent me a quick grin, one that I'd seen on a crappy video years ago when I stole a sneak at the C-tape. "I got this."

* * *

Click right here to grab your copy today!

Katie Cross is ALL ABOUT writing epic love stories and wild places. Creating new books is her jam.

When she's not hiking or chasing her two littles through the Montana mountains, you can find her curled up reading a book or arguing with her husband over the best kind of sushi.

Visit her at www.katiecrossbooks.com for free short stories, extra savings on all her books (and some you can't buy on the retailers), and so much more.